Also by Eliot Schrefer

GLAMOROUS DISASTERS

THE NEW KID

ELIOT SCHREFER

SIMON & SCHUSTER
New York London Toronto Sydney

SIMON & SCHUSTER
1230 Avenue of the Americas
New York, NY 10020

This book is a work of fiction. Names, characters, places and incidents are products of the author's imagination or are used fictitiously. Any resemblance to actual events or locales or persons, living or dead, is entirely coincidental.

Portions of Chapter 10 originally appeared in a short story entitled "BOSTON→OSAKA," published online in *Swink* magazine.

For information about special discounts for bulk purchases,
please contact Simon & Schuster Special Sales:
1-800-456-6798 or business@simonandschuster.com.

Designed by Julie Schroeder

Manufactured in the United States of America

10 9 8 7 6 5 4 3 2 1

Library of Congress Cataloging-in-Publication Data
Schrefer, Eliot.
The new kid : a novel / Eliot Schrefer.
p. cm.
1. Family—Fiction. 2. Love stories. I. Title.
PS3619.C463N49 2007 813'.6—dc22

ISBN-13: 978-0-7432-9909-1
ISBN-10: 0-7432-9909-4

for Barbara Schrefer

better than any mother this writer

could imagine

PART ONE

HUMPHREY

PART TWO

GRETCHEN

PART THREE

HUMPHREY & GRETCHEN

PART ONE

HUMPHREY

1

By the age of fifteen I've taught myself the essentials: how to walk cool, how to shave, and how to masturbate. The first involves spacing your feet wide and looking like you're about to fall sideways; the second, starting with your sideburns and proceeding with downward strokes; the third, the efficient application of saliva.

And yet, despite these skills, I have a number of strikes against me:

—My name is Humphrey.

—I'm overweight, with a lame haircut.

—I'm the new kid.

No one knows dread like the new kid. No matter how friendly we may try to be, we're none of us easy to talk to. We're all either snobs or assholes, because we're scared as shit.

Summer school won't start for a while, so all I do for the first two weeks of June is swim in the pool at the crappy motel my family has moved into. At first it's all bright fun, games of king of the dolphins with the girl with the wet band-aids from room 10. Then she leaves so I float lizards on leaf boats, collect the curled husks of drowned centipedes, or, finally, just stand for hours at the shallow end, my arms hitched over the wet concrete, and stare through the chlorine haze at the low palms at the edge of the parking lot. One day Mom comes home from work and finds me like that, my hair a greenish matted mess, both dry and wet like pool-hair gets, my shoulders peeling, and that's the day she throws her hands up and says I'm not contributing anything to the family and I call her a bitch and she says I'm ungrateful and moody so I wander off and come home late that night. She rubs my back and says she's sorry and I say I'll apply for a job the next day. I guess I'm ready to do something else. What I really hope is that I'll make a friend at work, at least one friend, so I'll know someone when I arrive at summer school.

The woman who interviews me is named La Toya, and she seems nice but doesn't say much, so I lead the way and tell her about how I worked at the supermarket back in Fresno. She chuckles when I ask if she wants references. I start the next day. My pay is $5.15 an hour, which means I can buy a new video game every couple of shifts. She makes me a bagger, but tells me that I could train on the registers and become a cashier in a few weeks. That comes with an automatic ten-cent raise.

My first few nights I'm bagging for Bernice. She pretty much ignores me (everyone at Food Festival does; I'm not really loud and also I'm white), but I really like her, because she talks back to the after-work assholes in suits, smiling the whole time, tapping her fake nails on the corner of her lips.

Even though the other baggers and cashiers live near me, they're mostly in their late teens, and moms, so I don't make any friends. I bet Bernice might hang out with me if we started talking, but we haven't yet.

I wish I could capture the moment for you, what it was like when they walked in. I was wearing the uniform: a red plaid button-down, black jeans, black apron, black Velcro sneakers that I bought down the street from my old school in California. Bernice was scanning a mound of tortilla packages for a couple of Mexican dudes. The air conditioner had just snapped off, so the fluorescent lights were brighter than usual, and they made the edges of everything sharp. I had just got back from asking the front end for a carton of Winston Lights for Michelle's customer on 2. Bernice slid the last plastic package down and placed the dudes' tomatoes on the greasy aluminum scale. She punched `5 8 9 [scale] [code]` and handed them to me.

So. `5 8 9 [scale] [code]` and the receipt printer's whirring and they come in. High school kids. The girl comes first. She's got one of those careless-yet-worked-on ponytails that hot girls wear—you know, where the hair has probably been blow-dried because it's perfectly straight and flying above her head, full inches higher than her scalp, and the tail fans out like the wash from some department-store fountain. She's got this tight army-green T-shirt with a little pocket over a nipple—no bra, I think—and this pair of khaki shorts that flare over her tan legs, and she's wearing flip-flops that are soft brown leather. I don't think I'm an expert on this kind of thing, but she's definitely pretty well-off, a lot richer than this neighborhood, for sure. She sails right past the bread aisle with this purposeful expression, looking like most dumb people do when they have something on their mind, like she's balancing all the troubles of the world on the down of her upper lip, and the solution to it all is somewhere at the back of the store.

He comes in after, but he's totally different. She's all directed, like she's on an errand that someone has the car idling outside for, but he comes in pissed and reluctant. The automatic doors have already half-closed and opened again before he makes it inside.

Hot air must have blasted in when the girl entered, too, but because of some chaos of wind currents in the rafters, I only feel a wave of wet heat when the guy enters. He's got Vans on (like he's a skater! like he's from California!), and these baggy pants that make it look like there's some other pair of pants inside trying to get out. He's also wearing—and this is what makes me think he might be a nice kid—a yellow tank top. I mean, what guy wears yellow? He's got these defined arms, so he's clearly got some social capital, but at the same time, I figure a guy who wears yellow has got to be kind, right? He doesn't seem really friendly, though. He scowls and saunters into the Food Festival like it's a pool hall. He's wearing a baseball hat, but the hair sticking out in the back is crusted with beach. He's got this small and intense expression that might mean he owns a shotgun. He disappears down the wine aisle, after the girl.

If I could be friends with them, it would be perfect.

I look down at the scored metal of the checkout. I could be as popular as he. If only I weren't wearing a plaid shirt embroidered with "Food Festival." If only I had gotten around to losing those twenty pounds. If only I weren't earning minimum wage at a supermarket.

"Hey, Bernice," I say. "Do you have any go-backs?"

She has been picking price-tag goo from beneath a lacquered nail. "Um," she drawls as she scans the shelves beneath the register. She holds up a box of tea like it's an artifact. "Yeah, I got this."

I take the box and head toward the aisles before La Toya can stop me.

I take the middle row and sweep the store, glancing left and right, just like when I was a kid and would lose my mom. Unless my potential friends happen to be passing an end cap, I'm sure to spot them. 4AB, jams and spices, no; 5AB, toothpaste, no; 6AB, paper goods, no; 7AB, cake mixes, no; 8AB, soft drinks, no; 9AB, cereals, toys, no; 10AB, frozen foods, no—or yes. They're in the dairy section, at the end of the frozen foods.

It has always been the most untamed section of the grocery store. The pastel purple gives way to stark whites and silvers; puffs of cold vapor make the whole area an arctic passage. And at the end of the aisle, leaning against the grill where the white and purple of the 1 percent shifts to the white and blue of the skim, they are making out.

He has her pressed past the half-gallons and into the gallons, her ass pushing so deeply into the containers that they seem to be fleeing her. His half-thrusts have pushed the plastic sliding tags over, so the milk prices are bunched at the yogurt. Her legs are spread around his hips, and her shorts are short enough that from my angle it looks like she's not wearing any at all.

Her eyes are closed—the rule of teenage kissing—and he's not facing me, so I can watch them in privacy. He's got her neck between his hands, and the frayed bill of his cap cradles the top of her head. He's going after her with such animal intensity that I feel anxious for the girl—if she's even a little bit not into him, she has to be really uncomfortable. But by all evidence, she's into him. I stare at the spot where the denim of his jeans presses against the smooth skin of her thigh, and then walk away. I have a box of tea in my hand, after all, so there is something to be done.

As I pass back down the cereal aisle, though, I wonder why they have come into the store. They lost no time getting to the milk section. Why head straight to Dairy and go at it? By the time I reach Produce I think I've got it figured out: summer break is weird like that. You slam against the emptiness of the suburb, and in order to relieve yourself of the boredom of hanging with your girl and yet remain into her you come up with challenges, ways to break the deadening feeling. Maybe getting it on in public places was the best solution this guy could come up with.

I've never had a girlfriend. Well, I had a couple back in California, but all we did was hold hands in the hallways and go to the mall after school. We made out a bunch and one girl gave me a blowjob but she had braces and it hurt. I can't help but feel that whatever I did with those girls is lily-white compared to what's going on in the dairy section. I wonder if this is what Florida will be like, all girlfriends and intense making out. I hope not. Hooking up was fun sometimes but usually I found it kind of boring, like playing a chess game by following the moves written down in some book. And when the ultimate thing turns out to be boring, it's really depressing. I put the tea back and return to Bernice.

I can see straight to the front as a couple more kids arrive. The door slides open, and in the wavering space of hot air outside the store I see their pickup idling. They have the yellow-tank-top boy's coolness but not his hotness. Their hats are at the same angle as his. They have sulky what-the-hell expressions on, like they're pissed off but not ready to fight about it, and they storm toward the back. I slot myself behind Bernice, fit another tab of plastic bags on the dispenser.

I know La Toya sees them come in. She's leaning against the front counter, with her ass out and both elbows on the ledge, the pose she always takes when she's at the end of her shift and wants to rest her tits, but she's got this preoccupied face on, like *why does this shit always have to happen on my watch?* She takes the public-address phone in her hand, presses the little button. She stares at me the whole time; I'm only a yard away. "Humphrey to Dairy, please. Humphrey to Dairy."

She's looking at me with one slick plucked line of an eyebrow raised: *That's right, boy.* She knows the power of loudspeakers on a kid; I can't say no. I angrily head to the back of the store. What the hell am I supposed to do? I'm fifteen.

I'm not dragging my feet, not exactly, but I'm definitely taking my time. I imagine that the hot kids will still be making out, that the two roughs will be hanging in front of the shredded cheese and watching. But that's not the case. They're all standing in a circle, the three guys and the girl. She's obviously peeved that she's sharing her boyfriend—she's toying with her flip-flop, letting it clap to the floor. The guys—and here's where I become intensely aware of my own name badge and uniform, my official position—have opened a carton of milk and are passing it around like a bong.

Their gulps are so carefree, so manly, that they could as easily be three frat brothers in front of the house fridge. But they're in a *grocery store.* I stand there, stunned by the impossibility of drinking milk in the store. One of the guys spots me. He's pale and beefy.

"What the fuck do you want?" Pale Beef says.

Anything I could say would put me in the straight-laced loser role, so I don't say anything.

"Are we in *trouble*?" Pale Beef asks. The guy in the yellow tank turns down the carton when it comes back to him.

"We're not in trouble, right?" the other guy says. He's wearing a tribal necklace. There's a touch of nervousness in his voice.

I smile. It does seem weird that they'd be in trouble. They are, after all, drinking *milk.* "No, I don't think so," I say. "I'm just supposed to check up on you guys. You know, store security, all teenagers are thieves, that sort of thing."

The girl tucks her hand around Yellow Tank's waist. He's smiling at me, and that makes me feel a little more sure.

"Are you callin' us thieves?" Tribal Necklace asks. His eyes are wide and his mouth is firm. He's not stupid. But he's mean and bored.

"No, of course not." I'm starting to get mad, too, because I want friends, dammit, and I was being funny and confident, and this fool won't let up.

Pale Beef moves toward me. "He's acting like we weren't going to pay for it."

"No, I'm cool," I say.

He takes another step closer. The girl is ignoring me, staring into Yellow Tank's shoulder, and he's smiling a little but not doing anything to stop the guys.

"There doesn't have to be a problem here," I say. "Make sure you pay for the milk, that's all."

Now the guys are near me and I'm pressed against a door of the frozen section. My hand grips a pizza sale sign.

I've been bullied before—back in Michigan I used to get shoved around at recess, until I hit my growth spurt—and I'm used to the routine: a few stupid words, then a push and nothing more as long as I haven't lashed back. But these guys are pressing into me, and the bigger one, as cleanly as if it's a dance move, takes my head in his hands and slams it into the freezer door. His palms slapped on my ears, and I'm so shocked by the noise of my head against the door that I just stare back. It's like I can't hear anything, like I'm stuck somewhere within the glossy unreality of a television screen.

My nose is bleeding—how did that happen if he slammed the back of my head?—and I dab at my bloody shirt with one hand and plug my nostrils with the other and yell at the kid, "What the hell do you think you're doing," then I see he's got his hand back like to punch me so I swing around with my foot out. I kick him in the thigh and he falls back a little, but his friend grabs my foot and suddenly I'm on the ground with my leg twisted in his hands and I'm yelling and he's yelling, and the girl's like, Let's get out of here, okay? and they're all heading out, but not before the guy in the yellow tank holds out his hand and helps me to my feet and maybe even says he's sorry, I still can't hear anything. I've kind of teleported away and watch them leave from a distance, both hands on my nose because it's bleeding more now.

I go back to the front and La Toya asks what the hell happened and I tell her and she gets some ice from the deli department because apparently I'm going to get a black eye even though I don't remember being punched. She couldn't be more sorry for not going back there herself, and if she ever sees those kids again she doesn't know what she'll do and she lets me off early, without even having to clock out, and drives me home. She's being motherly, which is exactly what I want, and she's a lot more concerned than my own mother would be, though maybe she's just worried my parents are going to call corporate. I tell her I'm fine, and I do feel fine except for the crust of blood on my nose . . . except that summer school starts in a week, except that instead of having friends I might have a couple of full-on enemies.

I have La Toya let me off before we get to my block because I live in a motel and that's embarrassing. I must be disoriented because I've told her to let me out blocks away. I walk beneath the power pylons, on the sidewalk covered in dirt and sharp palm fronds. I've been the new kid all my life and I promise myself that this will be the last time. If I have to run away and rent my own place, then fine. My half-sister ran away, after all, and it worked out for her.

Places I've lived: Duluth, Detroit, Coeur d'Alene, somewhere else in Coeur d'Alene, some suburb of Vegas, Fresno, and now Haven Township, Florida. We got here at night. I sat wedged in the backseat of the minivan in the middle of my stuff, my eyes closed, the streetlights of the interstate regularly flashing my eyelids purple, my dog Citrus licking Doritos dust from my fingers, and I imagined what it would look like in the day.

I figured everyone lived on the beach, came home to high-rise hotels or huts along the water with sand between their toes and turquoise bathing suits under their work clothes. But you know what?

People who live here don't go to the beach; they drive around and shop or stay home and watch television. All the stores are new. No homeless, no corner tobacco shop, no dilapidated anything. Target and Starbucks and T.J. Maxx. With so much sun-bleached concrete the heat and light hit the ground and stay there, and we all walk around like we're being pressed down by some heavy, luminous gas. When we first arrived and I opened the car door and stepped into the parking lot, even though it was midnight the air struck me like a hot wave. We're all sluggish and unmysterious here.

My parents didn't have any money for a deposit to rent our own place, so Dad worked out some deal with a motel. It was June, so he got a cheap rate. We could stay six months for "practically nothing" and pay by the week. Mom didn't agree that the motel cost "practically nothing" and she was mad that she'd have to ask for a transfer to a Florida Arby's after all. She had started working at one of their California restaurants when Dad started losing jobs. She was a manager or something important like that but did sixty hours a week and hated it—always came home smelling like urinals and whatever grease they put on the bread.

I always wondered why rich people didn't live in motels instead of in houses—there's no clutter, there's a little fridge with food in it, someone else *makes your bed.* But actually it isn't that awesome. Sure, it was cool at first—there's a pool, and at night no one even notices if I bring Citrus swimming—but when the motel became home, it began to suck. The bedspreads smell bad. The tables are smooth on top but rough as broken plywood where your knees go. The kitchen only has a coffee maker and not much else. I eat my cereal out of a coffee pot because we couldn't fit our dishes in the van. The first time I poured my corn flakes up to the 2-cups line it felt weird, and after that just plain bad. Then Dad finally stopped watching TV and unpacked all of his stuff. He programs elevators, and he's got so many motherboards and other sharp green cards covering the industrial carpet that to make my way across the room I have to jump from bed to bed.

My mom's home and although I wiped away the crusty blood and took off my work shirt apparently my eye's already black because she asks me what the hell happened to you. I tell her that I was beat up on the way back from work because made-up bullying is less embarrassing than real bullying. She lets me off picking up dinner, even though it's my turn. I go to bed early and hang out with Citrus and play a video game at the foot of my cot in the walk-in closet and listen to her yell at my father that he's the one who made them live in this shitty neighborhood so what does he expect?

2

Finding a seat on the school bus. This is impending doom.

First day of summer school. One fifteen-year-old named Humphrey (how I wish my mom had never watched *Casablanca*!), now only a few pounds overweight, and with a better haircut, or at least a less conspicuous one. One black eye that has almost faded. One bus stop along an oily side road.

I moved every two years while growing up (no, my dad didn't work for the military; he just wasn't ever any good at his job), and so I have the first-day thing down. But it still unnerves me. Waiting at the bus stop can't be too bad, I tell myself. No one's going to pick on you or make any important social decisions because it's seven in the morning and no one's awake enough to do anything but stare at the asphalt. This girl, probably pretty popular, is picking at a scab on her ankle. Some guy, probably not popular at all, is chafing his apple against the curb, trying to flay off the skin. I open my bag and check out the five crisp, bright folders. I don't have any reason to open my backpack, but I want to do something other than continue making myself nervous. I give myself an intense expression in case anyone else is looking, as if something vital is being broadcast inside the bag.

Adults can be alone when they really want to be. They can drive themselves to work. They can eat their lunch by themselves. They can decide to stay home all day. But teenagers are forced to enter enemy space. By law, we have to go to school. By law, we have to share bus seats and face one another down at the lunch table. I'm slow to get my backpack on so that I will be last onto the bus, because getting landed with a bad seat is infinitely preferable to taking a seat that someone more established wants. The driver presses a silver button to swing a lever to open the door, which makes the whole boarding operation seem industrial, like I'm entering a slaughterhouse through the animal entrance. I stare at the steel trim behind the driver and give him the standard teenage-boy smile, the slight clenching of the corners of my lips, in case he expects me to acknowledge him. He slides the door closed, hands me some form, and then I venture a glance down the ribbed rubber aisle.

And there it is, the immediate decision: the driver has closed the door, and he can't move until I find a seat. The hardest challenges of school are these split-second ones. Academic tests, no matter how important, can be completed over a number of minutes. But this is the toughest exam all year, and I have only a few seconds for it.

I first scan for a seat that is totally empty, but there are no such seats. The back of the bus, of course, is completely occupied—there's even a pair of girls bobbing on guys' laps. The front of the bus is filled in equal parts with the freshmen and the eager, everyone from the unpopular to the half-popular. I'm left with the middle section. Only two spots are open: I can sit next to a guy snoozing in a weathered Billabong T-shirt, his leg covering the rest of the seat, or with the girl across from him, who is staring angrily out the window, her new lavender backpack propped too neatly next to her. I make my way down the aisle, practicing my cool walk. My plan: by the time I get to their row, one of them has to flinch, move either leg or backpack.

While I am still two rows ahead, the girl reaches for her bag. But she just leaves her hand on it, as if for security. The Billabong guy does nothing, and since the girl is actively against my sitting next to her, I choose to go with him. Apparently he is authentically dozing, because when I nudge his leg he doesn't move. An adult would have said "Excuse me," but for a high schooler that shows deference, and deference is doom. I just sit down on the triangle of vinyl left to me.

The crappier parts of Haven Township are near the high school, so my trip is short. I grip the handle of my backpack (Invicta, cool in California but apparently not cool in Florida; JanSport still rules here) as if it's an anchor and as we ride I wonder where my homeroom classroom will be.

The scene earlier this morning: me at the desk/table, eating my cereal and inspecting my folders. Dad's still asleep, snoring heavily a foot away, Mom is taking her mug of coffee into the bathroom—she's late. I'm nervous so I'm aware of the texture of the cereal but not the taste. "I'm off to summer school," I say as I rinse the coffee pot in the sink. "It's my first day."

"Oh, honey," my mom calls over the running water, "good luck!" Mom was working hard last week, so we didn't get a chance to check out the school.

Dad used to be something called a contractor, but since we lived in a town that was "full of the suckers," his contracting stopped, which I think means he got fired, and we had to move. Mom pitched a fit, of course. She was making dinner at the time and threw a bunch of celery across the kitchen. It hit Dad in the face but he just took the abuse, because "What are we going to do, stay in California and starve?" so he chose a state that he thought wouldn't already have a load of computer experts. It was Florida.

Moving is really expensive. We didn't have that much money to start with, we didn't own our own house or anything, "we were renting life," as my mom often said with her sad smile, so I don't know where they found the money. We didn't get a truck, we just drove in the old Aerostar, which means we didn't take any furniture. We removed the far backseat and left it in California. I got the space above one of the rear wheels for all my stuff. All I had were a couple of suitcases, a duffel bag, my computer, and Citrus. He's awesome.

We moved as soon as my freshman year ended. One hour I was sitting in American history, watching *Good Morning, Vietnam* and eating candy with my friends. Then the next I was sitting in the backseat with Citrus on my lap, my dad edging the van onto the interstate ramp, scanning up and down the highway and sweating at his temples. I was ticked that I couldn't chill with my friends for even one day, but I didn't say anything because Mom and Dad were already really pissy, and I knew it would be best to put my headphones on and hang out in back with Citrus.

I only really turned my music off to tell my dad that Citrus had to pee. I *get* my dog. Once there's enough urine in his bladder his nose twitches, even if he's asleep. The little guy's on a roughly three-and-a-half-hour schedule between intake and peeing, which in the big western states meant every fifteen exits or so. I counted because, really, what else was I going to do?

Poor dad, he's huge and so he kept squirming in the bucket seat of the van, and so we had to stop all the time to stretch his back. My mom got huffy about the delays. I can still see her, hurled back in her seat like a bad kid in a boring class, her hands wedged in her hair like the plastic combs in Bernice's 'fro, staring out the window at a gas station in Oklahoma, Missouri, Georgia. She's always made it clear that she was meant for something better. One time my dad left the parking brake on near Tallahassee, and these big plumes of blue smoke came out of the van on I-75 and we had to stop for a few hours so it could cool down. She crossed her arms and leaned against the hood and then hit Dad once, hard, when he came back from taking Citrus to sniff out a patch of grass. He was mad but he didn't hit her back or anything, he just accepted the slap. They stood and stared at each other in the middle of all the fumes and bad smell. Then Mom started crying and my dad hugged her. Why does he take all her shit? There are a lot of complicated reasons, I'm sure, but the basic truth is that she's beautiful and he's really fat, so they both know she's got an advantage. You know how there are these weird points when you realize what your parents are, outside of what they are to you? Like, beyond being strict or distant or whatever, but what the rest of the world sees them as? I realized on my way to Haven Township that it's like my half-sister Gretchen once said—my mom is a bitch and my dad is weak. They just are. I love them, but they are.

When the school bus pulls into the parking lot, it is totally clear that we bus riders are an underclass. The parking lot is full of red and gold and silver SUVs and Ford F-150s and BMWs. The air brakes of the bus squeal. Since I don't really have any seat to get up from I'm already halfway in the aisle. But when I get up I feel this swift kick against my thigh and spin around. The Billabong kid is reclining on the seat, still in the same pose, only now his eyes are open and beaming fire. "Don't ever sit next to me again," he mutters. "Faggot."

I walk off. The kids are bunching up behind me; what else can I do? But if only I wasn't new, if only I had established myself somewhere in the ranks. I could lash out at that kid. He isn't that much bigger than me. And *he* was the one who dug his foot into *my* leg, practically my butt. Who was acting like a faggot? The thought does cross my mind—do I look gay? Black boots, camouflage shirt held together with safety pins—that doesn't fly in Florida? I pause before the smudgy double doors of the school entrance. Of course. Haven

Township is too close to the beach. Surfer is the look here, not skater. It will take weeks to recover from looking weird on the first day. Unless I carry it confidently. Acting sure of myself is my best hope. I throw open the doors and slam my way inside, as if barreling backstage after a rock show.

My class for the first half of the summer is *Care and Prevention of Athletic Injuries*, which is what they call health here. It makes me nervous, like maybe everyone in Haven has to either play football or tend to football players. Everyone in Florida took the course in ninth grade, which is why I have to take summer school with all the failures.

Haven Township High is one central concourse surrounded by a dozen spokes, like a squashed concrete bug. My classroom's at the end of one spoke. I arrive there early, since stalking through the halls is the best way to avoid revealing that you don't know anyone. I just have to make it through the day, I remind myself as I open the door. My old English teacher had a cheesy poster like that, a kitten trying to get onto a branch One Day at a Time.

M. Torino of my schedule, Coach Torino, is a nearly bald man with the sweet and blank face of a slow child, and is disinfecting a dummy when I enter. It sighs mechanically as he swabs its lips. I pick a desk halfway down against one wall. I will be conspicuously invisible. When the coach smiles at me, I nod back, fractionally. I'm desperate to smile back at him, to feel the shared warmth, but I'm not sure yet if teens here are supposed to smile at teachers.

The other kids file in, mostly in twos and threes. I concentrate on those who enter singly, because they're easier targets for friendship. But those kids who aren't already attached to friends don't sit near me, or near one another, for that matter. We've all decided it's safer to be hermits, I guess. Only the popular can assume that someone else would want to sit next to them.

The bell rings and the coach hands out assignment lists and a floppy textbook. I take bored jabs at the book with my pencil, feigning important thoughts, as though there is a party somewhere where I would much rather be. The coach is one of those Teacher teachers who believe in building suspense and selling students on the course. He announces that this very day! This very period! We will! Cure an injury!

Only one kid looks excited, and it's not me.

Apparently we are to splint legs. Not our own legs, someone else's. My breath catches. Group work, the bane of new students. Hopefully he'll assign us partners.

No such luck. He asks us to pair ourselves off.

The class is suddenly on its feet. All the students, even those who regularly flunk math, are suddenly doing massive calculations, determining rank, how high they can reach, who will be the safety choice if the reach target doesn't pan out. I spend too long doing my calculations, and soon everyone else is paired off. I'm left standing at the side of my desk, looking like I'm the lamest kid in the room. *But it's just because I'm new!* I want to say. *I promise.*

The coach looks at me concernedly. "It looks like you're without a partner. What's your name, son?"

"Humphrey."

The class is silent. My name is weird, but apparently not weird enough for them to tease right away. Coach Torino pats the table. "Okay, Humphrey. You can be my demonstration buddy. Come on up to the front."

"You want me to sit on *there*?" I ask. Someone snickers.

"Yes sir, come on up."

I sit on the edge of the table. I feel like I'm on a gurney, waiting to be inspected by the doctor. All that's missing are the crinkly paper and the exposed testicles.

Coach Torino tugs on my legs. "No, up up."

The coach arranges me on the table. I'm flat on my back, my boots against the tabletop and knees in the air. He tells me to take off one shoe and sock. When did I last cut my toenails? I take off a boot and a sock, then realize that all the cool kids are wearing flip-flops. My feet are pink and corrugated from the pressure of my socks. Definitely not tan and sandy. I look at the coach, who is holding up the textbook and spouting off about something. I turn my head toward the class. Even though I'm lying down, because of the table I'm at their eye level. And suddenly it strikes me—being supine on the table, immobile and stared at like a buffet, makes me really horny. I turn my head back so I stare at the cracked surface of the ceiling panels, try to quell the rising in my pants by scouring for patterns.

The door opens, and in walks the yellow-tank-top guy from Food Festival. What he's doing in a freshman class, who knows. Probably failed a couple of times already. "You're late," the coach says, with that resigned yet deeply scared tone teachers take on with bad kids.

The guy crosses to the back of the room and sits next to a kid who, I realize with shock, is Pale Beef, the one who slammed my head into the freezer. "What are we doing?" Yellow Tank whispers loudly to the kid. It's a smart move—he hasn't openly disrespected the teacher, but he gains points for turning to his friend for info instead of the authority figure. For a few seconds all the attention in the class is directed on him.

"Wade," the coach says. Wade. The yellow-tank guy's name is Wade. "Come on up to the front. I have a partner for you."

Suddenly Wade's attention is on me. I find it impossible not to squirm. I swallow my spit, straighten my shirt. Lying flat on my back, my head turned against the cool slate, looking at this potentially violent stranger, is tripping me out.

"I'll work with Wade," Pale Beef volunteers.

"You've already got a partner," the coach says. "What do you want to work with Wade so much for, anyway?" The class titters. This teacher isn't weaponless, after all; he knows how to play our game.

Pale Beef relents. He's not as bad-ass as he might seem to be.

"What do you mean, you've got a partner for me?" Wade asks. He has this slow but deliberate way of speaking, like he's confident but not intelligent, his power entirely outside schoolwork.

"You're working with Humphrey," the coach says. "Come on, get up here."

I hear Wade shuffle across the industrial tile. He's got the equivalent of a zombie's lope—sluggish, impressive, and, to the sacrificial new kid on the table, scary as hell. I stare at the ceiling. I'm kind of shutting myself off, like I'm in the doctor's office. This is happening to my body, not to *me*.

He's at the front of the room. I tap my fingers against the slate.

"So what do I have to do?" Wade asks.

"Take his ankle in your hands."

"For real?"

"Yes."

I don't look down when Wade takes me in his hands. My ankle is slender and lost in his callused grip. He holds it firmly but disdainfully in one hand. "Now what?" he asks.

"You need to move him so that the leg and foot are in a normal position."

"What's normal?"

I lift my head. "Normal. Like straight up," I say. Some girl at the front laughs. I lay my head back down.

Wade has his other hand on my foot, now. He's intimidated by teachers, I can see—he looks to me beseechingly, almost, as if hoping I'll keep telling him what to do. I shift my foot from side to side in his grasp and then bring it down in what seems a neutral position.

"So what's next?" Wade asks. He's got this little spark in him, like he's getting into it. I like him, I decide. Even though he stood there while his friends were beating me up, even though he acts like an asshole, I can tell he's really not. This childlike gleam, this unembarrassed excitement I glimpse inside him, is really cool. I also like that he has kept his hand on the top of my foot while the coach is giving the directions for the next step. I look down at his hand, this proof that he thinks I'm okay enough to touch. His tan is peeling at the bases of his fingers. His nails are recessed where he's been biting them. He's got a silver ring on his thumb and a couple of pieces of fluorescent nylon cord as bracelets. There's a rawboned look to his hands, as though he's been scrambling up mounds of dirt or searching beneath paving stones. His fingers rest on the thick veins that rib the top of my foot. When I flex my foot, just a little bit, his middle finger falls so that it's resting on the smooth white middle plane between my tendons.

As he binds my "broken" ankle to the good one using a rag, I absently press my big toe against the dirty plastic of the sole of my booted foot. It feels obscurely unlawful to touch the bottom of my shoe with my bare foot in front of so many people. It's like I'm stretching the limits of logic, like I'm bringing together two objects that some physical law says can't come into contact. Like something's going to touch that never should have, and then something crazy'll happen.

The class gives a couple claps for me and Wade when we finish and I go back to my seat and stare at my notebook for a while until I feel like a normal member of the class again. I watch two girls do the same splint, then two guys again, and then a guy and a girl.

The rest of the day is a typical first day for a new kid. I eat lunch alone between two banks of lockers, suffer through the end-of-the-day anticipation of the final bell, and then go home, watch a cartoon because it's like being ten again, then cry a little and take Citrus for a walk. We wander for a long time, because no one's home and I don't want to hang around computer parts for hours. There's a huddle of palm trees in a Chick-fil-A parking lot and Citrus and I take a break there. When I sit down my pant leg rides up and I stare at my ankle, there where it lies in the sand and grass.

3

Wade's mom! How random.

We're both staring at Wade as he stretches for gym class. She's by her car on the other side of the fence and I'm next to the tetherball pole and he's between us, the sun backlighting his ripped T-shirt and outlining the frame beneath, dappling his body. They say she's got some court order against her. That's what I hear. All I know for sure is that she's not supposed to see him, and that she's hot. I'm supposed to be touching my toes, but I can only really get partway, so I'm bent over watching her, seeing her and him framed by my thighs. Bounce, bounce, stare.

She's wearing the work uniform for some cheesy kids' restaurant, and the orange rayon has gone wet and caked at her armpits. She plucks the fabric away from her skin. You can almost feel the breath of Florida air when her shirt snaps back. I watch her flat-out spying on him. She's not built for being sneaky—she's too tall, and her hair is really large. She slinks down the side of the car.

Wade himself, well, he's standing relaxed and unstudied, as if gym class might actually be a parking-lot party on Friday night. He's with the most important kids, the rude but outgoing boys, in board shorts and T-shirts gone yellow. They're making fun of each classmate in turn and scanning one another with admiring eyes. I, of course, am standing by myself, practically with the girls.

Wade looks like he could be the gym teacher; he's impossibly large. He is a demigod of high school, a broad-framed, alert *man* who would intimidate anyone's dad. He already towers over us—another year and he won't look like a high schooler at all. His shorts reveal rippling masses of muscle, and the tan and black down of his tree calves. He has a chest and arms. None of the rest of us guys do. Pale Beef and Tribal Necklace know this—they've positioned Wade as their center.

I wonder if Wade's mom has come by the school because he's already failing summer school. Word is he hasn't gone to elementary Spanish even once yet, now or any of the four years he's been here.

She rotates her wrist absently. There's a catch in the motion, a wince on her face, and I notice an Ace bandage. Maybe she's out sick from work. That's what makes me pretty sure she's his mom, because of course—what would a mom do with free time but come check up on her son?

Class starts and the coach makes us sit down. The sun has broiled the tar of the parking lot, heat rising in waves. It feels like when you get up the wet hot blackness will still be on you.

I watch Wade's mom watch Wade as the coach takes roll. I try to see what she sees: his old Converse are unlaced and his arms are crossed; he looks like we all do, like he is trapped in the first instant after waking from a pleasant and preferable nap. His only expression has been to give a few of those almost-silent smug laughs that all of us teenage boys know, that one violent rise and fall of the shoulders; he only listens to other kids' stories, never contributes his own. The girls—those who are secure enough, at least—have formed an impromptu semicircle around his inner ring of boys.

A triangle of sweat marks the hollow of Wade's chest, and his thick eyebrows glisten. He gets to his feet, absently cuffs a friend on the shoulder. The coach went back inside without ever telling us why; where are the "team sports" of the course title? So much of high school is this—doing nothing—only this time it feels weird, because someone from the outside is here to witness it.

Every one of the girls, even the nerds and the fatties, has rolled down the waistband of her shorts to expose her hip bones. So many of them are sexy; not pretty but porn-sexy, with skinny arms that make any breasts look huge. Everyone knows, even if they'll never say so, that fifteen-year-old girls are hot. I see Wade's mom look at them and then slide a hand over the mass of her own dandelion hair, rub the muscles of her neck. She looks nervous for Wade's well-being among the hotties. What of her son, she's probably thinking, who only a few years ago traded game cards and watched cartoons but is heavy-limbed and glowers, and looks like, well, sex? What danger awaits such a body owned by a kid?

An old lady walks by, pushing a beaten-up grocery cart full of soda cans, and fixes Wade's mom with a suspicious look. Wade's mom gives her a look back that says *you're the bitch pushing a grocery cart along a high school* and flicks her off.

The period bell rings, which immediately causes a pang of anxiety to rise in me. I hate bells and passing periods, those times when everyone's jumbled and you can't avoid the kids who spit in your hair or try to trip you. Some of the nerdier girls cry out—where's the coach? He left us no time to change! Wade lingers, and therefore so do his admirers. We stand nervously, waiting for his lead. Then some quiet charge passes from him to the rest of our herd and we lumber toward the building.

I see Wade's mom get caught in the turning of the moment. She slips through a gash in the fence and steps toward him. But our group is almost at the door.

"Wade!" she calls.

He keeps moving. Maybe he just didn't hear her; he wasn't necessarily ignoring her—being unaware is, after all, what makes him cool.

"Hey," says a girl with an expensively ripped shirt and tan abdomen. "Wade, there's some lady calling for you."

All the boys, of course, stop on the word *lady* and turn. The girls twist more warily, flank Wade like lionesses. Wade is expressionless.

The hostility of the girls flusters Wade's mom. I see her falter—the girls aren't putting up the cold walls children put up for parents, but rather the hot barbs shown to a rival.

"Wade," she calls again. She jangles her car keys, as if to announce that she is there on important maternal business.

"That's his mom, guys," one of the girls announces.

For a moment his mother is facing us all down, a foreign champion. We are all charged for battle, but then Wade takes a step toward her. The moment breaks, and the girls lead the retreat for the doors. We boys follow more slowly. Pale Beef and Tribal Necklace stare over their shoulders and whisper. Even in her work uniform Wade's mom is a "hot mom," and we all know it. The name we whisper is Brandy.

I engineer it so I'm the last to go inside.

"What are you doing here?" Wade asks her.

"Hey, honey," Brandy says.

"I have to go to class. What are you doing here?"

"You only have one class left? It's almost the end of the day?"

A shadow passes over Wade's face. The shadow is: *you're not supposed to be here.* But he would never say *you're not supposed to* about anything: his popularity is rooted in not supposed to. "Yeah," he says.

"I was going to buy you something. Like an ice cream or something."

He appraises her, slides his lower lip between his teeth. He leans on the outside of his foot. "I'm still in my gym clothes. I don't have my books and stuff."

"Oh, come on. Just come. Don't be lame—I'm taking you out!" She looks cheap and desperate, heartbroken and unmotherly, and I feel really bad for her.

Wade runs one leg behind the other, scratches at a fire-ant bite on his calf, and a bright splash of pink gum flashes from the sole of his shoe. For a second he looks like a child. But the foot falls and he is a man again. "Yeah, let's go."

"There! You can get your homework from your friends."

"I think you have to sign me out or something."

Everyone else has gone inside. I'm tying my shoe to buy time, the door closing against my back—I look ridiculous. But Brandy and Wade don't notice.

Brandy snorts. "I don't need to sign you out. I'm your *mom.*"

"No, I'll be marked absent. You really do. One more absent and I'm screwed."

Brandy stamps a foot and scowls in mock outrage. Going to the principal is going to the principal, at any age, and she clearly doesn't want to do it.

"Mom! Are you taking me, or what?"

"Yeah, let's go. Can't believe I have to sign out my own damn kid." She was totally about to say *fucking kid.*

I go inside and the door closes behind me.

The air is still, as the next class period has just started and bathroom passes have not yet been issued. I pass the lockers mounted three high along the wide central hallway, the cinder-block walls slathered in waxy flesh-colored paint, the maroon industrial carpet as damp as moss. I am alone in the school, even though it is full of people. My skin tingles at the thought.

Brandy is standing at the entrance of the school when the end-of-the-day bell rings. I step to one side when I see her. She's immobile in the flood of shouts and backpacks, momentarily stricken as the mass parts around her. The kids pay her no mind, nor she them.

No Wade. She got ditched. I wonder how it came down.

The crowd thins. Here are the stragglers, those last to emerge, the band nerds and drama geeks, the girls with sticker-covered clarinet cases and boys with buttoned shirts. And me.

"Isn't that the waitress chick from MegaMouse?" one loser mutters. He's the kid I got stuck with at lunch—a frenzied redheaded boy who stripped his sandwich of planks of bologna and sketched intricate war diagrams on notebook paper. Brandy must've heard the comment and looks down at her top, as if she has forgotten she's still in her work uniform. A leering mouse is emblazoned over her breast. I want to beat that kid up for making her feel bad, but he soon passes, and me and Brandy are alone.

She walks to her car and sits behind the wheel as I pretend to search through my bag for a cell phone, which I don't own. She lights a cigarette and rolls down her window, stares dumbly at the empty playing field. The cicadas are buzzing. A sign by the creek reads DO NOT MOLEST THE ALLIGATORS, a famous source of humor at the school.

I wonder what she thinks of me. Me, Humphrey, not a geek and not a cool kid but somewhere in between. Hip jeans but also a cowlick. Maybe she knows me as the sorta interesting-looking kid who watched Wade in gym class. Without the porn-star lionesses to guard us boys, Brandy is bolder—she stares at me as I lope toward her, gauging whether I think she's attractive. I do think she's attractive, so I smile. She smiles, too, but it's half-done and twisted, like she's equally struck through with pride and loathing. I know why: I haven't given her the kind of look given to mothers. But how am I supposed to look at her? I know she's got a court order not to see her kid. She's not really anyone's mother.

She continues to fix me with a lazy stare. I straighten and slow when I approach; I'm jerky, suddenly wound up.

"You smoke?" she asks me, holding out her pack of Pall Malls.

"You looking for Wade?" I ask.

Brandy takes a long drag. "No, I'm not looking for Wade."

I accept the cigarette, something skinny and menthol. I don't smoke usually, but no one has offered me anything in a long time. Brandy pushes in the car's lighter. "It'll be just a sec. Or you can just light off mine," she offers. Her yellow hair has fallen in her face, and she looks sexy.

"I'll hang here for a while, it's cool," I say, standing awkwardly, the unlit cigarette slack in my fingers. "I think Wade left," I say to Brandy. "Like a while ago."

Brandy nods lazily. She has obviously gotten ditched, and is just as obviously pushing her rejection deep inside. "You can sit in here," she offers.

"No, I'm cool." I pause. "It's too hot to sit in a car."

"Suit yourself. Wish I had air-conditioning." She holds out the glowing lighter and I lean forward, the cigarette loose in my lips. I can feel her gaze pass over me as I do. My neck is covered with freckles. I like her attention and arch my back, push out my small chest. I know I'm still gangly but hope I look like a heron: awkward, yes, but lurching and beautiful. I'm wearing a leather bracelet and my fingers are adult, brown and long. When I look at her, Brandy's concentrating on my fingers.

"This is kind of messed, huh?" I say. "Smoking outside a high school."

Brandy laughs. "Yeah. Whatcha up to? Need a ride somewhere?"

I'm nervous, but not scared. I feel like I might be about to sit down for a test. I'm also preparing the story to tell my friends once I have them (*in her thirties, but so hot, like H-O-T. Uh-huh, Wade's mom*). "Yeah, I could use a ride, do you mind?"

Brandy opens the door and I slide in, dropping my backpack between my legs. Brandy stares over at me with a mock-chauffeur expression, a look any dissatisfied mom might give. "Where to, sir?"

I don't want her to see the motel where I really live, so I pick a nearby subdivision. "Weatheridge."

She pulls into the street and whistles. "You've got like one of those huge houses there?"

I pause before I answer, look at the cigarette I've been holding near my lap. I'm fake smoking, just filling my cheeks and letting the fumes float back out. I don't ever want to be the kid who doesn't know how. "Yeah. Not huge. But I guess."

"You shouldn't accept rides from people, you know? They might not all be like me. Moms like me."

I look at her and bounce my hand on her gearshift. "You offered me a cig," I explain.

"You're a friend of Wade's?"

"Yeah, sorta."

"What's your name?"

I smile—I'm nervous, so I know it comes off smug—and take a

long puff. She waits for me to say something but I don't. I don't want Brandy to make fun of my name, so I just shake my head forlornly, as if she wouldn't understand what I'm called, as if nobody would, like it's French or something. I can't help it. I always come off as an asshole when I'm unsure of myself.

"I'm down this street," I say.

The house I choose is gray and imposing and dull. She stops the car and I sit there, waiting for her move. She makes as if to brush my hair out of my eyes but she just holds onto the steering wheel.

"So," I say, my lips slack.

"So!" Brandy says brightly.

"Thanks," I say, suddenly nervous again. I unlatch the door and get out. As I adjust my shirt I can see Brandy's hand still gripping the wheel, tinted blue by the windshield.

"Thanks a lot, see you around," I say.

"Bye, honey," Brandy says. I'm already at the front door. I can't ring the doorbell or anything, of course, so I just stand waiting uncomfortably, like I'm there to sell something. A real mother would wait to make sure some other mother's kid gets inside safely, but thankfully Brandy takes off. She probably doesn't want to be seen on the driveway in a rusty Pontiac, staring after me like she's some pervert.

I put out my cigarette when she leaves and stand in front of that house for a while, the big magazine-spread-looking one I said I lived at. I wonder what it would be like to live there, a life of multiple bathrooms and balconies and beige carpet. I rap the aluminum FOR SALE sign and it rings out down the street. If Brandy noticed it, she didn't say anything.

Since the development is called Weatheridge, I figure Weatheridge Drive must be the way out. I track down the winding street, past the identical homes. Brandy seemed pretty nice, like she really wanted me to like her. And I did, even though she offered me a cigarette, which was weird. I know how hard it had to have been for her, to cross the field to our gym class, to call to Wade in front of all the kids. She's famous among the guys for being fine, and she's famous among the girls for being the bitch who caused all of Wade's shit, all his bad grades and constant detentions. All I know for sure is that she's Wade's mom, and riding home with her will give me something to talk to him about tomorrow.

When I get home I write in my journal. I like it when no one's around because I can hang out on Mom and Dad's bed, and it's a lot of space so I can spread out and jerk off while I watch the cable stations that come in all scrambled but on which I can see glimpses of flesh and at least hear all the voices and moaning. My imagination fills in all the bits I can't make out, which is more of a turn-on than if it came in clear. Anyway, Brandy's made me think about my mom and I write about her, mostly how she's not around much and I miss her but then when she's around she's totally too much, like eager for me to tell her all these details about my life and treating me like a friend and confiding in me, making me into her husband more than her son.

My mom's an odd case. She used to be an actress, and lived this whole other intense life in New York. But then she met this guy who was intense and an actor, too, and their relationship was messed up so she finally left him, like in the middle of the night, took her baby and everything. She couldn't act anymore because of Gretchen, so she had to get a job fast, and she's been working ever since. If she ever decided to get a career, that would've been something, but she's been doing "temporary" jobs forever. Eventually she married my dad, who was really nice and wouldn't fuck her up like the other guy did.

So my mom always carries herself with this attitude of being better than she seems on paper, you know? She's always grinning slyly, like *if only you knew.*

She really had it in for Gretchen. By the time Gretchen was a teenager they fought all the time. I think Mom held the loss of her acting career against her, thought that if she hadn't had a kid she wouldn't have married Dad and wouldn't have ended up working at Arby's. And then Gretchen became an actress herself, and a much better one, and got a few commercials, so *bam!* She's sort of a minor star, my sister; and my mom saw her as intentionally going after the one thing that would hurt most. I've always been mad at my mom for that, for chasing Gretchen off. She really got me, and when we were hanging out it felt like there was no one else in the world but us. But she was brilliant, like my mom, and that made her sorta crazy. She got a scholarship to go to boarding school and the two just wiped their hands of each other. I only saw Gretchen at Christmas, if that much. She's been better about staying in touch recently, but it's still pretty rare that I get an email from her. Now the only one who's around and constant is Citrus. I love him and all, but he's still a *dog.* I'm writing all of this in my journal. I know my mom reads it (it's in a slightly different position every time I pick it up: one time she left a coffee stain, marking a ring of words brown and warped), so it's like an open letter to her. I even write "Mom read up to here" in the margin so that she'll know I know.

The motel phone rings and I pick it up even though I don't feel like talking, because otherwise that little red siren light will blink all afternoon and that drives me crazy.

"Hello?" I say.

"Hi. I'm calling for Humphrey." It's Wade's mom. She pronounces my name like it's "hum-fry."

"This is me."

"Hi, um . . ." I can tell she's thought of a couple things to say and she's choosing between them; her breathing is too quick to be simply at a loss for words. "You left your backpack in my car. Your phone number's on your schedule."

My eyes dart around the room. Crap. No backpack. "Oh yeah, I guess I did. I'm sorry."

"Don't be sorry, honey." She sounds weirded-out that anyone would apologize to her. "So what do you think we should do?"

I'm at a loss. No adult's asked for my lead before. "Um, I dunno."

"Do you want me to run it over to you?" Of course I can't say yes. She thinks I live in Weatheridge. Besides, I can tell she wants me to say no.

"You don't have to do that," I say. "Maybe I can pick it up from you, or something like that."

"Yeah, okay, that'd be nice," she says.

"Where do you live?"

"Two-one-one Baywood Road. In Harbor Oaks."

"How do I get there? I'm new."

"Oh! Where are you from, honey?"

"Lots of places. California, I guess."

"Oh, how great! My place's off State Road 570. A few blocks before it hits the reservoir."

I think that's pretty near me, actually. I can walk there in half an hour and be back before either of my parents gets home.

There aren't any oaks in Harbor Oaks, and definitely no harbor. It's a decaying older development, full of wet little homes and streets choked with pine needles. Weedy trees lean over the fences. The neighborhood may be made up of real houses instead of motel rooms or trailers but it's still pretty crap. There's all sorts of lawn furniture rusting on porches. Most of the cars are from the early nineties and covered with bird droppings.

I've brought Citrus with me, and I've attached two leashes end to end so he can reach the mailboxes and get excited over other dogs' piss. There's lots of Spanish moss hanging from the trees so the road is spotted with shade. One moment Citrus is blinding white in the afternoon sun, next he's in twilight. He doesn't even notice, but I'm kind of fascinated by him, my shifting dog.

Brandy's house is deep in the subdivision. Me and Citrus start walking up her driveway. I've pulled him close because I don't want Wade's mom to think I'm going to let him poop all over her lawn.

Good thing I did.

We're halfway up the driveway when all of a sudden there's this cloud of snarling fur at my feet, like in a cartoon fight. Something's growling from under a truck and Citrus is yelping and screeching like he's being killed, so I yank him away. He peers up at me, trembling and freaked out, with a little trail of blood on his beard. I pick him up and all I can see is a snapping set of gray jaws coming from beneath the pickup truck. If Citrus had been any closer, he might be dead. I hold him up and examine him. It's just a surface scratch, I think. But he's trembling all over, poor little guy.

Wade's mom is at the front door, pulling her hair behind her head. She's wearing a tank top and shorts. "Oh," she exclaims, rushing over. She's got bare feet, and I stare at them as she runs heedless over clods of dirt and sharp seeds. "I didn't know you were bringing a dog. Carl's got his pitbull tied up under his truck. We call her his bitch. I don't let her in the house."

I nod. I think she's being funny, but she hasn't said anything I can reply to.

"Is he okay?" she asks, standing next to me and stroking Citrus's shivering head. "He's so cute. What's his name?" She's got this mad strong Southern accent.

"Citrus," I say.

She nods blackly like I've told her a riddle and leads me inside. The light in the living room is bright stained with darkness. There's an old yellowed computer in a corner. The couch is green except for oily dark streaks from years of hands and necks. There is no airconditioning, and the whole place seems damp in the Florida air. She runs a hand over the cigarette-burned armrest of the couch. "You should call me Brandy," she says.

I sit down as she goes into the kitchen. The dirty soles of her feet flicker at me. Being alone in the room feels off. I hold Citrus tightly on my lap and stroke him.

"You want somethin' to drink? My housemate, Dee, just bought a bunch of sodas," Brandy calls.

"Um, no, thanks," I say.

"You sure? She won't mind. How 'bout a Coke?"

"No, that's okay."

She comes in with two cans of Diet Coke and sits beside me.

"So you've got my backpack, right?" I say.

"Yes, of course, your backpack." She looks like she's about to get up and get it, but she doesn't. She glances down at the cans in her lap, and hands me one. We open them at the same time and smile at each other when the snapping sounds overlap.

Two hours later and we're watching TV. She can only get two stations to come in, and we settle on the one that comes in better. The antenna keeps slipping so she has to get up to adjust it every few minutes, until I start to do it instead. She smiles a lot the first time; something about my getting up for her really fires her up. But then she gets used to it and stops smiling.

"Will your parents mind that you're here?" she asks during a mouthwash commercial.

I shake my head. "They won't even know. They're not home until like nine. Well, maybe my dad's home, who knows, but not my mom."

She smiles at me, a little smile that makes me feel like I've just been deep. "Same with me, home all afternoon. We're like latchkey kids." She says it slow, like she's teaching me a phrase only fancy people know. I nod like a student to make her feel good.

"So tell me about Wade," she says during the next commercial break.

"Umm . . . he's cool. I like him."

"He *is* cool. Huh. Are you two tight?"

"Kinda. We don't hang out much, but it's like we're always friendly. We were partners for a class once."

"He should hang out with you. You're a sweet kid. You'd be a good influence on him."

"Well, I'd be happy to." I feel goofy and hopeful. Can she make me and Wade friends somehow? But of course she can't. Neither of us can hang out with Wade. Me because I don't have much history with him, her because she has too much.

"Hey," I start. I'm perched on an edge, totally excited and totally scared, like the time once when I was goading myself to launch off a half-pipe. But when I'm being indecisive I should go for it. I should always go for it. "Hey," I say, "how come you don't see Wade anymore?"

Sadness transforms her face from calm to something intense and mournful, like the way sunlight changes to orange and black oblivion when you drive into a tunnel. And then the daylight's back. Brandy recovers and watches the TV like nothing's happened. For a second I think she's going to ignore my question. Then she says, "I made a mistake. I didn't have a real good home for him for a while. I do now, but it's like that doesn't matter. There's no going back to being a mom."

"Yeah?" I say. "That's awful."

She stares deep into the space between the couch cushions. "Yeah, it is. That's why I'm asking you about Wade."

I don't have anything really interesting to say about him. But I see that she'll be thrilled with whatever I tell her. "He's tall," I say. I look at my Coke can. "He gets a Dr Pepper from the machine between third and fourth period, always with the right number of nickels and dimes, never quarters or dollars, like he's thought about it and took the exact amount from some coin jar at home. He's taking some junior and some senior classes. I'm not sure what grade he's actually in."

"He needs to study more," Brandy says. She's lying back on the couch with her feet resting against my thigh, clutching a soft old pillow to her chest, like I'm telling her a bedtime story.

"He's smart, though, you know," I say. "He sells these nylon bracelets and everyone buys them because they like him. He's a really good businessman."

"What all classes is he taking?"

"Umm, Personal Fitness and Care and Prevention of Athletic Injuries, definitely, because we're in them together. It's still summer school, so we haven't begun our real classes yet."

I search for something else to say, but I don't have much. People were comparing their fall schedules after class yesterday. I'm in all average classes, Wade's in all basic. It's hard to know about someone in a different track.

Citrus has been sniffing around the room and then he comes back to me. I think about the pitbull out front. "Someone else lives here?" I ask.

Brandy shrugs. "Yeah, I've got a roommate. And sometimes this guy Carl. He's gone right now. Borrowed my car."

For Citrus's sake, if nothing else, I don't like the sound of Carl, so I don't ask any more about him. But later, when I hear a car cut off in the driveway, I start. I'm about to ask Brandy what to do, like her parents are coming home and I'm not supposed to be there. But the front door opens before I can find any words.

He's kind of an ogre, with a trash can of a torso and lots of slick curly black hair that's down to his shoulders. "Who's this asshole?" he asks. He's smiling really big when he says it, but the words aren't friendly so I'm on my feet right away with Citrus in my arms. "Hey, settle down," he says. "What's going on here?"

Now he's suspicious because I stood up so suddenly. Brandy shakes her head a little. "Nothing," she says. But she's scared to look at him, so she says it to me.

Carl's got one of those orange boxes from the car parts store, some filter, and puts it down on top of the TV. "What's up?" he asks again. I'm not sure if he's being friendly or if he wants to hurt me and I really just want to leave.

"I'm going to go," I say to the wall.

"Love 'em and leave 'em, eh, kid?" Carl says. Then he says "Kidding" but Brandy says "Shut up, Carl" at the same time and we all fall silent. He looks down at the orange box and smiles but I know it's totally the quiet moment before something big's going to happen, like he's pulling back a bowstring. I'm closer to the door now. I have to pin Citrus under one arm to grip the knob.

"I'm going to go," I repeat.

But Carl's got his heavy arm around my shoulder. His fingers reach down far enough to stroke the top of Citrus's head. "Don't go, little guy," he says. "Brandy wants you here, can't you tell?"

He turns us so we're both facing her. She looks apologetic but mostly exhausted, like she's about to pass out.

"I'll see you later, okay?" she says. "Bring Wade around sometime."

Carl laughs. "Yeah, bring Wade around sometime."

I nod and I'm out the door. At least I remember to grab my backpack. I hold Citrus tight in my arms and don't let him down until we're far away from the pickup truck and the pitbull underneath.

4

We're deep into the summer term now, and although I'm not the new kid anymore I'm still not fitting in much. I had a sleepover once with this guy who had two different game systems, but I'm more or less hanging out with just Citrus, and that's okay. I'm biding time until the next stage in my life, and I know I'm too young to be doing pathetic stuff like that and the next stage won't be for a while, but I don't really have any other option. Whenever something big happens to you, like starting a new school or going to another country or something, I think you're supposed to think of it as some fantastic life-changing thing, "wouldn't trade it for the world" and all that, but I don't feel that way about coming to Haven Township. It's trippy to think that your life just plain got worse. People always say "Whatever doesn't kill you makes you stronger," but that should mean everyone just goes through their lives getting stronger and stronger, and from what I've seen the opposite is true. Like my parents. They've lost the energy to even pose; they've given in to being unfulfilled, no longer pretending that life's going to look up real soon.

I'm sitting here on the grass in front of the school, one leg against the sticky graphite of my skateboard, rolling the wheel until my hand gets as dirty as the blackened plastic and looking at kids go past. It seems like everyone's in groups, tan and happy and chatting, but I make a little experiment and look for the people who are walking alone and it turns out there are more of them, I just didn't notice them before. It's like in the mall when I was back-to-school shopping with my mom and everyone seemed so good-looking until I decided to search out ugly people to make me feel better and suddenly everyone seemed ugly instead, only wearing hats and jeans that lied.

I feel like I'm turning into an asshole, that I'm a little nasty when I never was before. When a teacher walks by she sees me sulking and gives me a look that's condemning and high-minded, like just by glancing at me she's fixing my life or preventing me from spray-painting my initials on the gym door. I stare down at my skateboard, at my lame California Invicta backpack. The bag's empty and it hits me suddenly that I've become a kid who doesn't do homework and that makes me even more depressed.

Huge air conditioners and hedges block my view of the parking lot so I stand and when I do I see that most of the school has gone home. It's always the crappy cars that are left in the parking lot at four P.M.—all the SUVs are out as soon as the bell rings, seniors hanging out the windows, on their phones or yelling, and I guess the only ones left are the band kids and the kids who don't really have anywhere to go. Our cars suck. Or you're me and you don't even have one.

One of the cars is this old black pickup truck that Wade and his girlfriend Chantal are in. There are two other guys there, the ones who roughed me up in the Food Festival. They've left me alone since then—I'm not weak enough to be bullied, and not cool enough to be a rival.

I've still been trying to figure out how to become friends with Wade. In movies adults just introduce themselves, but kids in high school don't do that. For a new kid, making friends is a fragile, multistep process, guarding yourself at each moment and being prepared to drop all aims at any slight rebuff . . . it's only because there are so many of us crammed into one school that you wind up with any friends at all.

If I walk slightly out of my way to Food Festival, make a little loop at the start, I'll have to exit the parking lot in front of Wade's truck. I shoulder my bag and square my shoulders and then I'm crossing the sunny pavement. I've met the guy's mother, so I have something to say.

My Vans are barely staying on my feet because they only had big sizes on clearance and I have to shuffle but I figure shuffling probably looks cool. I've got one hand hitched on the strap of my backpack and my skin feels gritty where the sand and dust have been blowing on it and I know that if I rub it little tan peels of grit will come off. I'm holding my skateboard by the axle and I realize it's also so totally me to be carrying a skateboard when everyone here surfs and I like that.

So I'm almost alongside the truck now. The gate is down and they're all lounging on the back. Chantal is drinking a soda and I want one, too, and the other guys are just lazing about, catching the sun and shooting the shit. Someone says something and no one responds, then someone else says something and no one responds, and I can see they're comfortable with one another and I want to say something that no one responds to, too.

Tribal Necklace sees me and says something and Pale Beef barks one word. The other guys don't acknowledge him so I start to feel there might be room for me in this group, that maybe I could take Pale Beef's place. I'm a few feet past the truck, dragging my feet, when Tribal Necklace says, "Hey, do you know any tricks?"

I say, "What?" and turn around and the sun's full in my face so I put my hand up like a visor and I like the pose because it makes me feel invulnerable, like these guys are so much smaller than me that I have to squint to see them. Chantal smiles at me and I want her so much, she's so pretty and rich, like a queen with suitors.

"Can you do anything with that skateboard?" Tribal Necklace asks.

"Yeah, I can do some stuff," I say, but Pale Beef interrupts and says, "Yeah, like stick it up your ass and spin?" and someone laughs. I check my progress with Wade. He's sitting on the corrugated bed of the truck, staring at his hands. He might be asleep; the sun dazzled me and I can't make him out; whenever I try to look at him he's electric purple.

"Shut up," Chantal says. "Come on, let him do something for us."

My hand is slick on the axle of my board, and I realize I'm nervous, which makes me more nervous. "You're going to have to get off the truck."

"The fuck we are," Pale Beef says, but the other guys have gotten up so he follows them. They're standing around the opening, all of them smiling and confused, their arms crossed. I've got them off guard. I try not to look at Wade.

I hurl my backpack to the pavement so that it lands near Wade's feet. A grind is pretty easy and looks cool and makes a lot of noise.

So I pop an ollie when I'm near the truck gate, and then the front of my skateboard is riding the gate, and then I exit backward because it's actually easier to do a fakie and I'm back on the ground and I do another trick to finish off and I stare back at the guys. They're totally jazzed except for Pale Beef, who's freaking out. I guess it's his truck. He's staring at the gate, running his finger along the edge. It does look pretty silver, and the truck's supposed to be black. "What the fuck, man?"

I stand there with my board, staring back. I guess I should have thought of that.

Pale Beef is looking at me and heaving and isn't really so pale anymore. I step backward. But Tribal Necklace says, "Chill, man, it's the inside of the back, and what the fuck's your brother going to care, anyway?" Wade's smiling and I realize I've scored by scraping the truck. I don't think they like Pale Beef too much.

All the guys start riding on my board except Wade and Chantal, who hang back and make fun of everyone else. I stand next to Wade. He's got these small black eyes and trails of little pimples where his beard would go if he had one. His cheeks are wide and brown and I can see all the muscles at the base of his neck rearrange when he claps after Tribal Necklace falls down.

"Have fun, guys. I'm out," Pale Beef says. He's got his keys in his hand.

Tribal Necklace looks over. "Like hell you're out. You're my ride."

"Then, get in, asshole."

They bitch for a while but I can tell the party's breaking up. Pale Beef and Chantal are already in the cab and bass is thudding out the windows.

Wade knocks his knuckles against the truck window and Pale Beef rolls it down and I feel a wave of cold air conditioner as they talk. Tribal Necklace is staring at his feet and I realize I'm being left and it doesn't feel good but I know I'll get over it because the small success of having hung out with these guys will stick.

Then Wade withdraws his head from the window. "I'm going to hang here and go to the weight room," he says to the guys. "I'll see you later at Virginia's." I can't believe it's just a Wednesday night and they have plans. I was planning on going to work, getting home, and jerking off.

Tribal Necklace gets in the car and Pale Beef peels out and suddenly I'm alone in the parking lot with Wade. Being with him in the empty humid space is so unexpected that I'm bugging out a little, like I've been teleported into a movie. I stare around: at the traffic light, still green from releasing Pale Beef and Tribal Necklace; at the steel Indian '99 gave as a class gift; and eventually at Wade. I wait for him to start toward the school, but he's just standing there. He's pulled out a cigarette and asks if I want one and I take it (I'll quit once I'm not the new kid, but everyone smokes around here) and we stand there puffing.

"I met your mom," I say.

He mumbles something that I don't hear but he repeats himself without being asked, like he knows he always mumbles, and says, "She's hardly my mom."

"She's pretty nice."

"She's nice. And a doormat."

I stare around the parking lot, at the splashes of gum turning shiny on the concrete. For some reason I can't make myself look into Wade's eyes. I realize he's being quiet so I risk looking at him. He's staring right at me. "You're not, like, into her, are you?" he asks.

I laugh. "No, I'm not into her. I mean, she's . . . really pretty, but I'm not into her."

He laughs and then the laugh falls away so suddenly that I see he's actually a shy kid, and sad. He spaces his feet apart and leans down to stretch. "I wanna work out. You wanna?"

"Um," I say. I've never worked out in my life. "I don't think I have the right clothes."

"It doesn't matter. Coach Torino has already gone home. All the guys are wearing whatever. You can just spot me, if you want."

"Yeah, okay," I say.

We cross the searing lot and then we're through the glass doors and into the cold of the school. We walk down the linoleum wing where the guy classes like shop and gym are. Wade opens the door and then we're inside the weight room.

The machines stand empty, all ripped vinyl and shiny aluminum, torture instruments from a past decade. A boom box rattles out staticky beach anthems. There's no one else there, thank God. Wade pulls off his T-shirt and he's wearing the yellow tank top beneath. He sits on a bench, the stuffing bursting out between his legs, and stretches forward, hugging his torso over his thigh. I pick up a free weight and heft it. It's far too heavy, and I hope Wade doesn't notice that I only lift it once. Now he's lying back on the bench and has got his hands on those severe-looking silver grips in the center of barbells, the ones that look like metal sandpaper. He shifts from side to side, then looks at me. "You gonna spot me?"

I stand behind him and place my hands on the shiny part of the bar, outside his palms. He tugs the barbell off its guides and I'm resting my hands on it as he lowers it to his chest and then back up. It's an odd feeling, carrying none of the weight and yet being part of it, like I'm a redundant piece of a machine. I think I'm supposed to be groaning or yelling like guys in weight rooms do, but that seems to be crossing some line so I don't. Wade lifts the bar only six times, then lets it slam back into the guides. I wait for him to begin another set but he doesn't and I say I didn't feel like working out anyway as he puts his shirt back on. We leave the school and start walking home. We have to walk down SR 570 together and it's just us, the brown grass on either side, and occasional cars that push hot air on us and make me sweat even more. The wave in my hair is wet and Wade is back down to his yellow tank. We don't talk much and that's fine by me.

As we cut through the parking lot of a multiplex and a Big K, I find out that Wade's an only kid like me (I never tell anyone about Gretchen—it's too complex). I tell him his mom's been wanting to see him.

"My dad would kill me," Wade says, his fingers twitching in front of his lips even though he's not holding a cigarette anymore.

"But she's, like, your *mom.*"

"So what? Pansy," he says, but I'm not hurt because I think he's being friendly. "I'm not *allowed* to see my mom, anyway," he says. "There's like a court order."

"Jesus." But I knew that.

We walk some more. He balances like a gymnast on the curb of the exit from the strip mall and I do the same thing after him. "Did she . . . do something to you?" I finally ask.

"Nope. But yeah, she kind of did. Carl sucks."

"Yeah. I was kind of scared of him."

"God, I didn't know you met him, too. That's so fucked up. What were you doing there?"

"She gave me a ride home from school. I left my backpack in her car. I had to go over there to pick it up."

Wade stops walking. I guess we're near his dad's apartment. He sits on the stone wall in front of the complex, and I sit next to him.

He pulls out a cigarette and I take one, too, and we just sit there, staring down the disapproving looks of the old people pulling into the subdivision. We're just peacefully being next to each other, and it's nice. Only when Wade gets up and leaves do I feel a release of pressure and realize that his foot was resting on mine the whole time.

5

Brandy's still out on workers' comp, so most days after summer school I go to her place and watch TV before my shift starts. If I bump into Wade as we're leaving school he'll come along, too. I feel proud for bringing mother and son back together, like it's been a community service project.

Me, Wade, and Brandy are sitting on the couch and watching TV. Brandy's sipping a beer slowly, like she doesn't really want to be drinking it. Maybe it's because we're there, or maybe it's because we just returned from getting supplies at 7-Eleven and the beer got warm on the walk back. We're halfway through a rerun of some show and I know I'm not going to be able to catch the end because I have to go to work. I've already got my Food Festival shirt and apron on—I've been promoted to cashier, so there's a gold star on my name tag. When I get up Wade gets up, too. Brandy waves good-bye wistfully like it's going to be a hard night ahead, but there's nothing either Wade or I can do about her loneliness so we ignore her.

We don't really have places we want to go to, Wade and me, so he's happy hanging out with me even if I'm working. I'm definitely cool with that. La Toya doesn't care if Wade keeps me company while I cashier. He doesn't bag or anything but just stands at the side of the register and reads *Car and Driver.*

Chantal comes by a half hour into my shift, and she and Wade disappear to wander the aisles. La Toya stares at me meaningfully, like I'm responsible for whatever they steal, but I just look back at her like she's crazy, because she's let them hang out in the store tons of times, so she can't start getting bitchy about it now. La Toya knows that there's nowhere to hang out in Florida, no parks nearby and no cafés or anything, just grocery stores and Targets and the mall, and we're going to get into less trouble hanging out by the meat counter than skateboarding on some construction site.

Wade's never really introduced me to Chantal. All I need to know I learned that first day, when she came in with him and they made out in front of the milk. She's still pretty, she's still into him, and she's still distant, like she knows she doesn't really need to talk to me. She and me, we're both Wade's one-on-ones. We know we're not supposed to meet.

I'm on Express, which means I spend a lot more time doing the money part of the deal and less scanning, which will make my items per minute lower so it'll be harder for me to get a raise. It also means I'm lodged by myself near the candy display far to one side of the store. The bus from Fawn Village just dropped off a load of old folks, so they're wandering around and bumping their electric carts into the end caps. I've got one in front of me who just put at least twenty things down on the belt, but she seems sweet and a little confused so I'm not going to say anything. I wonder what it would be like to go live with my own grandmother, although I haven't seen her for years and I'm actually not too sure where she lives.

The guy after the old woman gets cranky and points at the UP TO TWELVE sign as I scan his items. I wonder what makes him so angry. The after-work crowd is piling in and we're understaffed as usual and as I help the guy slide his card through I glance at my line, which is getting huge. It's about six people deep, and the last one is Chantal.

Wade and me've taken to splashing through this creek behind the railroad tracks. But last time we went Wade told me that water moccasins were poisonous so I made us get out. We lay on the grass with our bare feet pointing to the clouds and watched the dragonflies as we tried to muster the resolve to go back for our backpacks and shoes. We worked out earlier that afternoon, so we each kept passing our hands over our own pecs and arms. That's all we work out, really, because we agree they're the only parts girls really look at.

"Hey, do you think it would be weird to invite Chantal to Brandy's house on Saturday?"

"Weird? Why?"

"Well, you know, inviting my girlfriend to a party my mom's at? There's something fucked up 'bout that."

"Yeah, it's fucked. But fucked is okay, right?"

"Carl always used to call Chantal hot. Not in front of her, but to me." Wade adjusted himself in the grass, wedged his hands into his armpits. I love when we're lying on the grass and not looking at each other, because Wade will *talk*, and I know he doesn't talk to anyone else this way, so I'm his only confidant. I'll never be one of the coolest kids at school. But I can be a supporter of a cool kid, and that's good enough for me.

"That must have really pissed you off."

Wade had rolled over and was looking at me. "Yeah, it did. I coulda kicked his ass."

I looked back at him and I couldn't take the intensity of it so I concentrated on the sky instead and laughed like I was lighthearted. "I don't know, dude, he's pretty huge."

He put on a fake voice that I guess was supposed to make fun of me. " 'I don't know, dude, he's pretty huge.' Shut the fuck up!"

I was laughing up at the sun and then suddenly it was all dark with little flashes of light because Wade was on top of me. He rolled me onto my stomach and in a moment had my arm behind my back. He was laughing and I was laughing but I was surprised at myself because when it came out it sounded like crying.

"Take it back!" Wade said breathlessly.

"No way, man, he could totally kick your ass."

Wade had my arm wrenched tighter and his weight on me was heavier. "Shut the fuck up!"

I didn't shut up—instead I was singing, because I felt like it and also because it made it sound like I was totally ignoring him. I raised my head from the grass and his was next to mine, smirking like I was a pansy, but he was also smiling wider than he does with any of his other friends and laughing at me really hard. I tried to heave myself up but I couldn't and was kinda glad I couldn't.

"You gotta hope I can take down Carl, 'cuz you're gonna need me for protection." He said it low and deep into my ear.

"I could take Carl," I said. "I bet he fights slow."

Wade flipped me over so he was sitting on my chest. "You'd be toast," he said.

"All right, I'd need *you* to protect me from your stepdad," I said, rolling my eyes. "Now get off me." But I didn't move. My abs were sore and sensitive from my recent workouts, and I could feel them rise against the sides of his thighs.

Wade didn't get off. He sat up, suddenly outside the moment and bored, stretched his arms behind his head, and scanned up and down the tracks. His gaze moved evenly and without reaction—there must have been no one else around. I would have preferred he got off me, now that the energy was gone. But maybe he thought releasing me would be some kind of defeat.

I was thinking that my shorts must have been getting muddy, and how Wade and me were still wet with river water and the water was mixing between our leg hair, when suddenly Wade's face was moving toward mine and my cheek scratched against his neck hair. He held his throat there, and I didn't know what to do but then he pulled away and his face was in front of mine and his lips were full and red. I got panicky and my head jerked, which made our mouths graze. I smelled Doritos and felt the bristle of his chin rough over the smooth skin of my own.

He pulled back, breathed at me, and stared with his dark-hooded eyes. I couldn't put an expression on my face—I was too shocked and freaked, I must have looked like I just got stabbed. He straightened my shirt and got up and started walking away. I wish I had been looking at his face so I could know what this was about. I started to follow and tried to think of something to yell after him but I couldn't. He didn't slow or look back so after a minute I stopped and walked in the opposite direction, toward our backpacks. I couldn't think about any one thing—it was like what happens when I'm watching TV and listening to music and trying to read at the same time, when I finish a chapter and realize I haven't taken in a single thought. Nothing was any clearer by the time I got to our backpacks. I guessed Wade had forgotten about his and I wondered if I should pick it up for him but that would've probably made things weirder, like I wanted to take care of him, so I left it there in the mud. I shouldered my own and hurried home because it was getting dark.

Chantal's at the front of my line now. She's standing at the edge of the conveyer, leaning against the fingerprinty metal with one hand idly tapping the rubber belt, holding her head so that her hair falls flat and gorgeous away from her face, and she's looking at me and smiling nonspecifically, like I might be on the other side of the screen from her personal shampoo commercial.

I've been kind of fixating on her. She and Wade are pretty similar—dismissive, confident. And she has this awesome body, because she's a softball player, but the season hasn't started yet so she's got the muscles but not the bulk, and she tans all the time. When I jerk off at home, if the TV's not on I'm probably thinking about Chantal. I remind myself about that sometimes. It's a relief.

Then she's up at the register and she looks at me and I look back. It's the first time I've ever interacted with her, except for that day on Wade's truck. She's still smiling at me and it's suddenly clear that if she seemed distant before it was only because she didn't know me.

"Hey, Humphrey," she says, pulling her hair behind her ear.

"What's up, Chantal?" It feels fake to say her name back but I want to prove that I know it. I'd say more to her but there's a line of customers waiting and it seems rude.

"Humphrey," she says coolly. "Want to get me a pack of Marlboro Lights?"

I stare back. Of course she's not eighteen. She's a rising junior; she's probably not even seventeen yet. But she's Wade's girlfriend, looking at me nicely, and I'd like to help her out. But at the same time I'm mad that she's chosen a time when there's a ton of people watching. All the cigarettes are behind the front end, so I'll have to go back there and ask La Toya and she'll probably see that Chantal's a minor. Meanwhile Chantal's all-out staring at me. Her eyes are going *c'mon, please* and her lips are twitching like she's going to say it, too, but she can't because of all the people lining up behind her.

I figure why not, I should, because my job doesn't matter much to me, because I find it hard to say no to hot girls with buttery tans and pleading expressions, and maybe also because I feel bad for sorta kissing her boyfriend. So I lift the metal gate and squeak across the white and purple linoleum to the front end.

La Toya's running someone's lotto numbers and doesn't even look up when she asks me hard or soft pack and I'm sure as hell not going to ask Chantal from across the store so I say hard. La Toya glances at my register as she hands the cigs to me and reminds me to card the girl and I say I already did. I walk back to Chantal. She's been reading a little astrology book but not really. She's really thankful when I give her the pack and she pays using a credit card with someone else's first name on it and I'm realizing I could get in shit a dozen different ways. There's even a ten-dollar minimum on credit cards that she's not gonna make. So I'm happy when she walks out, all the more so because she squeezes the spot where my shoulders meet my neck and mouths a thank-you. The pinch hurts and lingers.

I see Wade leave soon after Chantal, ducking past the old doughnuts at the front of the deli section and lingering one second on the rubbery *thank you for your business* mat in front of the automatic doors to shoot me a *see ya* look. I turn back to my next customer and see I've charged him for all his coupons instead of debiting them.

My shift goes pretty fast and I'm ringing up everyone so quickly that I have to do cash drops every couple of hours.

I get a fifteen-minute break between the third and fourth hours, and I've already asked a customer to put the CLOSED sign at the end of the lane when I see a police officer come in and start talking to La Toya. Of course I immediately think that he knows about the cigs, or maybe even about me and Wade, but he walks in pretty casually and just starts chatting. I'm ringing up a customer so I can only look around once in a while but when I do I see a receipt in his hand—maybe he's returning something. He's gone when I pull out my money tray and go to the front end. La Toya presses the creased receipt on the counter when I put the tray down in front of her. "What's this?" she says, in the tone my mom takes when Citrus takes a poo on the rug.

I look down. The only thing on the receipt is a pack of Marlboros. "What happened?" I say.

"You know what happened. You didn't card that girl. She's sixteen. She goes to that cop's church."

"Oh, shit. I'm sorry."

"You're going to take your break now, and you're not coming back."

"I'm fired?" I felt powerful before but suddenly I'm fighting tears.

"You broke the law. You're fired or I'm fired. So yeah, you're fired."

"But I carded her!"

"What you say 'I'm sorry' for if you carded her?"

"Because." I realize I'm looking at my feet, so I force myself to look up at her. "This sucks."

La Toya looks at me shrewdly. I can tell she's trying to tell exactly what I think sucks, and that she doesn't much care either way.

Suddenly I realize how tired I am, that I haven't done any of the summer school assignments from last week that I said I would do this week, that the pay sucks and my parents won't even know I don't have a job anymore if I keep out of any other trouble. Wade and Chantal are probably still nearby if they just got busted. I undo my apron very dramatic-like and La Toya sighs and says something quiet and severe but I can't care about that, because there's too much to care about already. I go outside to meet up with Wade and Chantal because we sure have a lot to talk about now.

6

Brandy once gave me her keys so I could mow the lawn for her, and I've kept them. She's standing at the sink washing dishes when I let myself in, and I don't think she heard me enter because the water hits the cheap metal so hard, so I just sit on the couch and watch her. The window she's in front of is overgrown with palm fronds and lets in daggers of light so the kitchen looks the way a pond does, bright spots within the dullest glow. The sponge has gone old, its cheery fluorescence speckled and marbled with crud, and she's washing gray-filmed glasses with that thing, and it's so gross. She stops and leans against the sink and stares out the window at the patches of the backyard that show through the vegetation. The water is still spraying into the sink and it sounds hollow, like a downpour hitting a can. It's the sink a trailer would have, and suddenly I see how angry she must be at her house, at her life, at its shallow and hard-to-win pleasures. She curls her false nails against the sink rim. The slide of acrylic against metal focuses her attention. She peers at her nails in sudden irritation and then seems curious and pleased, like she has been reminded of how lovely they are. She's always talking like she's ugly, but sometimes she seems totally transported by the reliable beauty of her body.

The TV goes to commercial. Brandy downs the last of a beer, picks up a box of Rice Krispies Treats, and scans the back, obviously reading none of it. She puts it down and wanders into the far side of the house, scans the bathroom, and steps over a wet towel into her bedroom. When she returns she sees me watching her.

I'm not wearing any product in my hair today. She likes it when I don't, says it looks boyish. She looks like she wants to ruffle my hair and rest her hand on my shoulder, but when she finally decides she can the right moment's passed and her arm feels awkward so I shake it away. She sits next to me, I kick my flip-flops off, and we start watching TV. I can't tell what's happening on the screen—some show about eating disgusting things—and I feel a roiling in my belly and a quickening of my pulse. I stare down at my legs and see her red nails on the couch cushion next to my thigh. They look trashy but she obviously put time into them so I want to say that they look sexy. But that's just creepy, so I get up to go to the bathroom and when I come back she's gone into the kitchen and gotten the snacks. She's standing in the doorway and shaking the box, like the mom in a commercial saying *who wants treats!* I give a little thumbs-up, so she pulls one out and tosses it to me.

I bite off a piece as I'm watching TV, then I see Brandy still in the doorway and staring at me so suddenly I have to really concentrate in order to keep looking at the TV and then I look up at her anyway. "What's up?" I say. "Is Carl here or something?"

Brandy shakes her head. "No one's here. How do you like the treat?"

"It's good. I've only had them homemade before."

"Well, it's practically homemade. I mean, you're eating it in a home and all."

That's just stupid so I turn back to the TV. Brandy stands in the doorway looking for more attention from me and I'm getting tenser so she goes back into the kitchen and finishes swiping the dishes with that nasty sponge. I still feel the boiling in my abdomen, and a tightness in my throat, like I've got something huge to say and can't stop it from coming out anymore, but I really can't think of what it could be. She finishes the dishes and leans against the sink again, and some bleakness hits her. I knew she was lonely doing the dishes when I came in and I know she's lonely now. She's leaning against the sink staring out the window again because I'm a kid and there's nothing she can really say to me.

"You want a beer?" she calls from the kitchen.

She's not supposed to ask that. "Huh?"

"Do you want a beer?"

"No, I don't think so."

She pulls two cans from the fridge, I guess in case I change my mind, and sits next to me on the couch. She opens hers and lays mine on the coffee table. I look at it, look back at the TV, cross my legs and lace my hands on top. My thumbs tap. There's some commercial on about health insurance and I'm watching it like it's breaking news. She lays a hand on mine in a sort of maternal way, like to say *you can tell me anything you want, pumpkin,* and lets it lie there. I think about what I look like to her. I've been working out after school and have lost the fat but haven't replaced it with anything yet. I feel loose in the frame of my T-shirt. I don't like how my thin legs rise from the wide lip of my shorts, like pencils in a jar. My cheesy leather belt rises and rings my hips. My boxers have attached to the fabric of my shorts, a lining of the denim. Does she notice that kind of thing?

"I need you to show me," I say.

I don't know what I mean. I mean a lot of things.

She takes a swig of her beer and watches a black-and-white lawn mower on the screen. Finally she gets up the nerve to look at me, pulling her hair to one side as she does. I'm looking back at her, feeling feverish and nervous, aggressive and insecure, and there's no mistaking what I meant. I'm coming on to her. It's something other than that, too. I really just want her to talk to me intensely, to say she wants me there every day. Sure, I'm a hornball and think about sex all the time, but I don't really want to get off with her. I just want her to be something big to me.

"Is everything okay, honey?" she asks.

"Yeah," I say, but my voice cracks and I'm about to cry.

"Something wrong at home?"

I shake my head.

"You in trouble at school?"

I turn back to the TV.

She stares at me intently, eyes wet. I'm afraid of what I've led her to think.

But then she asks brightly: "Where's Wade?"

I shrug.

"You boys in a fight?"

I look at her blankly. "No, we're cool. He'll be here in a sec. He's just hanging out with Chantal for a while."

And then, like he's been waiting for his cue, Wade pushes open the front door. He's flushed and panting. He whizzes into the center of the room and dives for one of the Rice Krispies Treats. He bites into it, smiling, watches the TV for a minute, then glances at me and Brandy and picks up on our weirdness. "What's up?"

Brandy smiles, and she's pretty convincing at it. "Not much. How's everything with Chantal?"

Wade piles on the couch so Brandy's in the middle, and stretches his arms along the back, the way men on top of the world do. He's so much larger than her or me, and I think we look almost like a little family, Wade and Brandy as the mom and dad and me as the son, and I'm creeped out with myself. I feel both agitated and fulfilled, and in the strangeness of the sensation I can't think of anything to say to either of them.

Wade has kicked off his sandals and placed his big feet on the coffee table. The toenails are cracked and small, buried in the callused flesh of each toe. His feet look like a dockworker's next to the feminine painted arc of Brandy's and the avian slope of mine. Brandy laughs and says that Wade smells, and looks at me to share the joke, and sees that I'm already looking at Wade's legs. We all turn our gazes back to the TV and fall silent, waiting for whatever comes on next.

7

It's Saturday night and we're playing airport tag. I'm hiding out with Chantal in the old terminal that has all the crappy airlines. Most of Wade's friends are total assholes when they play, hurdling luggage and knocking over those plastic WET FLOOR signs, screaming through bathrooms, and chasing one another up and down the baggage belts. Chantal and I have been avoiding them, deciding that to be lame but never "it" is just fine. We share a cinnamon roll as we wander the shadowy corners of the terminal. Wade and his friends have been roving like a gang of rapists and pillagers, while we've been nothing but polite tourists.

There's a pleasant ping and then a woman's voice comes on: "Wade Dixon, please pick up the nearest page telephone. Wade Dixon, please pick up the nearest page telephone."

Whenever someone gets tagged, his name gets paged. Chantal and I look around, but we're still alone. "I'm sure he's out for us," Chantal says nervously. "We're the only ones that no one's got yet."

She's generally totally up for being in the middle of the fray. But she's got these new strappy shoes that have turned the backs of her ankles chapped and red. As for me, I don't think any of Wade's other friends really like me all that much yet, and I don't feel like having them chasing me down. "Let's go to the parking garage," I suggest.

"It's off limits," Chantal says.

I nod.

Standing at the edge of the roof and looking at the winking, foggy orange lights of the city, I kiss Chantal. I knock a beer bottle off the ledge as I do, and we break off and watch it plummet, gold and occasionally silver, the beer spreading out in wide globes, until we hear a thunk when it lands in a bush. I press my lips to hers again. She's been checking me out for weeks (I've been working out, I have Florida hair, I've been going shirtless and tanning whenever I take Citrus out; I'm not hot like Wade, but I'm looking pretty good), and I know she wants to. But she turns her head and licks her lips and smiles into the concrete of the ledge.

"What's up?" I ask.

"*What's up?* What would Wade think?"

"Wade's way off in another part of the airport. It's not as though I'm moving in on his territory. I just wanted to kiss you."

" 'Territory.' You're a talker, Humphrey."

"Come on," I say. We kiss again. Truth is I've been freaking out about my kiss with Wade. Lips are lips; boys' are different from girls', sure, but not *that* different, and if you enjoy one you're going to enjoy the other. I know I like kissing Chantal, but that doesn't prove anything, really. I keep going at her with a purpose until she pulls away and looks at me like something's really not right.

"I could fall in love with you," I say. I don't think I could, but it sounded so perfect in this movie I saw that I want to try it out.

She looks at me, her eyes suddenly shining. "Nobody's ever said that to me before," she says.

"Wade doesn't tell you stuff like that?"

"No," she says. "He doesn't."

She runs her finger around the wet circle left by the fallen beer bottle. "Look. You're cute. A lot of my friends would say I was crazy to pull away. But I like Wade. Let's call it a drunken kiss and leave it at that."

I pull away. She's always saying phrases like "a lot of my friends," like she has that many.

We take two cars back. I'm stuck in the middle backseat of the more crowded car (I'm still the new kid; this is my place). Wade's in shotgun, messing with the radio and gulping from a two-liter mixture of Diet Coke and rum. We're racing over the causeway and the streetlights are flashing like strobes. I'm laughing and joking with the guys but my thoughts are racing in other directions. I don't want to do anything but hang out with Wade. I'm still definitely into girls. I just liked Wade on top of me. That shouldn't ever happen and yet it did, so I can't stop thinking about it. I felt possessed by him, that for the first time all I had was the place we were and what we were doing, that there was nothing more for me to worry about.

Maybe whatever you're thinking about when you come forms whom you're attracted to, so if you think of girls when you ejaculate then girls are part of pleasure, and you'll start to want to have sex with them more. And I do want to have sex with them. I just don't want to want to have sex with Wade, too. So every time I jerk off I think about girls, about remembered porn babes, about Chantal, about Brandy. I feel jazzed now, drunk and jazzed. I could jack off right here in the back of the car. I take a swig of rum and Coke with one hand and keep the other close on my thigh.

We arrive at Brandy's place, because she and Carl will let us drink and it's become our default party headquarters. She's turned the pool light on (all Florida houses have a pool, even the crappiest ones), and opened the sliding doors, and it looks almost like a swanky place, like something movie stars would be passing through with real drinks, cocktails and stuff. We get beers or punch and crowd around the bright green water. Of course someone gets pushed in—it's Chantal—and then we're all stripping off our shirts and piling in, except for a couple of pudgier guys who keep their shirts on. Brandy's standing at the edge, holding an iced tea and looking nervous even as she's smiling widely. She takes big gulps and gives me too many winks. She's put on sweats, but tight sweats, and looks really good in her white tank top. "Come on in, Brandy!" I yell, and then I smile because of all people Tribal Necklace picks up the cry: "Yeah, come in, Wade's mom!"

She's shaking her head and smiling even wider and saying no, but she's put her iced tea down on the table as if she knows what's inevitable. I get out of the pool and so does Tribal Necklace and we're standing on either side of her. Everyone's cheering and raising their drinks. She's shrunk away but still facing us, as if she's backing into some powerful wind. I reach my arms around her and whisper in her ear, "Do you really not want to?" and she says, "No, I don't." I don't really believe her tone, though, and besides, Tribal Necklace has already got her under the arms. He's grinning at me and that's a rush, so I bend down and grab her legs. I feel her heavy under my hands, with the weight of a real person, and then Tribal Necklace has started to swing her and count to three. She's squealing something horrible but we release her into the pool anyway. Everyone yells, and Chantal gets so excited that she drops her cigarette into the water. Brandy stays under for a few seconds and then comes up, smoothing her hair behind her ears. My jaw drops. She's not wearing a bra. The roundness of her tits, their size, the way they have their own life and heft and go in opposite directions, the whole round redness of her nipples, has me struck dumb. She's heading right back out, away from the other kids, so I'm the only one to see them. She walks toward me, with her arms over her chest at first and then back down at her sides. When she comes really close to me, she leans into my ear. "Can you grab a towel from over there?"

I go get one. Everyone's kind of staring, stunned, and Wade's looking at me with curious, smoky eyes. The towel's damp because someone already dried off with it, but I bring it over. Brandy's facing away from everyone, and her tank has turned flesh-colored and adhered to the curve of her back. I drape the towel over her shoulders. She whispers "Thank you" and tucks it in the front, like she's just come in from the shower, and then turns to the crowd. She looks really serious for a moment, and I can see a tremble in the drops of water falling from her jaw, but then she grins and makes a running leap into the pool. She's holding onto the towel when she surfaces, the other hand pushing water off her face. Everyone cheers, "Go, Wade's mom!"

"You'd be surprised," she says. "You'd be surprised by me."

She beckons me back into the water and as I do a cannonball I catch a glimpse of Wade, treading water in the deep end. He's staring at me like a riddler, his eyes golden in the pool light. Chantal's leaning over and whispering something in his ear.

Later that night, probably two or three. Cell phones have come out and so a bunch more people have arrived, and Brandy's house has filled enough that suddenly it's not a group of friends hanging out but an anonymous party, with pockets of conversation and the potential to get yourself lost if you want to. I've been talking to some of Chantal's friends in the kitchen. This is only my second time getting drunk and I'm on an extra high just from the newness of the sensation. These girls have caught on to my energy, and we're laughing and then we all take a walk and talk about Very Important Things. When we get back we disperse until one of the girls finds me again while I'm heading out of the bathroom. "Wade's looking for you," she says. Her eyes widen dramatically as she ducks into the bathroom. I just puked in the toilet and feel embarrassed for a moment that she'll see that I left chunks on the rim, until I hear her own retches and realize she's not going to notice anything.

I avoid Wade for the next half hour. I'm sure Chantal's told him how I came on to her, and I don't know what he's going to say to me. I'm desperate not to lose his friendship, desperate not to make him hate me. I wander between other people's conversations, get myself another drink (someone's made punch with Kool-Aid and Sprite and Everclear and it tastes fantastic; I fill myself a big plastic cup, chew on the edge until the red plastic turns white), walk around outside some more, keeping to the shadows, and then head back to the kitchen.

Brandy's house is pretty tiny, so they've had to open up her bedroom. A bunch of kids are sitting on her bed watching the TV and talking. Brandy's housemate's bedroom is closed, so I crack open the door. Since I don't hear anyone hooking up, I let myself in.

All Dee's got in there is a bed, a cheesy bureau with bright gold fixtures, and clothes everywhere. I sit on the unmade bed and stare at the wall. It's tilting at a crazy angle, and when I close my eyes the tilt turns into a spin. I open them until the world rights itself, and then close them again and brace for the dropping away of my stomach. I don't know how much time I spend that way, blissfully and uncomfortably aware of nothing but my own centrifuge.

The door creaks open. I've been lying down, my face on the pillow, staring at the exposed part of the mattress. I look up and see Wade. "Hey, man," I say.

He doesn't see or hear me because he's busy tugging someone into the room. Finally he outright yanks and Chantal tumbles in. They both fall onto the carpet. She's been protesting, but it was fake because now she's laughing. I stare at the wall, my eyes wide open. Do I say something or not? The decision process seems weird and long—I can think of the implications of everything but can't reach a conclusion. I really wish I wasn't drunk anymore.

They're quiet, which fires my curiosity. Wade's lying back, and his fly is down and Chantal has pulled his cock out of his pants, and she's bobbing her head up and down on it. I watch, repulsed and turned on and scared, and I can't turn away. Wade's squinting and then opening his eyes wide, staring at the ceiling and then staring at Chantal. He puts his hand to her head and pushes a little bit, and then just puts his arms on the floor, his fists clenching.

She keeps going, always the same mechanical motion, and I've seen this in porn all the time but it's the imperfection of this moment that gets me, that Chantal's not smiling or cooing but going about it like it's her minimum-wage job, making these gross slurping sounds. But Wade's loving it: his legs are trembling, he bobs his torso up and down like he's back in the gym doing crunches.

They're going to do this to the end. I can watch it happening, but the idea of seeing Wade come in front of me totally freaks me out. I decide I'll just stare at the ceiling. The slurping slows and stops. I peek again. Both of them are staring at me, quiet like wild animals discovered.

"Humphrey?" Wade says.

Chantal starts laughing, no warm-up, just sudden hysterical laughter.

I keep on staring at the ceiling. I'm desperate to know their expressions, but at the moment I can't really lift my head. I feel the bed depress next to me, and see Wade's wet shorts before my eyes. I sit up. He's looking murderous. I stand, barely.

"I'm so sorry, guys, I must have fallen asleep. What's going on?" The question sounds totally innocuous, except Wade's dick is hanging out of his pants, which kinda punches a hole in the whole charade.

"Holy shit," Chantal says in between fits. She's standing by the door, her arms clasped around her waist.

Wade tucks his dick into his pants and looks at me totally normally. How can he do that? "I've been looking for you," he says darkly.

"What did Chantal tell you?" I whisper. The easiest way I can think of to move us past this moment is to tease out his anger.

"What do you mean?" He's drunk, probably as drunk as me. I can see a halo of red around his lips, from the punch. He lies on his back, rests a hand on his chest. "Chantal didn't tell me anything."

"Yeah," Chantal squeals. "What would I have told him?"

"Oh," I say. I laugh. "Oh."

He turns his head and looks at me. "Come over here."

I already am "over here"; he's right next to me. My heart is racing and I don't know why. He's lying back and looking at me, but it's not a look for friends. He runs a hand from the side of his head all the way down his torso until it rests nestled against the bulge in his wet shorts.

Sometimes you find things attractive that you're not usually attracted to. Same way, you can be unattracted to something that you always fantasized about. Wade is lean, muscular, confident, and he's looking at me like he's waiting for me to take him. Even though I don't really want to, somehow the option of refusing doesn't occur to me. For him to want me so frankly—it's a moment full of possibility. I can choose the safe route or I can go for it. So I go for it. My lips are on Wade's. There's little romantic about the kiss; his lips are muscles fighting against my own. I can hear him gulp for air around the edges of my mouth.

He calls Chantal's name and she suddenly stops laughing. "Come here," he repeats, stern and masterful. Then she's on the bed next to us, still holding herself tightly, like struggling to keep her body inside itself. When I put my hand on her thigh she jolts, and then lets me run it down. She's brown and smooth. The impossibility of what's going on disappears; lust takes care of it.

Wade has me bent backward and all of a sudden I'm lying down. He's fiddling with the band of my shorts, his mouth near my crotch, and he's looking up at me as he wrestles with the knot. I lean my head back and stare at the ceiling. This is the most shocking thing ever to happen to me but the room won't stop reeling. I can't separate the filaments of the moment; it's the punch and the beer and Wade on the bed and the fact that the pool water has tightened the knot of my drawstring and Wade might not ever get it undone. I see his head down there and simultaneously know that I'm finally with Chantal. She lets my hand go under her shirt and I cup her breast. To have her next to me and Wade down there, desperate to please, him with all the power in the world, God this could be over in seconds.

Wade has given up on the knot and is running his hands up and down my legs, just kind of breathing on them, which should feel erotic but feels odd. I'm turned on and excited, but at the same time I don't think I even have a boner now. I don't feel much of myself, really, just a general warmth. He rolls me over and I'm on top of him, which means my hands aren't on Chantal anymore. I want to kiss her neck, but she's not here so I kiss Wade's, and realize I've wanted to kiss his neck for some time. I press against the stubble beneath his jaw, breathe into his ear. I run my hand slowly down his throat—his Adam's apple bobs nervously—and down his flat chest, along the lines of his abdomen. Desire rises in me and fills the room. I'm too curious and too freaked out to be a lover, I think. I just want to explore, to play with him, to investigate our bodies. But I also know Wade's more experienced, and feel the need to make this go like the seduction in a movie. The Velcro of his fly, a ripping and then it's open. He moans in anticipation.

And there it is. A penis. For a guy it's something to be glimpsed but never looked at; we see plenty, only incidentally. But this time I'm supposed to interact with it. It's only semihard, and rests against his thigh. I wonder what he wants me to do, if I'll do whatever that is correctly. I kiss it once, and wonder how girls can do it. It freaks *me* out, and I have one. It sticks out of the body, it changes shape and size, it's really ugly, blue and gray and surrounded by black hair. I kiss it again. The skin is tight and dry because of the pool water. I feel like a first-grader who's been dared; there's nothing erotic about it. I don't know if I'm attracted to Wade. I don't know if I'm attracted to guys at all. I do know that I would do this for him, just kind of as a favor, but we'd have to talk about it first. I look up at him. That's when I realize Chantal's gone. "Hey, man . . ."

When he looks at me his pupils are chasms. "What's wrong?" he says, his tone half concern and half annoyance.

"We're guys. And Chantal's not even here anymore."

Wade lays his head back. I wonder what's going on in his mind. I'll never know.

I sit on the edge of the bed, my hands in my lap, like I've been scolded. I feel like I need to puke, but I don't want to go to the bathroom in case Wade'll think I'm puking about him. I hear a rustling noise, look over, and Wade's jerking off. His eyes are closed, he's running one hand over his chest, and he's jerking off. I don't mind his doing it; it's a relief to see him taking care of it instead of me, but I don't really know what to do with myself. I get up and stand by the window. The dusty old venetian blinds are closed and I don't dare open them in case anyone's outside, so I just stare at the plastic-metal pieces and the nylon joining them.

I risk a look at Wade and see that he's staring straight at me as he yanks. Not idly, not curiously, but intense as all fuck. "Stop it, man," I say.

He starts going faster. "Keep telling me to stop," he moans.

"Jesus. I'm serious. Stop looking at me."

"Yeah," he says, in that drawn-out way of porn actors. "Yeah . . ."

I'm mad now, not that he's into me, but that my first real sexual experience is going to be this fucked up. I kick the mattress. He just goes faster. My fists clench. I'm reluctant to throw my hand in, like it's a moving machine, but I put my hand over his to make him stop. I pull it away and say "stop" again. I've got his hand pinned against the bed. He's a lot bigger than me and could easily resist more, but he doesn't. I'm just holding him down on Dee's hairspray-smelling sheets and he's still staring at me, his lips parted, his boner pressing against my side. "Just touch it," he says.

I don't touch it.

"Make me stop, then," he says.

"You're fucked up."

He closes his eyes and nods, rubs his boner against my hip. "Jesus!" I say, almost crying now. "Stop it, stop it!" He just goes faster, and I can feel the wetness of his precome against my side. And then my fist is clenched and I punch him on the chest. He's got his hand on his cock and is gyrating again. I punch him again, harder. I leave a mark and he gasps, but he keeps going and he's making the same motions I do when I'm about to finish. I reach down and pull his hand off again and it's at that moment that he comes. It's on my hand, my forearm, his chest, the sheets. He's grunting and I'm stunned by the process of it.

He lies back on the bed, breathing hard, his eyes closed. I lie next to him and stare at his beauty, his familiarity, and try to figure out if I hate him or love him, if what I just went through was trauma or ecstasy. I lay my hand on his chest, like we're lovers rejoining after a fight, then I withdraw it. I want to back away from it all, stare at darkness and take in nothing more for days until I've sorted it all out. I close my eyes and the room spins and I let myself fall this time.

Later, while I'm recovering, I have plenty of time to imagine what's going through Brandy's head. The party's broken up, and she can't believe she ever let it happen. Now that the kids have left, all that remains are the things that prove what a bad parent she is: plastic cups, beer bottles filled with cigarette butts, an Evian bottle bong in the bathroom. Piles of vomit along the pool, bright red from the punch, blue wads of gum in the centers of most. She'd throw out the makeshift bong and the plastic cups. She'd hose the vomit off the grass.

What would she have done if the police came? Said that she felt safer having the kids over here drinking, rather than off on some isolated causeway somewhere? Played it off as the responsible act of an irresponsible parent? The police didn't come, but still. No wonder they took Wade away from her. Carl or no Carl, she makes some fucking piss-poor decisions.

But imagine how she felt when the kids were arriving, thronging her house. Not sizing it up the way adults her age do, not judging her and wondering why she couldn't do better, but thinking she was awesome for having them over. They said they wished their own parents were like her.

She's working on a sticky stain on the coffee table when the front-door lock slides over. She shoots her head up—is it Carl, who has been coming unannounced recently after hitting the bars with his workmates? But, then, maybe she could tell by the slower slide of the bolt that it's her housemate, Dee, back from her late shift. Dee'd come in and drop her bag, look around the place. Luckily Brandy would've almost finished cleaning. Dee'd sniff the smoke-scented air. Cigarettes, pot, and something more. Sex? She'd smile, a little worriedly. "Party?"

Brandy would nod. "Sorry you had to miss it. It was something."

"Who came?"

"No one you know." Brandy would be glad that Dee was so tired, that she wouldn't probe further.

Dee'd shuffle into the bathroom. A beer bottle crashed to the floor, Dee cursed. I remember hearing that crash, because I was fumbling closer to awake. The door to Dee's bedroom opens, Dee sees me, then she's back in the living room. "Uh, Brandy," she says.

Brandy follows her to the bedroom doorway. There, in a fetal position, hair sweaty and eyes slowly opening and closing, is me. Picture me outside of me: I'm shirtless and the comforter is wrapped around my lower body; Brandy can't tell if I'm naked or not. They stare at me for a few moments, then start talking, and I'm dreaming about what they're saying even as I'm hearing it. "Who is he?" Dee asks.

"Friend."

"He looks like he's thirteen."

"Fifteen. Wade brought him over. Friend of Wade's."

"Jeez, Brandy. Jeez."

"He'll be fine. I've been checking on him," she quickly lies. "Why don't you take my bed tonight?"

Dee gives her a judgmental look and then it passes—it always passes, with Dee—and clumps into Brandy's bedroom.

Brandy doesn't enter Dee's room until she hears the door close. She approaches me where I'm sleeping in the bed. My head is pressed into the pillow like a child's. She holds her hand against my forehead, because that's what parents do. No fever; of course there wouldn't be a fever. When she arranges the sheets about me she probably senses odors she knows well, semen and armpit and a hundred other body things. She pulls the sheet away from the bed and drops it to the floor, looks at me. *What has Humphrey done*, she's wondering, or *What has been done to him?*

She sees that my swim trunks are still wet. It's unhealthy, she knows, to let the moisture sit there, but she also knows she can't possibly take my shorts off. She sits on the bed and stares at me, wonders what she should do. A real parent would know, she realizes.

It occurs to her that my parents must not know where I am—they're probably worried sick about me. She should give them a call, at least. She certainly doesn't want them showing up at her door. She nudges my bare shoulder. "Humphrey, baby," she says. "Baby, wake up."

I turn away in my sleep, then turn back. I remember wondering why colors would want to wake me. She gives my shoulder a tiny squeeze. Suddenly I'm staring at the wall. The colors are gone, replaced with Brandy, and I'm totally nauseated. "Oh, you're awake," Brandy says dumbly.

"I'm," I say, sitting straight up in bed. "I'm . . ." I can't get my eyes to focus.

Brandy puts her arm tighter around my shoulder. I shrug it off. "You're in my house, baby. It's okay, you're in my house."

I look at her, and really see her for the first time. "How long . . ."

The words won't come out correctly, until I bully them into order. "How long have I been sleeping?"

"I don't know, baby. It's six in the morning right now."

I lie back against the pillow. "Is it okay if I sleep here tonight?"

"Of course. Of course. Just make yourself comfortable." Brandy stands up. "Let me get you a pair of Carl's sweats to change into. Your shorts are all wet."

I look down at my shorts for what I know must be an oddly long time, even for a drunk person. So much has hinged on my shorts. Who was trying to unfasten them before? To change them for Carl's sweats seems to rip apart the world. "My shorts . . . thank you."

Brandy starts for the bedroom door, but I stop her. "Wait. Come back here." I feel like if she leaves I'll fall deep into the room, too far to come back out.

I'm authoritative, in a way that I never was before. Brandy is at my side before it comes to her that maybe she shouldn't be taking orders from a kid. "Lay down," I instruct.

She looks at me suspiciously. "Really, baby?"

I nod. I'm pleading with her. I'm worked up and horrified and want to be held. I can see her think: *Mothers comfort children, don't they?* She sits on the bed, folds me in her arms. "What's wrong? What's happened, Humphrey?"

We lie down like that, with her hugging me. I'm totally still for a few minutes, and I just feel my blood pulse through my body, rapid and forceful, feel the tremors of my rib cage against her arms. She coos soothingly in my ear. This moment could go on forever; it's the slower pleasure of warmth rather than the bliss of fire. I start to shudder beneath her. Her arm's slick with tears and drool. "Please tell me," she says, crying now, too. "Please."

I turn so I'm facing her. What do I look like to her? "I'm here for you," she says.

Then I reach a hand out and place it on her breast. She stares at the hand in shock, like it's some growth her own body has produced. She removes the hand, places it on the sheet. "No, baby, I'm a mother."

I shudder again and the tears are full this time, not dramatic little streams but great inarticulate sobs. I didn't want to grope her, I just wanted to be part of her. I close in on myself and howl. She doesn't dare put a hand on me so she just lays there, breathes on me as I turn on my side and rock. "Shh . . ." she says. "Shh . . ."

A year's worth of anguish and insecurity is pouring out of me. Even through the deep and giddy detachment of the alcohol, I feel rational shock. Everyone says teenage girls are the moody ones. My exterior never betrays the fighting inside except at moments like this, when I'm crying, I tell myself, and that's okay. But it doesn't feel okay.

Brandy jerks her head up. The front-door bolt is going again. The only person with a key other than Dee is Carl (how I bet she wishes she had never let him back into her life), but he's supposed to be staying at his own place this weekend, had told her she expected too much of him, that he was his own man. The front door is open and we both can hear his heavy thumps across the living room floor. We sit there in silence and hear her bedroom door open, hear Dee and Carl's muffled exchange. Then Dee's door flies open. "What the *hell* is going on here?"

Brandy stands and crosses to the middle of the room, her arms out like she's going to block him. "I had some people over, Carl, that's all."

"Did you think you were gonna tell me?"

"It's nothing, it was nothing, just Wade and some of his friends."

"Yeah, Wade told me you had his friends over. He came and found *me*, told me just what was going on. And there's the little asshole right now."

Brandy glances at me—I'm staring at them, still crying but quieter—and crosses her arms. She's probably wondering, and I'll be wondering when I wake up later in the hospital, whether Carl is lying. But how would he find out otherwise? "Wade did what?"

"Wade felt he had a duty to tell me when my own woman is fuckin' around. He's seen what's been happening with you two. He *knows*."

Later I wonder: Why would Wade ever tell Carl that I was staying there? He hates Carl, and I'm his friend. The strange impossibility of it boggles Brandy even though it will eventually resolve itself to me. "The kid got drunk, Carl. He's just here sleeping. He passed out."

"And you're what, sleepin' with him?"

"I was going to make up the couch. I'm just making sure he's okay."

"He's half-naked. He doesn't look okay. You scared of me, boy?"

I don't say anything. It's hard to speak, and I don't think it would be a good idea anyway. I just lie there, curled up and trembling. "You *should* be scared of me, boy."

Carl grabs Brandy's arm. "At least Wade has the fuckin' decency to tell me what's going on here. I leave for the weekend and you run around like a fucking teenager, huh?"

"Shut up, Carl," Brandy says. She cringes like she knows what's coming next, and sure enough, there it is, his palm across her mouth, blood on her cheek. She heads out the bedroom door to the living room, trying to lead him away from me. "Shut up!"

But Carl doesn't follow her, and now he's alone in the bedroom with me. She returns and hurls herself at his back. "Get the hell outa here," she screams. "Get the hell outa my life!"

Carl throws her off and she lands hard on the floor, struggling to regain her breath. I'm scared and pissed as hell and standing now, swaying. I'm wearing only damp shorts, my boy's body insignificant before Carl's bulk. "Leave her alone," I say. My words were large in my head but come out small.

"Stop," she gasps. "Just let it go." But her voice is twisted by the rasps of her breath, comes out in moans. We're so feeble, the two of us.

Carl advances toward me. "What did you say?"

"Get out of here," I say. I've pushed forward to some edge, and I can't think why I'm acting so crazy. My emotions remember something that my drunken reason doesn't.

"This is my house, boy," Carl says, and his fist cracks into my chest. My body creaks once, awful, like a battered door. I drop to the floor. "This is my house!"

"It's not!" Brandy tries to yell, but she can't, she just wheezes loudly.

Carl is collected the whole time, goes about the beating like something premeditated. His foot strikes out and catches me in the stomach. My arms flail as I try to get up, but I'm a pile of limbs on the floor, moving uncoordinatedly. I don't feel the pain of his blows, but I know their force. It feels like roughhousing, except my blood is on the floor. Carl picks me up and sits me on the bed. He's just standing over me and we breathe at each other for a while. Then I flail and strike Carl a glancing blow on the nose. It's enough to draw his blood.

He's suddenly bent over me, going after me furiously. I distantly hear a thud, another thud, and then a wet crack. My knees are branches crushed under boots. Carl looks like something supernatural; the background that contains him is gray and white and full of sparkle. He stands back, shaking his fist, his eyes ablaze but with a new hesitance in his stance; he's scared of what he's done to me now.

Brandy stands and throws herself over my body. It's only when I heave against her that I realize I'm sobbing. "Dee!" she screams. "Dee! Please!"

Dee is there in the doorway, darts in and joins her. Carl does nothing to stop them as they drag me across the bedroom floor. Half the room is blocked out for the blood in my eye. Brandy takes the fouled sheet from the bed and wraps it around my head. Later I try to reassemble the moment: Carl does nothing as they cross through the house. He does nothing as they place me in the passenger seat of Dee's rusty Pontiac. He does nothing as we drive away.

8

I've never been in a hospital before. I was born in one, sure, but since then I've been pretty safe. Now it feels like I've been lying here and healing forever, in this narrow bed with the metal rails and the empty room after that car-accident kid got to go home. My mom was here for the first couple of days, but then she had to get back to work. My dad comes between jobs, but we don't really know what to say to each other, anyway. *Sorry, son, about your sleeping with that woman, even sorrier that her husband found out.* I don't think so.

They all think I did it, that I slept with Brandy. And it's not as though I'm that positive about my own memories of that night. I remember the gleam of the sides of the toilet, I remember feeling Wade's come on the sheet when I wrapped myself up, remember being too tired to do anything about it. I remember Brandy comforting me. But I'm almost certain we didn't have sex. I still don't know what it feels like to be inside someone. I think I'd remember.

But I still find it hard to convince anyone. "You're an attractive boy," my mom says. "Older women can have desires." The way she says it creeps me out so I refuse to talk. It's like she's not angry at Brandy because once we understand what Brandy's thinking, it's okay. And it's true that *I'm* not angry at Brandy, because she didn't do anything. So Brandy gets off scot-free. It's the fact that I'm not angry at her that makes everyone think I did sleep with her, that I had some thing for her. I do wish she'd visit me; that's the only thing I'm upset at her about. I know it must be weird for her, and she's feeling guilty, and maybe she's not even legally allowed to come see me, but still.

My mom is pissed as hell at Carl, though. If my dad weren't such a wet blanket she might have sent him to go beat him up. Luckily she doesn't know any details about Carl, not where he lives or even his last name. So there's not going to be some bitch-slap and more broken bones. There's totally going to be a lawsuit, though. A police officer came to interview me and everything. Mom keeps bringing it up, even though I tell her not to. I don't want to think about court for a few months, at least.

What happened to me. Broken nose, twenty-five stitches on the side of my face where Carl kicked me into the corner of the bed. Something complicated but temporary with my knee. No internal damage. I'm going to have a scar on my head, but it's going to be mostly beneath my hair. If I ever go bald I'm going to look like a wicked pirate, but it'll be hidden until then. It's a little image change waiting for me when I get old.

Honestly I'm not mad at Carl, not much. I'm more just frickin' scared as hell that I'll ever see him again. I don't want revenge; I just want to get away.

This period in the hospital sucks because I know it's going to cost my family a lot, even though we get emergency Medicaid. The most they make you pay is something like three hundred a day; I asked the nurses. But when I'm not worrying about the money it's not too bad here. It's not as though there's anyone on the outside whom I would be seeing; I don't have any friends or anything. I thought I had Wade and Chantal, but I don't want to see them again. Wade's a fucking nutjob. I liked him for his rough upbringing before, but it's screwed him up. I think I figured out why Wade told Carl I was at Brandy's: He was freaked that I would tell his friends what happened between us. He wanted me to pay for what he himself had done. Asshole.

No, all I want is time by myself to think about everything, and now that Mom has gone back to work I have it. It's just me and the TV and my cast and the food, which isn't so bad. I like chickwiches. I like pudding and I like Jell-O. And the nurses love me. When they come in they lean against the door frame and smile at me, *what a sweet kid.* They're like rented moms.

I'm tempted to say that these past two months have been a scratch. Friends made and lost, summer school failed, job at Food Festival gone. But it's been worse than that; I'm lower than just the new kid now. I have a history. I can't imagine what the other kids at school will be saying about me in the fall. And who knows what else Wade's going to pull. And Chantal's his girl, so she'll back up whatever lies he tells. No, it's a crap situation. I'm going to have my cast off by then, but I'll have this bright red scar, and I'll still be the new kid with the funny name. That's not going to change.

I've been doing some reading. Magazines mostly, crap stuff, and my summer reading, and some books I picked out from the hospital book exchange. I read them while the TV's going and my headphones are in my ears, and the nurses think it's hilarious. They think I'm doing three things at once but really I'm doing four, because I'm charming them at the same time.

It's my last day today and, like the motel, the hospital has gotten a lot less fun. The food doesn't change very much. TV is just soaps from eleven to three. *The Awakening* is boring. Even after a week stuck in a bed, I haven't finished it. No wonder everyone just reads the Spark-Notes. No one's been visiting, except for my dad for twenty minutes in the afternoon (I'm happy when he comes, but I'm even happier when he leaves, even though I miss him immediately. Go figure). I turned sixteen a couple of days ago, and my mom came for a special visit after her shift. She had to get permission because normally you can't come by that late at night.

She's been really distraught: *Dad's not working enough. Her job is hard, and it's harder because she's thinking about me all the time instead of Arby's. No one else seems to think this beating is as serious as she does. She's suffering and doesn't know what to do.*

I'm really ready to go to sleep whenever she leaves.

Then it's the morning, with a new lineup of talk shows. Lunch is different today, beef. I'm chewing and watching TV when one of the nurses comes in, carrying a card-sized envelope. Like an invitation, maybe. She shakes it at me as she would a rattle to a child and I can't reward stupid behavior like that so I keep my eyes on the screen. "You got a letter," she says. I nod, never looking at her, and she just leaves it on the stand and goes. I'm trying to act like Wade today. Seems to work for him, better than being Humphrey has worked for me.

As soon as she's gone I pick it up. It's this rough paper, really high quality, and I don't recognize the handwriting on the front. It's addressed to me, Humphrey Baxter, care of the hospital. I'm desperate to open it, but I know it's my only afternoon entertainment once the soaps start, so I just leave it on the bed and wonder about it. I don't have any pen pals.

The Young and the Restless comes on. I open my card.

It's a letter, really. Well, a card plus a letter. The handwriting starts out big and then shrinks, becomes almost unreadable by the end of the card and spills onto a piece of notebook paper. I study the front first. It's some charcoal sketch of a big temple with a hole in the roof. There's all these cafés in front. Some place in Europe. I put the piece of notebook paper to one side, and when I do a picture falls out.

It's a girl, probably in her twenties. Gorgeous. She's wearing a flowing white skirt and sunglasses pushed back in her hair. She's one of those people you pass in the street and think, *Jeez, she tries really hard.* She's got this pink-tan face, a big white smile, hair that's been highlighted in chunks and thrown all over the place like in a wind machine and then smoothed back. Lip gloss. There's a fountain in the background, something pretty grand and famous, I can tell. There are lots of tourists around. She's leaning on this cream motorbike, blowsily and dreamily, like she's actually on some fiancé's lap at a picnic. She's got dirty feet. You can see this arm at the edge of the photo holding a helmet. It's probably her boyfriend or husband or something. The arm's got this short black sleeve, and the forearm is muscled and deep brown.

The girl is my sister.

Humphrey,

How do you like the card? I'm in Italy right now, and I have to speed-write this because the "ufficio postale" closes really soon and I've got to make it in time. I've been traveling around with my boyfriend's parents this summer. I'm in a hotel lobby right now, sitting next to the front desk. A nice big potted fake tree is next to me and all these Italians are going by in front. It's awesome here.

So anyway, I've been back in touch with Mom because I've been going through some weird times. Not bad, just weird. And she emailed me an article about you (just a few paragraphs, have you seen it?) from the local paper, along with a picture. It's so terrible what happened. I honestly can't believe it. I don't know the details, I feel like no one really knows all the details, maybe not even you, but I'm just so shocked and saddened. My thoughts are totally with you. You were only nine when I saw you last, you know that? And now you're the age I was when I left. So much time has gone by. I'm not going to harp on it, but I'm really mad at myself and I wonder how to make it up to you. We're blood.

So! This is all leading somewhere, I promise. I don't know how to phrase it, because you'll think I'm being all dramatic, the histrionic and selfish older sister I always was (histrionic, btw, means "over-dramatic"). Maybe I still am. Did you see the TV show I had a lead role in a couple years ago? Mustang? *Anyway, I made some money from that, and I have some leftover college financial aid, and put it all together and I've got a little ducket right now. Not a lot, but more than Mom and Dad have. So I wonder: when you get out of the hospital and are feeling better, do you want to come stay with me? You could travel with me and the Lansings—they heard what happened to you and are totally willing to do what it takes to help, they're really great. You could enroll in school here for the fall semester, if we decide we want to stay on. I don't have a home of my own or anything, but we could be roommates and I would look after you!*

Whoever beat you up is still there. I want to see you come over here.

I already mentioned it to Mom and she wasn't thrilled. Something about a lawsuit in the works, and they'll need you around. But the court case wouldn't be for a while, and if you tell her you want to come I bet she won't say no. My boyfriend's parents will buy the ticket. We'll figure out some scholarship to pay your tuition. Think about it. You'll get to see Europe. You'll get out of Haven Township (where the hell is that, anyway?). I'd love to have you.

Your sister always,

Gretchen

I fold the card back together and look at the sketched ancient building on the front. I examine the picture of my sister. The motorbike, some older guy holding a helmet. Maybe I can bring Citrus. This all means I'll be the new kid again. But for the first time I feel I've gotten totally used to it, that new is the best thing to be.

PART TWO

GRETCHEN

9

Gretchen met Rajan when she was a guest star on *Mustang* and he was just a production assistant because he couldn't get a part. The show was on the cool network in primetime so, as she figured it, the teenagers of America would obsess over her for about six weeks. At this summit in her life she was `LUCIA`, back from boarding school for spring break and determined to become a cowhand.

```
                    LUCIA
So she finally roped you into her party. Did
you think she was hot?
                    TRENT
                   (lying)
Of course I didn't.
                    LUCIA
Yeah? Kiss me, jerk, and make me think you
mean it.
```

Gretchen's training had provided her various techniques to access her characters' cores: typically she pictured their childhoods or imagined the books they read. She discovered the inner life of LUCIA residing in her thighs. LUCIA's grand entry to Colorado ranch society was to recline on Trent's diving board and dangle an apple martini so precariously that it dropped rings of green into his pool. She had only two words in the scene: "Hey, Trent"; audience gasps; there's the girl Trent's been talking about for weeks; credits. She was the cliffhanger! But even in such a vital role, Gretchen's primary responsibility was only to hold her knees at the correct angle. She performed this duty (admirably, she felt, considering she had just arrived from L.A., her suitcases hurled to one side of the set) under the gaze of a director, his assistant, and a half dozen production assistants.

One of those PAs was Rajan. He wasn't as lackeyish as the others—he never got coffee or touched a sandbag. He just sat with his feet hitched on the back of the director's chair and periodically scratched into a spiral notebook.

"Who's the guy in back?" Gretchen whispered to makeup Lonnie.

"Rajan Lansing," Lonnie said, an eyebrow pencil bobbing between her teeth as she slathered foundation on Gretchen's calves. "His dad's a friend of Sally Blumenfeld. He's wandering the set for the summer, pretending to be her intern." She took the pencil out of her mouth and snorted. "Apparently he was supposed to get a bit part, but you try working a half-Indian into a dude-ranch subplot."

"Almost done, Lonnie?" called the production manager.

"He is handsome, though, isn't he? And going to Harvard in the fall," Lonnie whispered as she applied powder to Gretchen's ankles. "You got it!"

The next shot required Gretchen to lower her head so her cheek rested on the diving board. On each take Rajan slowly came into view.

His face was obstructed by the glow of a diffuser, but she took in his hair at the edges of the blinding fluorescence—thick and black, wiry except where he had overly slicked the part. As they filmed her head lowering she traced the swaggeringly upturned collar of his polo shirt, the triangle of his chest, his expensively tattered jeans.

By the third take she began a process that, repeated throughout her life, had gotten her a boarding-school scholarship and a college acceptance letter: she made a plan and executed it.

Gretchen hadn't ever really been on a date. After she left home she had wandered into brief liaisons with various older men (when she touched them their skin moved more than she thought it should), then finally landed a six-month relationship with a French-Canadian her own age who kissed aggressively, cried when he came, and was now rumored to be dating men. She felt that starting to go on dates was vital to the adult woman she was soon to become. It was certainly something LUCIA would do.

When the production manager called lunch Gretchen knew she should go drop off her bags (all her possessions in the world fit into two suitcases; she tried not to contemplate it), but instead she found herself sliding one glistening leg and then the other off the diving board and approaching the half-Indian in the polo shirt.

Gretchen would have found a side entry into conversation, asked him where she could find Sally Blumenfeld and her trailer key. But LUCIA said, "Hey, I hear you're going to Harvard."

He blinked as though trying to figure out who she was, though he had been staring at her for the last two and a half hours. "Yeah," he said, sitting up in his chair and then forcing himself back into a slouch. "Are you?"

"Cambridge College," she said proudly, as if her school weren't third tier. "Right next door."

"Oh!" Rajan said. Then: "Can't say I've heard of it."

"Look," said LUCIA. "You're going to think I'm forward, but I just flew in and I don't know anyone on the set except crazy makeup Lonnie. Do you want to show me where we can get some food?" The line was poorly constructed, too rapid in its turns, but she felt she had delivered it admirably.

They had lunch (he a burger, she a melon with cottage cheese), and after she had worked her food down he swiped his card to pay for her. When he asked her to meet him for dinner that night—and she knew he would—she said she had plans. Preposterous, since she had just arrived, but it flew. When he wondered if breakfast would work instead, she conceded with a sense of benevolence. LUCIA didn't need to be going out with any interns.

She located him in the dining tent, perched before a glass of milk, which he was pouring over a colorful dune of sugary cereal. She placed her tray at the other side of his table.

"Hey," he said, running a lazy hand over his torso, which made her figure he wanted to impress her. He had a hard and heavy form: he actually had to dig when he scratched between the twin mounds of his chest. "How've you been settling in?"

"Oh, I don't know." She laughed. "Life in a trailer isn't as glamorous as I thought." Actually it felt more glamorous than she had ever imagined, living in a cube trucked in just so millions of people could watch her in their living rooms. She had barely slept for the excitement.

"You should see the assistants' housing. They rented us a nasty motel. You've got it made, trust me."

"I'd like to see it sometime," LUCIA said, then quickly added, "Why don't they give you a role and throw you in a trailer? I bet you'd be a great actor."

Rajan's spoon flung flecks of milk as he pointed it at his face. "They hadn't seen me before I arrived on set. My stupid dad talked me up, promised I could play Hispanic extras. I'm lucky a PA ducked out last minute, so I could stick around at all."

Gretchen peered at him. Dark skin offset by green eyes and a tidy patrician accent. What a set of contradictions. She could feel herself falling for him, as she had predicted. But LUCIA snickered flirtatiously. "You'd make one funky-looking Mexican."

Rajan laughed, broadly and helplessly, in a way that promised he wouldn't cry when he came. He sifted the bent spoon through his cereal. He was avoiding her eyes: a moment of self-revelation was surely coming. "I want to be an actor, but all I ever did at Dalton was Shakespeare. I can do that stuff fine, but some of these *lines* in television. What is it you have to say today, 'This horse is your bitch'? I don't even get what that *means*."

She let her hand touch his for a moment and spoke in meaningful tones. "This stuff is all about faking. It's not real acting. Not like what *you* do." He looked at her with a flicker of needfulness. His gaze caused a breathless feeling to rise, like speeding. If they were at a club he would ask to take her home. She concentrated on not running her hands through her hair.

He watched her shoot her crash scene and helped unbuckle her from the prop stretcher afterward. She joined him in front of the chrome and glass doors of the equestrian arena set, wearing jodhpurs and a crash helmet and bruise makeup. They laughed at LUCIA's fate, and then he opened up to her: he had never taken acting lessons and probably should if he ever wanted to get cast in anything; he had failed a practice math-placement test the night before. She had taken similar practice tests for Cambridge College and had passed easily, but said she failed all the same. He leaned in as he spoke, pressed her into the glass. She felt the cool clear surface against her shoulders and her ass and she wished it would give, softly, that she and Rajan could ease into it and be wrapped into its clearness like cellophane.

She spent that night in the PA motel housing.

Gretchen had another big shoot coming up—some hospital scene involving a bottle of pills and an old girlfriend—but for now LUCIA was in a coma and Gretchen had a couple of weeks off. Her agent had lined up a few gigs back in California: a callback for the *Quixotica* cable pilot and a follow-up print ad for *Wet 'n' Wild*. Though she would be provided housing while she was working, for the other days she would have to crash with her gay ex. No one on the *Mustang* staff ever seemed to realize that she didn't have a home. They just sent her away for a couple of weeks and expected her to return grounded and ready to perform. God, she was lucky for that gay ex.

When the gigs were over she was so excited to return to Colorado and Rajan that she arrived at LAX three hours early. When she got to Boulder, though, she found all was not as it should be. Her usual car service wasn't there, for example, so she had to take a cab to the set. Once there she found that her trailer had been shoved a dozen feet to one side, and when she went to unlock it she saw some unknown bitch's name was on the door.

"Oh, Gretchen," Sally Blumenfeld said once Gretchen tracked her down in the producers' office. "Don't you have a cell number? The one I kept trying was disconnected."

She hadn't been able to pay that bill in months. "I told you guys to email. I check email all the time."

"This is all very last-minute. Email seemed hardly appropriate. So you didn't get any messages?"

Gretchen shook her head.

"How do I explain this? Ratings took a dip, and you know how some executives overreact. Despite my protests, they've had the writers do a bunch of last-minute rewrites. And, well, LUCIA's dead."

"Dead?" Gretchen said. "But when does she come back to life?"

Sally Blumenfeld considered it for a moment. "I don't think she's going to. But—God, I wish I had more details, the writers are being so secretive—I think there might be a Trent dream sequence in a few weeks, which we'd need you for. I wish your cell were working, I would have told you to delay coming back."

"So where do I stay in the meantime?"

"Well, since you're dead, it's hard to arrange housing!" Her laugh rang out in the tin trailer. "Why don't you go back to L.A. for a while? We'll email if we need you to come back out. Rajan can call you a car service."

Gretchen left Sally's office and stood in the dust of the ranch set. She had gained and lost enough parts that she wasn't desolated by LUCIA's death. But the real issue was that now she had six weeks until college started, and nowhere to stay. She had decided long ago that going back to Tricia, George, and Humphrey wasn't an option, and she couldn't put upon her gay ex again. She couldn't even afford her own plane ticket, and while she could probably talk *Mustang* into paying for her flight back, it wouldn't endear her to them. She might as well stay around here—but where? Some "Natasha Piers" chick had taken over her trailer.

He said yes—of course he said yes.

Rajan's motel was indeed nasty. He shared a musty room with a grip who wore grimy berets and left tighty-whiteys hanging over the tub sill. But she had a bed, a bed she would gladly share with Rajan, a bed they had already shared the night after LUCIA's riding accident, a bed that provided a way to steal even more time with him. She stashed her suitcases to one side of the TV stand.

The next two weeks were a grand experiment: she felt the usual alternating urges to love Rajan and to flee him, only she had no option but to stay. By the time she received the sides for the promised dream-sequence script, she felt she and Rajan had already been together for months.

LUCIA

Trent, Trent, I'm back for you.

TRENT

Wha?

Trent sits up in bed. Lucia, back in her jodhpurs and carrying a riding crop, towers over him. Her riding vest falls open to reveal a BIKINI. She's wearing the stolen Canyon Company PEARLS.

TRENT (CONT'D)

Nuh-uh. Emily'd kill me.

She flipped through the green pages and then lowered the script to the bedside table. "Trent, Trent, I'm back for you" would be the sum of her part. But at least it was something.

The scene was done in one take. She overacted it, she knew, but what was the harm in making a lasting impression on her way out? As they finished the shot she studied the face of the writer on set, tried to gauge whether this was truly the end of LUCIA. He was inscrutable.

Afterward she and Rajan went to the town's only diner, and he waited until the waitress had brought them their diet sodas to break what he had overheard Sally Blumenfeld say.

Over! She was sure they wouldn't have canceled *Mustang* if she had been in it longer, if the writers hadn't decided that having Trent's mom place a burr in LUCIA's saddle was a good idea. But God! They had Buckie buck her (fated from the start?), LUCIA broke her neck, and that had been what marked the beginning of the end. Rajan agreed.

He looked taken aback when she ordered pie, and that was enough to throw her over the edge. Her tears left wet spots on the powdered crust.

She watched Rajan try to help in his own stunted guy way, and that made her cry harder. Oozing tears, she knew, was not something LUCIA should be doing.

"They're still going to air the dream-sequence episode," Rajan said. "If I were you, I'd be happy the show got canceled. After they killed you off and all."

Finally she worked to the climax: she had no money, and nowhere to stay until college began.

After the cancellation news officially broke, they rented a car and drove to Rajan's family's summer house in the Hudson Valley. Along the way they drank plenty of coffee, bickered between highway exits, and had frantic sex on beds with headboards bolted to the wall, sex that Gretchen was sure she enjoyed. A *TeenSmack* article mentioning Gretchen came out while they were on the road, and she exploded into peals of blissful laughter when Rajan held the photo against the car window to show a passing trucker.

She would meet his parents. Wow. From all she had heard from Rajan, the Lansings were a Family. Their country house had a wooden fence with the "Lansing" name branded on the gable, along with "Established 1998," so cute. Gretchen and Rajan arrived late morning, sighed to a stop along the gravel driveway. His mother promptly emerged with a tray of biscuits. A tray of biscuits! She kissed Gretchen as though they were already halfway to mother and daughter, as though Gretchen hadn't just emerged from a filthy rental car, the scent of Mrs. Lansing's only son upon her.

"Gretchen, this is my mom," Rajan said after emerging from beneath his mother's embrace and nabbing a biscuit. "Mom, this is Gretchen."

"So pleased to meet you," she said, standing back and smiling, as if Gretchen were a piece of art she'd previously only been able to admire in catalogs. "I'm Gita."

Rajan's mother really was Indian. It seemed both impossible and perfect in the context of the gabled house. Her skin was the color of tea-stained paper, her nose a stub before two round eyes. The clothes were a very domestic Ann Taylor—no saris for Mrs. Gita Lansing.

"Rajan has told me so much about you on the phone," Gita said.

"Oh, now I'm nervous!" After winning an approving smile for the suitable sequence of pleasantries, Gretchen followed Gita inside.

Some events pass as though unimportant and live a fuller life in memory. That month Gretchen was endlessly entering the Lansing house: the creak of the rain-wearied boards of the two steps up to the porch, the smells of citronella and fresh tar from the neighbor's roof work, the white paint of the door frame, worn away at the edges to reveal wood gone dark brown. The front door that needed to be lifted slightly to open, releasing when it did a profusion of fragrances—sandalwood, perfumed wax, cumin—and odors—rich and rotted soil, air shut into antiqued rooms, the red-brown scent of Mr. Lansing's sweat. She remembers entering that first time, dodging the repeated offer of a biscuit as she stepped over the threshold and placed her bag on the blue and brown rings of a tufted rug. The home managed to exude a sense of having been lived in for centuries without having suffered for it. It was the home of decorating magazines. For the first time Gretchen wondered not how long it would be until she tired of Rajan, but how long she would have to wait until she could make herself a Lansing.

Gita put her hand to her throat and made a great show of fretting over their having driven through the night. But when Gita directed her and Rajan up to the bedroom they would share, Gretchen realized that Gita was no prissy aristocrat mom.

"Your parents are okay with us sharing a room?" Gretchen said, throwing herself facedown on the bed. Rajan kicked the door closed as he lowered himself onto her. She loved his weight, being half-crushed by the intensity of his desire.

"Of course they are," Rajan said. "They're cool with girlfriends staying in my room. What would we do otherwise, sneak down the hallway in the middle of the night?"

His lips were lost in her hair. She giggled as he rooted for her ear, and tried to ignore the gray bloom of depression over his having mentioned past girlfriends. "My mom married a white guy," he said. "That already makes her a total radical in her family. And Dad . . . yeah, I guess you don't know the half of it."

Stable and unconventional. It seemed an ideal combination to Gretchen, magical in its improbability. "We shouldn't stay upstairs too long," she whispered as Rajan slipped his fingers under her bra strap. "Maybe your mom wants help getting lunch ready."

Rajan refused to let Gretchen go down and help make lunch, but that evening—and every other evening of their stay—Gretchen was in the kitchen with Gita. Indian cuisine was apparently never prepared in the Lansing kitchen—the cumin smell Gretchen had first detected actually emanated from take-out containers sitting on top of the trash. Instead, Gita taught Gretchen how to cook Italian. "The garlic sticks on your fingers, yes," she said, her accent slight but unflagging, "but in Indian cooking you smell like samosa for the whole day. The chef in my childhood house in Calcutta, he was walking food smell. I do not know how his wife suffered it."

Gretchen had longed to have a home someday in which the oven was used. The closest she had ever come was to watch food shows for hours at a stretch. When Gita handed her peeled cloves of garlic, she cradled the slick roots. Gita placed a knife in her hand and, on cutting into the cloves and revealing the green bud at their core, Gretchen felt as though she might as well have spent her life in a kitchen. If she had a gift for this, she told herself (and who was to say she didn't?), it might shine through even in her first meal.

She longed for Gita's praise, and it came with a hand at the small of her back as they carried the dish out to Rajan, seated at the head of the table, still sweaty from a tennis set with his father, his muscular legs splayed to the ends of the table. "What in the world . . . ?" Rajan said as he saw Gretchen approaching with a ceramic bowl. "Mom, you didn't make Gretchen *cook*."

"She wanted to," Gita said. Gretchen caught a look pass from Gita to Rajan—*she'll do.*

"Your supper, sir," Gretchen said with a dip, which she aborted, struck by the fear that she had obliquely insulted the family's Indian background. She eyed the decanter of wine at the middle of the table.

"I'm scared," Rajan said as Gretchen placed his dinner in front of him.

"Oh, Raj!" Gretchen said, playfully cuffing his shoulder. If they were alone she would have added "fuck you."

Mr. Lansing was taking a long shower after the match, so they began dinner without him. Gretchen downed a glass of wine and enjoyed the dulling of her edges. Some gloss of LUCIA had to still be upon her, after all, some patina of stardom. And to Gretchen's delight Gita seemed fascinated by *Mustang*—both in Rajan's production internship and in Gretchen's big break. Did Gretchen have any more acting leads, she wondered as she passed the bread basket.

No, Gretchen didn't. But she wasn't concerned—surely the casting agents knew that she was entering college and were wise enough not to call her in for auditions.

The table fell silent once they heard Mr. Lansing's tread as he descended the stairs. They watched one another wait for him, their smiles stretching while his steps grew louder. Gretchen wished they had kept talking.

"I see you're eating away your huge loss." Mr. Lansing laughed at Rajan as he pulled out a chair.

"Great, Dad, real sweet," Rajan said. He had rarely spoken about his father, and whenever he had Gretchen had detected neither intimacy nor animosity.

Gretchen watched Rajan's father sit down. He wore a tailored jacket over a rumpled T-shirt, both of which strained over his beefy shoulders. The iron-perfect part in his hair produced two waves of silver-flecked black that landed at the ends of his eyebrows. "What have we got here?"

"Risotto," said Gita. "Rajan's new girlfriend made it with me. Gretchen."

"Of course. Gretchen. I'm Joel Lansing."

Gretchen allowed her hand to be lost in his. She found herself not quite able to meet his gaze.

"You," Mr. Lansing said, "must be the famous actress."

"Hardly," Gretchen said, as if her lack of prospects weren't actually the case.

"No, really," Mr. Lansing said, pausing until Gretchen had to return her eyes to his, "a television show and then college. You've covered all your bases. No wonder you've snared my son. I hope you feel very welcome here."

"I hope so, too. You're just darling. She's just darling, Raj," Gita said.

"Way to take away my game," Rajan said. They all laughed and picked up their forks before the mirth had a chance to die down.

* * *

The month was a succession of genteel activities (they rode horses! they played badminton! they sipped aperitifs on the veranda!), and Gretchen left with the heady sensation of having planted herself into a family she adored. But when she arrived at Cambridge College she discovered it was full of societies that would never accept her. The folder Gretchen was handed at orientation was thick with applications: *write for the official paper; write for the independent paper; play in the orchestra; show your body for the crew coach; apply for a special major; be cool enough for a sorority.*

Gretchen didn't try out for much. She got a work-study job, but there was no tryout to that. She figured she'd spend most of her free time with Rajan instead. She did get a part in a Harvard-student-written musical about urban planning that required her to channel Le Corbusier's girlfriend. She soon realized she was no academic; over the four years she botched her chances of graduating with anything nearing honors. Really the only thing she had tried out for were Rajan and his parents. With qualified success.

They went to his country house for the stray times between semesters, the days before and after internships or small acting gigs. Gretchen began to crave the home visits more and more. Gita became a confidante; Mr. Lansing was affectionate on the rare occasions when he was home. When Gretchen crossed the threshold of the Lansing house she began no longer to see the parents as obstacles to be overcome, but rather as sources of comfort. They were reprieves from—yes, she could admit it—her flagging relations with Rajan. She and Rajan still shared a bedroom at the house, and the proximity of his parents was no longer a restraint to their longing for sex but rather a needed charge of danger, without which they would have spooned for a minute before retreating into slumber.

But surely this was normal couple behavior. When Rajan fell asleep first she would sometimes lie awake and stare at his bare back, whisper "I love you" into his ear, and see how it made her feel. She had been taking him for granted, she knew. But they'd been dating for four years. Weren't you *supposed* to take someone for granted? Isn't that what unconditional love is all about?

In Cambridge she could chalk it up to wandering attention. But during a holiday break at his parents' house, could she really say that her courses were taking too much of her energy? And the love of the Lansings, much as it gave her security, threw the increasing tedium of her and Rajan's relationship into clarity. Gretchen had become the daughter the Lansings had never had, yes—but didn't that make her and Rajan siblings, make Rajan the new Humphrey? Could her love for him, deep as it might have been, have gotten serious enough that it was no longer sexy?

One night she got up and went to the bathroom, not because she had to go but because she knew it would wake him. "You know what?" Gretchen said when she returned, "we don't talk about *us* much, you know?"

He pulled in close behind her, laid his body alongside hers, and cupped her breast. She could feel the muscle of his stomach against her back, sense the hints of an erection against her thighs. "That again? Do you *want* to talk about us?" There was a smile in his voice, and she could imagine what it looked like: a little sexy and a little condescending.

She put her hand on his. She touched her own breast at the gaps between his fingers and it felt odd, like she was copping a feel of herself. "I feel a little . . . guarded around you," she finally said. "Do you know a reason why I should feel guarded?"

He sighed against her. "You're feeling guarded and you want *me* to tell *you* why?"

"Yes," she said. "I'm feeling whatever this is and it can only be because something's still not right. So tell me, is there a reason everything shouldn't feel right?" She sounded as if she were parroting someone on daytime television.

"I don't know," he said. "I hadn't thought anything was wrong until you said that." She could no longer feel him hard between her legs.

Why couldn't she get him to tell the truth? Didn't real adults fess up about bad feelings? "Okay, then," she said. "Cool."

"Cool," he drawled, squeezing her to him. He'd given the word an odd emphasis, as if he'd said "yummy" instead, and she knew what otherwise inexplicable emphases indicated—he wanted sex. For the sake of their relationship, to prove that they could still have fun together, that she hadn't leadened their relations, she should pounce on him. But she didn't want to. She wanted him to hold her against him and tell her that he would love her whether she wanted to fuck him or not. But she knew he wouldn't say it. She was struck by the desperation of it, her need to have him be everything to her, family and husband.

He kissed her neck. She felt his belly against her back. She was frustrated that the nerves there were so inarticulate, that she could feel nothing more specific about his abdomen than a general heavy pressure against her. She wanted to feel his body hair with her back. He didn't even know where his viscera were, she found herself thinking. He used his organs every day, without knowing where they were or how they worked. She was the same, she knew, but it still struck her as sad that she knew so little about what maintained her very existence.

And there, she had done it again; she had gone away.

"Where *are* you right now?" he asked. There was reproach in his voice. She wasn't making it up, right? He was irritated with her for thinking about him! If she had gone elsewhere in her head, why should he blame her for it? What's wrong with being alongside each other without filling the intervening space with words and sex?

"I'm right here," she said.

"You're beautiful," he said. He was erect again, then he was beneath the covers, his head brushing against the backs of her legs. She loved him and wanted to cry. She opened her mouth to speak.

She said what she said and when they returned to Cambridge they decided to take a couple of weeks without seeing each other. Gretchen didn't allow herself to leave him a message, yet checked her own inbox incessantly. Eventually Rajan showed up at her room and they had sex, his orgasm quick. She wondered how she had ever let him slip away and then, only a month later, she remembered quite easily.

Gretchen sneaked into Widener Library to find him in his usual spot, four levels deep, lodged in a study carrel at the dusty border of Italian and French literature. His back was to her. Normally the broad expanse moved so predictably and tenderly; it bored her. But now she heaved herself upon him.

She could smell the oil in his hair, feel the metal of his glasses behind his ears. Rajan held up a finger to delay her. They were in finals period; graduation was the next week.

"Rajan, please."

He turned and regarded her, suddenly curious: normally she called him Raj. Gretchen removed his glasses and took in the familiar wideness of his face, his handsome brow, the little pockmarks on his cheeks, as uneven and perfect as pottery. She kissed the space between his eyebrows. "What's wrong?" he asked.

She didn't know what was wrong, only that she felt like crying.

"Are you going to tell me, or what?" His sympathy had soured. It was always like this: any of his emotions could be milked only for a few moments before it turned to annoyance.

"Don't you know?"

Rajan sputtered. Gretchen waited for him to compose a response. They had sex here once, two years ago. The memory flashed for a moment and then skidded away.

"Come here," he said, although she was already next to him.

Maybe if she kissed him, she would start to want to kiss him.

Gretchen kissed him. She was infinitely aware of his taste buds.

She withdrew and stared around, desperate for a distraction.

He got up slowly. He sighed, as if facing an ordeal he was only just willing to go through. "Look, what you said to me last week—" Rajan said.

"There we go. *That's* what we need to talk about." That night at the Lansing country home, drunk and unhappy, she had told him that her trust in him killed her sex drive. They had been weaving a mannered dance since, taping together the fragments of their old intimacy, trying to remember how it worked.

"It's not that what you said got to me that much. I think all couples go through periods where they're, you know, less into it. But it's the fact that you felt you could say that. That you could just say you weren't attracted to me—"

"It wasn't that—"

"All it meant was that you think I'm so yours, that I'm so pathetically in love with you, that you can just say whatever crap you want, not try at all, refuse me in bed, and I'll still be around while you pull your dramatic bullshit and make yourself the focus of everything. Well, yeah, I am in love with you, so I put up with all your shit. But there comes a point, baby, there comes a point, where—"

She couldn't let him finish his sentence, so she hugged him, slid her hands over his back. She'd quiet him like a child, and he'd stay hers. "Stop," she whispered.

His muscles tensed. The thoughts that got pushed deep away, the feelings he thought he hid, were always betrayed in his body.

"I can't," he said. "I can't respect myself and stay in this. For you to lose interest just because I love you, that's such a *thing*, such an immature *thing*. The more you know me, the more you should want to have sex with me."

She blinked. Is that true? She hadn't considered the possibility.

"I love you, Raj," she said. "You know that, right?"

He nodded.

Their recent habit after a fight was not to see each other for some time. The Lansings were scheduled to arrive for graduation soon, and Gretchen consoled herself with the fact that her next occasion spending substantial time with Rajan would be under their defusing influence.

When she picked Rajan up at his dorm room the night his parents arrived, it was just as she predicted: he wore the resolutely cheerful expression he always adopted after they'd spent time apart. As they walked to the restaurant Gretchen held his hand limply; she would play the sophisticate newly fallen in love. She was thankful that, this evening at least, they wouldn't have to use the word *libido* even once. On the sidewalk in front of the restaurant he gave her a brisk rundown of what had developed over the last few days, as full of portent and clipped vagary as a prophecy: his father had ceased his consulting practice after rocketing up the number of Pennsylvania strip-mall cafés, and his parents were planning an extended vacation in Italy. He didn't know for how long. He pushed open the door and ushered Gretchen inside.

Mr. Lansing was tapping into his electronic organizer when Rajan and Gretchen approached the table, but he quickly put it away and joined his wife in greeting them. Immediately Gretchen saw that the veneer of his demeanor had changed; he was as tightly wound but had made some evident decision to relax. When he smiled, Gretchen couldn't recall having seen his teeth before. Gita asked Gretchen about her plans once she and Rajan hit L.A.

"None, really," she said as she smiled dryly into her Prosecco. "Who knows if I'll ever star in anything again."

All Harvard students seemed to have the professional lives of their twenties outlined, but all Gretchen and Rajan had secured was a two-week run of *Godspell* in the Berkshires. Gretchen promptly revealed that even that had fallen through. Mr. Lansing laughed broadly. Having caused such a sunburst made her lack of prospects suddenly feel like a success. Their conversation was soon loud and intimate.

For a time, the foursome hinged on the banter between Mr. Lansing and Gretchen. And then, two bottles of wine later, in the middle of recounting a failed audition, Gretchen realized that Gita had laid a sisterly hand on her arm. Startled, she saw on Gita's face both affection and some specific sorrow. Even as she longed to ask Gita what was wrong, Gretchen basked in the awareness that Gita valued her. *This is what a mother should always be,* Gretchen thought, as she laid her hand over Gita's. She would find an excuse to get her alone soon. She turned back to the men and saw them staring at her expectantly.

"Um, so I bombed it!" Gretchen said.

"Gretch, that's totally not the end of the story," Rajan said.

"It's not?" She was suddenly convinced she had been talking too much about herself.

"What about how the guy called you back anyway, for that live-action teddy bear movie?"

"Oh, yeah. I got a callback for some live-action teddy bear movie. Ridiculous. So tell me about your trip to Rome! That sounds like so much *fun*!"

The Lansings exchanged complex smiles. "It *is* going to be fun," Mr. Lansing confirmed. Then, after an evident hunt for something to remark on: "We've instituted a strict no-communications policy. No cell phones, as little email as possible. That's going to be half the pleasure of it."

"How long are you going for?"

"We don't know, actually," Mr. Lansing said. "As long as we care to."

"We think you should come to join us," Gita said suddenly. She spoke mainly to Gretchen, and Gretchen was struck, as she had been in the past, that Rajan's parents might prefer her to their own son.

"Oh, I'd *love* to," Gretchen said. "Doesn't that sound great, Raj?"

"Yeah."

"Are you really, honestly inviting us? Because I've never been to Europe, and I'm sure we'd have time to visit for a while before we start our real lives." She spoke too quickly; a bubble of saliva flecked her lip.

Rajan grunted. "Let's not get ahead of ourselves."

The table fell silent. Gretchen blinked into the candle at the center of the table, searching for a way to charm a retreat.

"Too late to say no!" Gita said. She nodded to Mr. Lansing, who extracted a travel envelope from a suit pocket and slid it across the table. "Graduation gift," Gita explained. "Since you have the summer free, we thought why do the children not come abroad and unwind before Los Angeles? You don't have to use them. But we want you to have the option. They are unrestricted. You can pick your dates."

"Really?" Gretchen said. Rome with the Lansings! She couldn't contain her excitement. Rajan just stared at the tickets.

"I don't think Rajan is too interested," Mr. Lansing said.

"That's not it," Rajan growled. "Let's just drop it."

"Children," Gita said. "What's going on?"

The love Gretchen sensed from Gita, the very real possibility that she would lose her new mother, made her eyes mist.

"Oh, Gretchen!" Gita exclaimed. Mr. Lansing looked from Gretchen to Rajan and back again, to all appearances frustrated by a delay of game at the U.S. Open.

"Why are *you* crying?" Rajan asked Gretchen, throwing his napkin on the table. It tipped the breadbasket, dusting the white tablecloth with poppy.

"I'm sorry," Gretchen said as the tears began.

"Raj, what do you mean, what do you mean to say to her 'why is she crying' in such a tone?" Gita asked.

"Nothing, Mom, just let it go."

Mr. Lansing avoided Gretchen's eyes and his wife's, reserving his attention for the wine bottle's label.

Gretchen excused herself from the dessert course and retreated to her dorm room. She wrapped herself in her bedsheets and pressed her forehead against the cool cinder block of the wall. When her cell phone vibrated she heaved a sob of relief to see Gita's name on the screen.

"Gretchen, honey. Talk to me. I'm all by myself in the hotel room—Joel is gone to get cigarettes. What's going on?"

"Oh, God." Gretchen willed herself to stop crying, with only minimal success. "I don't know. Rajan has it in his head that I don't love him enough."

"This is true?"

"No! Of course not."

"Why would he think that? You two are so perfect for the other."

She had spoken with Gita about many things, but never her sex life with her son. "I don't know."

"It's a tough time for you, trying to know what you're going to do after graduation. You're probably just in a bad moment."

Gretchen nodded into the phone.

"Do you want me to talk to Rajan?" Gita offered. "He's his father's son—it's so hard to get him to open. I might be able to help."

"No," Gretchen said. "But I love that you offered."

"Work on him. You are the only thing that can convince him to come to Rome, and I miss my son. Joel and I adore you, you know that. We'd do anything to help you two."

"I know, I know. That's such a solace, to know that you're out there."

"I hear Joel at the door. Do you want me to call back later?"

"No, I'll be fine," Gretchen said. She remembered Gita's distressed expression at dinner. "How are *you* doing?" she pressed, although through her sadness she had to fake the tone of empathy.

"Dear, don't worry about me. Just remember the longer story. You love each other—I've seen it. The hard moments can seem so long. Weeks and months. But they pass."

"I love you."

"You, too. Bye, dear."

Gretchen rubbed her face with her hands. She wanted to start sobbing again, if only to feel purged after, but her tears never came when willed.

Baby, her text message to Rajan read, *Let's have lunch tomorrow. I love you so much.*

* * *

Rajan called the next morning. He made no protestations or moves to forestall meeting her again, but she still felt she had obliged him to see her. She arrived at the dining hall first, snuck past the ID checker, and found a space next to the window. She watched students mingle in the courtyard and felt lost in herself. She had to be carefree. She rarely wore makeup but she was wearing it today, and it was an odd sensation for her, as though she were back in television again. She was further displaced when Rajan arrived. In the hard, brilliant light of the dining hall he was too perfectly in focus. She loved the sluggish way he tugged his tray along the guides, the way he lifted his foot and scratched inside his sock as he exchanged manly phrases with the guy behind him. But when he approached the table she could tell by the stiffness in his gait, the oddly rigid arrangement of his food, that he was breaking up with her, and for good this time.

10

It is Gretchen's theory—and she is a creature of theories—that young women who travel alone don't travel alone for long. Sitting on the curb in the early morning, she hopes her sense of isolation will lift by the time the airport limo arrives. She went to the Alitalia website the evening before, saw that her reservation was still valid, blinked at the screen, then poured her depression out to an Alitalia phone representative. Her request to confirm her and Rajan's seat assignments was fragmentary, unwarrantedly emotional, improperly worded—everything but tearful—but the ticket was verified.

It was another of Gretchen's theories that if she stayed up all night she would board her morning flight, fall instantly asleep, then sleepwalk through her layover and flutter awake just as she arrived in Rome, perfectly rested and adjusted to the Italian time zone. Executing the plan, however, is already proving difficult. After she gets in a cab for Logan Airport she tries to snooze against the vinyl seat, but can't keep her eyes closed.

She remembers the moment she hit on the idea: she was packing her suitcase (hurriedly purchased on a street in Chinatown), stuffing clothes into a black nylon contraption that had the heft and feel of a giant three-ring binder, when a fit of desolation came over her in the middle of packing her panties. She realized that she wouldn't need to keep packing that evening if she packed the next morning instead, and she wouldn't have to worry about getting up early if she never went to bed, and the lack of sleep wouldn't matter because she could sleep on the plane, thereby simultaneously escaping the tedium of the flight—it was genius. Her plan also had the blissful side benefit of preventing her from stewing over Rajan (she had been a fool, shortsighted and a fool, but she'd get him back somehow!). And so she celebrated graduation with her friends until four-thirty A.M., feeling miserable the whole time but acting ecstatic in case anyone cared to report her bliss back to Rajan, then at five stuffed her remaining clothes into the bag and hailed a cab.

She realizes, as she boards the plane, that she has forgotten to pack socks or tampons or panties.

No one could say she was in a fit state of mind when she was packing. It was the day after graduation, the day she had highlighted in fuchsia in her planner, when she and Rajan were supposed to put their stuff in storage and fly away together. As she was swamping the hallway with trash bags full of her possessions and slamming clothes into the suitcase, she couldn't stop the old schedule from unfurling in her head: now we'd be turning in the keys, now we'd be taking off, now we'd be landing, now we'd get some of Rajan's money out of the bank, now we'd argue about how to get to the city from the airport, and now we'd kiss.

But they had broken up and gotten back together, broken up again, gotten back together, and then again, once the charge of tearful sex was spent, broke up once more, only to get back together, until Rajan cut it off entirely, forbade her from calling him and blocked her from his email account. She sent him messages from her friends' accounts; she snuck up to his room and pounded on the door. But he never returned the emails; his roommates reported that he was never home. She tried calling Gita, but her away message said she was already in Europe. All Gretchen knew of Rajan she found out from friends of friends, the twice-removed gossips: he was wrecked, yet still vowed never to see her again.

She hopes Rajan might join her on the flight after all, might dash to fill the empty seat next to her just as the aircraft door closes. But no Rajan.

And so Gretchen has come to Italy to enlist the aid of his—their—parents. The Alitalia representatives—on the phone, at check-in, at the gate, on the plane—heard all about it.

A young woman hovers over the entrance to the Rome baggage claim, smiling beatifically at the arriving passengers. She is dressed in the Alitalia corporate colors: green, white, and red. She nods at Gretchen.

After a siren fanfare, luggage begins to parade along the conveyor belt. The suitcases, precisely rectangular incarnations of gray and green, file neatly past, shoulder-to-shoulder. Until, that is, Gretchen's nylon ogre barrels down the ramp and scatters a polite cluster. Gretchen muscles her bag over the lip of the conveyer.

The Alitalia representative glides over to her.

"I'll just check your claim," she announces, beaming.

Gretchen rummages through her pockets and produces a bouquet of boarding passes, her ticket envelope and claim sticker. The woman nods encouragingly as she checks the labels.

"Thank you!" she says. She gestures Gretchen toward a pair of frosted doors. They open of their own power, revealing a chaotic and expectant crowd of greeters. Gretchen is daunted; tears return to her eyes.

"Can I help you?" the woman asks.

Can she help Gretchen?

"Yes," Gretchen decides. In front of the smooth whir of the luggage belt, amid the controlled uproar of businessmen and schoolchildren claiming their bags, Gretchen explains her situation in slow, textbook-perfect English, as if conducting a language lesson. She dodges her sexual history with Rajan but conveys in repetitive detail the dilemma of knowing that his parents are the only way to win him back, but she doesn't know where they are staying, and they've been out of contact. The representative listens in rapt astonishment.

"I don't know what to do," Gretchen finishes with a hiccup.

The representative produces a cell phone. Gretchen takes it. The device is weightless in her hands.

"Call them," the representative suggests.

"I don't have their hotel number. Rajan was the one who knew it."

"No *telefonino*?"

Gretchen shakes her head. All she knows is that Gita mentioned that their favorite Roman hotel was near the Piazza Navona.

The representative leads Gretchen deep into the Alitalia offices.

Who arrives in Rome only to decide she shouldn't be there? It's not like she should be able to duck in, check out the scene, and duck back out. She's gone halfway around the world; she's in a new and fantastic land; she can't just plunge back into the rabbit hole.

She's in the Alitalia staff room, clutching a café mocha that was created, transfixingly, in the womb of a glass-walled machine. She can't make herself look up. All she can see are the four splayed aluminum legs of her chair upon a wide field of linoleum. She rocks her head in her lap. This is, she realizes, something crazy people do. She lifts her head.

The representative hovers by a console, glancing over protectively but giving Gretchen a cautious berth. The Italian language is thrown about the small room as she conducts Internet name searches and looks into ground transportation. "Is this a hotel *particolare*?" she asks.

Huh?

"Do you know what size is the hotel?"

No.

"Where it is on the piazza?"

"It's somewhere nearby, that's all I know."

The woman chews a pen as her fingers flutter over the keyboard. The screen casts her golden, gives her smooth forehead the glow of a new car's hood. "There are very many hotels near the Piazza Navona," she announces glumly.

Gretchen stares at her. "I guess I'll just have to go to there and poke around," she says, her voice quavering.

She wishes she had been able to speak to Gita even once since the breakup, that the Lansings wouldn't have gone abroad the very moment she needed them most. Would Rajan have emailed them since the break-up? Even if he's told them that the relationship is over, perhaps the Lansings will take her in with their usual unwavering hospitality, as they would receive any future daughter-in-law.

She remembers their discussing booking a house to unwind in before embarking on a sailing tour. They probably got one with an extra room for her and Rajan, maybe even with its own separate entrance. She can just hole up there and keep out of their way until Rajan eventually shows up.

She knows that appearing on their vacation doorstep is a shade more intense than romantic; it is psychotic. They might stare at the hysterical and bedraggled girl throwing herself upon them, smile a lot, laugh a little, take her to dinner, and then offer to drop her back at the airport. Gretchen would be stuck in Rome alone, with another failure to add to her recent list.

She wishes she had someone to call for support. Her own family is—where? Not Fresno, not anymore. Somewhere in Florida, maybe Tampa? She can't go back anyway. Her friends may say they feel rootless but she is the real thing, genuinely unconnected to anyone else. Back on the *Mustang* set her extreme independence felt indulgent, like she was a creature of the sky. But now she is crushed by her choices. Every place is the same because she will know no one everywhere she goes. Gretchen realizes with a start that she has been working through her concerns out loud. The Alitalia representative is studiously concentrating on her nails.

She'll be ambushing Rajan into seeing her again, but in a flattering Roman light. She'll have turned to his very parents for solace—he'll find it deeply odd, but endearing. They will be together again—or at the very least he'll have to talk to her! She can make all the apologies he hasn't given her the opportunity to make. This could be the remedy for everything gray and half-felt in their relationship: an astonishingly quixotic move, free of the gritless confines of Harvard intellect. She'll be crazy, yes, but, like black magic and white magic, there are two kinds of insanity, and she thinks the good kind may be the one source of spontaneous beauty in the world.

Gretchen wipes her tear-streaked nose as she grins, flushed with revelation. She may be miserable, seemingly ruined, but she will not stop herself from taking risks. Nothing will ever change unless she makes a change. It sounds reductive, but it has guided her life thus far. The only hope for living a life that isn't numbingly ordinary is to be new.

11

Gretchen's first impression of Rome is of sirens, of the flattened electronic honking of Italian ambulances. It's a more sibilant sound than in the States, weaker but more insistent, like a child calling for help. They seem to be saying "There he is! There he is!" the tones broadening as they pass.

Gretchen always thought of Rome, Italy, Europe—the world—as diversions for bored and successful American families, where those who have neatened the seams of their carpeted existence dipped into dark forests and pastries. Once, after finishing a spelling quiz back in elementary school, she stared at a laminated poster of the Colosseum on the classroom wall, that wonderful chaotic stone arena surrounded by cars turning so fast their lights blurred, and imagined herself and her mother and her father in yet another little black car whirling around it. They were crowded into the front seats, their faces larger than the windows themselves, gawking at the splendor about them. Her father, now just a remembered memory, fuzzy like any copy of a copy, was dark and threatening and exciting; her mother had her furls of curly hair restrained under a felt cap. Gretchen herself was younger and more lovely than she really was, a princess destined for rule. In Europe their family would become what it should become.

They never got to Europe.

Now that she is really here she has been guarding herself against loneliness, but what she feels is not desolation at all—it is the version of solitude that is exciting; everything is potential. In the train from the airport she uses her nylon suitcase to barricade herself into a row of seats, pulls her knees to her chest, and stares directly into the eyes of any Italians who pass her seat. It impresses her, the possibility of it all, that she could simply pick one of them, start a conversation, and, with enough hard work, become an essential part of his or her life.

Gretchen gets out at the *Roma Ostiense* station and steps into the street, sidles past an African guy selling clothes and trinkets, hitches her fingers over the handle of her suitcase, and stares at the Roman skyline. A throng of Fiats careens through a roundabout, then all is quiet, and then another throng descends before shooting out of orbit. In the glow of Roman midmorning the cars are white and blue and silver but also piped in orange light refracted from the nearby buildings. They are vibrant, nothing like the long-suffering little black car she had imagined carrying her family. The whole city is orange, she sees, apricot paint and warm diesel fumes and ochre ruins wedged between modern buildings.

She is tired, but more pressing are her hunger and a lingering fear that she is unmoored and potentially bonkers. She decides a beer and a snack are in order. Rome is clogged with Irish pubs. She passes three in her first hour of wandering, and decides to enter the fourth. The meat pie she orders is soggy but filling, and the bartender is helpful in getting her less panicked (via the beer) and giving her a sense of her bearings. She checks into the small hotel to which he directs her, then settles in at the lobby computer. She knows that, despite her exhaustion, she needs to send the email she has been mentally composing before she will be able to sleep.

From: Gretchenzbeanie@webfree.com
To: HumpSkate92@amweb.com
Subject: RE: Writing you back . . .

Humphrey!

I'm sure you're not expecting an email from me. It's weird for me, too, to be writing to you. Especially weird given where I am. If only you could see. I'm jet-lagged, and in Rome all by myself! I'll explain why later. But mainly I'm writing to let you know I've always been sad that I haven't been in touch. I guess it's come to a head now because of some personal stuff I'm going through. I want you to know that you've been in my mind, well, forever. I've imagined you facing the same kind of shit that I always faced, and I just left you to it. We should be looking out for each other.

Whew! How's that for an opening! Sorry. I don't really plan emails, they just happen. And I guess that was on my mind.

You probably feel like you don't even remember me anymore, but I want you to know that I totally get what you're dealing with. I usually ignore mom's emails, but I read the latest one just now and it says you're living in some place called Haven Township? They only name places like that when they're crappy. I can just imagine what it's like for you at home, or should I say "at motel." lol. Jesus.

Mom and dad never did anything wrong, nothing that could actually be called abuse. Some people really suffer for how they were raised. My good friend Alessandra missed a semester of school after she remembered her cousin molesting her during Bio class. She remembered it in class, not got molested in class! Creepy. Anyway that makes it seem like people like you and me can't complain, you know? But you know what, I don't know your dad well, but our mom's just a bad parent. It's not just that she worked too much, or didn't have time for me. She just had me way too young, never got over her own ambitions and so never really supported mine. I really needed someone, you know? And the weirdest thing is that I'm sure the worst times were the ones that are invisible now, that I was too young to remember. Who knows how much of an effect they had on me, the years mom and I lived with my birth dad in New York. When my dad left, I was like six or seven, and mom didn't leave her bed for a month. I was just a kid, Humph. I'm not trying to build myself up as a martyr or anything, but still . . .

I was in therapy for a while, did I tell you that?

I'm just going on and on, blah blah, but she's your mom too, I guess, so this should be interesting to you. It sounds petty now, but at the time everything was so huge. I was fourteen when I left. I was innocently bitchy. I hated mom because she stopped me from being totally focused on myself. I get that, now. I think I've totally gotten over that teenage crap. You'll learn about it in college if you study psychoanalysis – narcissism, too much ego. I can't really hold mom's wanting to fill her own needs against her. But god! She was suffocating. She could draw the focus of any relationship to herself. We were two children living together.

That moment, oh that phone call, when the agent called me with a part! Mom kept him on the phone for half an hour discussing her own acting ambitions . . . until he had to go and never called back. That was it. I was so done. The next week I made the deadline for that scholarship to the performing arts boarding school, and I was out. I was better off alone. I'm still better off alone. Everyone is, maybe.

And now I've graduated from Cambridge College and I'm in ITALY.

I'm going to make it up to you, that I've been so out of touch. Please write. You don't have to blab as much as I just did, but I'd love to hear whatever you want to tell me about everyone in your life. Like what's the new school like? Who's this friend Wade?

Love,
Gretch

With sleep and morning light on clean white sheets, her thoughts are first lavishly sensual and only gradually consumed by dread. What the hell is she doing in Rome—does she really think her plan will come off? But with the greater resolve that comes with rest she decides not to panic, simply does not allow herself the luxury. Enough time for hysteria tonight, when she is tired again. As she sinks her cheek into the crisp feather pillow, it comes to her that she feels beautiful this morning, potent and fortunate. She's been given an opportunity to keep her place in Rajan's life. She will strategize over lunch.

She takes a long shower, exfoliates, and moisturizes.

By the time she gets to a café and orders a pastry and coffee, she is apprehensive again. She's still very much in love with Rajan. It's not as though she thinks about him all the time, but when she does the sudden gloom is devastating. She stares at the brass-rimmed faux granite of the café table and then jabs her croissant into her coffee. She'll get a haircut before lunch. That will help.

She walks into Fashion 7 and, through gesticulations confirmed by the hairdresser in haphazard English, gets six inches lopped off. A thin halo of her severed hair layers the crimson satin of her smock, with a wider halo of brown shards on the marble floor. She watches her hair rise from the middle of her back to above her shoulders and can still imagine Rajan's hands in it. The cut alone is not enough.

The hairdresser sees her expression. "*Colorazione?*"

Battle plan of the newly blond: assume the Lansings are in Rome; assume they want to see her, that Rajan was not her only connection to them. These both simply must be true; if either assumption is false, then the whole precarious logic of her situation rips apart. She takes a wolfish bite of her sandwich.

She will do some Internet research after breakfast.

From: Gretchenzbeanie@webfree.com
To: Ale@post.cambridgecollege.edu
Subject: Rome?

Hey Alessandra,

what's up? or should I say ciao? :) how's the internship going? any pics from graduation yet? anyway, you're not going to believe this but I'm in Rome! it's a long story. Obviously you remember my craziness over the breakup, and I'm here now and I need to find his parents and you went to high school in Rome (Naples?), so do you know how I can find a pair of twenty-first century American aristocrats here? Write back soon, because I only have like a couple hundred Euros and they're getting spent fast. I know, I'm f*ing insane, but that's why you love me, right?

Luv G

Gretchen does some research at the Internet café. On an expat website she turns up an English language opera society (she hopes she won't have to go there to find them; she imagines matrons in quilted sweaters covered in mats of cat hair), two English language bookstores, the embassy, an American university, and five international high schools. When the enormity of her search threatens to overwhelm her, she watches a music video online and has a gelato lunch. She is still licking *panna* from her fingers when she returns to the computer.

From: di Mauro, Alessandra ‹ale@mailworld.com›
To: Gretchen Baxter ‹Gretchenzbeanie@webfree.com›
Subject: RE: Rome?

U R insane. I mean it. What do u think ur going to do, get them to call him or something???!! Honestly hon, I think Rajan's secretly crazy too, so this might mean ur perfect together. But ur really not supposed to DO shit like this!! Why didn't u just write him a pathetic "come back to me" letter like the rest of us would? it's just so U to go and find his parents. u should try English language bookstores. But it's a long shot. ur stuck. And ur crazy. And I do love u. Tell me if you need money.

—Ale

Gretchen googles Joel Lansing. He was once a member of an office softball team. He studied social sciences at Washington University in St. Louis, and graduated in the seventies. His name is mentioned on some other guy's résumé. His birthday is in two weeks. She finds the name of his company and goes to its website. An internal search for Lansing lands the real estate development department. Joel Lansing, VP. God, there are a lot of VPs. No email address for him, but there is one for his assistant.

To: denise@cockersecurities.com
From: gbaxter@cambridgecollege.edu
Subject: Urgent

Ms. Campbell:

Rajan Lansing, Mr. Joel Lansing's son, suggested I write to you. Rajan and I are planning on throwing him a surprise birthday party here in Rome, but Rajan's misplaced the name of his hotel. Could you please remind us?

Thank you,
Gretchen Baxter

She composes the email half in jest. But with a click, it is irrevocable. A moment later, brooked by the jolt of that reckless connection, she writes to her mother with all the reduced inhibition of the newly drunk.

To: Triciaonstage@amweb.com
From: gbaxter@cambridgecollege.edu
Subject:

Mom,

Whoa, surprise. Not expecting an email from me, huh? I've been thinking about you guys, about you and dad, wherever he is, because graduation was just last week. I've attached some pictures.

From your last message Humphrey sounds like he's doing fine . . . in yet another new school.

So, I'm in Rome! I guess you didn't know that. I had money left over from school, and so I just decided to come here. Crazy, right? I'm going to start a real job soon, probably go to

New York like all the rest of my friends and sit in front of a screen, but I'm not rushing. Are you still at Arby's? How's George's computer stuff going?

I'm also here because I'm in love with this guy and if you had come to graduation you would have met him, he's so great and you'd love him.

So what a surprise, huh? An email from me. I don't expect you to write back. It's ok if you don't. I probably shouldn't have written.

Anyway, I'm feeling kind of wild right now, and I guess it shows. I'm probably not even going to hit send.

By the way, this school email address won't work soon.

—Gretch

Why didn't she at least delete that sentence about not hitting send? A pang of bad feeling hits her as the browser returns to her inbox. She's usually the one to delay communications with her mother, and she always relishes the feeling of not having written back, that it gives her a power she never had as a child. But as soon as she sends an email that power is lost. For the next hours, days, weeks, she will be a needy child waiting for her mother to respond.

To: Baxter, Gretchen ‹gbaxter@cambridgecollege.edu›
From: Campbell, Denise ‹denise@cockersecurities.com›
Subject: RE: Urgent

Ms. Baxter,

Mr. Lansing no longer works at Cocker Securities. Surely his son has told you? But I'm glad to get your email, as he is actually writing a reference letter for me, and I'd like for you to send along my best wishes and (politely!) remind him for me. I made his final travel arrangements, which I've attached to this email. Please note that he's only booked this hotel for two more nights. He might just be changing hotels, but I'd suggest you throw your party well in advance of his birthday.

Sincerely,
Denise Campbell
Cocker Securities
521 5th Avenue, 26th Floor
New York, NY 10021

The Lansings' hotel is small but presides over a Fendi store on the *Via del Corso*, its façade gold-trimmed glass and fresco. As she takes in the imperial little building Gretchen buys a *panino*, dodges the flirtations of a man in a gladiator costume, and installs herself at an outdoor café across the street. She has purchased large purple-tinted glasses from a street vendor and, decked out as she is, imagines herself a pop star come to Rome to convalesce after a torrid and public affair.

She folds a paper placemat and begins to fan herself. Flirting with the boys at the front desk only earned her the knowledge that Mr. and Mrs. Lansing went out separately that morning. Surely they'd come back for a rest in the afternoon?

After pretending to involve herself in a magazine, she writes a postcard to Alé, thanking her for her attempt to help. She gets a beer, then a coffee, then another beer, then a sandwich. Multiple times the same two Italian guys approach her, and as they try different languages she mentally changes her identity: "*Ciao bella!*"—she is American; "Speak Eengleesh?"—she is now German; "*Bonjour?*"—she is still German; "*Bitte, frau?*"—she is Russian. They don't get to Russian before giving up.

She escapes the boys, but the Lansings escape her. The day is a failure.

She catches a few sights in the evening, returns to her pub, and chats with her bartender, Pietro. He's cute.

The next morning she installs herself at the same post. She brings a book this time, and glances up between paragraphs. By late morning she spots a Lansing; it had to happen eventually. Mr. Lansing stalks down the Via del Corso like it's a corporate hallway. He gives off the preoccupied air borne by most tourists during the first days of vacation: habitual anxiety not yet undone by the lethargy of sun and sleeping in. His hair is the same meticulous wave that it was in Cambridge, but in the context of khakis and Rome it looks architectural. He is hemmed in by the intensity of his thoughts—he doesn't look up from the ground—and Gretchen feels safe gawking at him.

He hesitates in front of his hotel, looks quizzically at the sun and his watch, then strides down the street.

Gretchen leaves a coin on the table and starts to follow. She will announce herself soon, but for now she can't think of the words to use. They were expecting her to arrive two days earlier, if at all; she can't recall the monologue she constructed to explain herself.

She has never given chase to anyone, and tailing Mr. Lansing thrills her. The rush of street traffic between them only heightens the illicit fizz, makes her feel both cosmopolitan and anonymous. She follows him to the Piazza Vittorio Emmanuele, dodges the cars thronging the busy square, skirts a Benetton window moments after he does. When Mr. Lansing pauses to glance inside a shop, Gretchen involves herself in examining the motorbikes in the street. What would he say if he saw her? She can't force his hand yet—she would be devastated if he were upset.

He has a muscular frame, but it has been iced with fat so that his V-shape has squared into one solid block of flesh. Gretchen may be in better shape, but Mr. Lansing has dressed more appropriately; Gretchen has worn jeans and is sweating heavily by the time Mr. Lansing ducks into a *farmacia*. She leans against an iron post across the street and catches her breath.

He emerges carrying a plastic bag. Gretchen follows him along the Forum, and then to the Colosseum. As she tails him, Gretchen removes her sunglasses to better scrutinize his bag. Whatever he has purchased is light, two glossy boxes. She dares to shorten her following distance. The initial thrill of standing so near her quarry is paled by the shock of discovery—in the late-afternoon sun arcing through the portals of the Colosseum, flooding the slate cobblestones and bouncing off the silver of the vendors' carts, she can see silhouetted within the plastic bag the unmistakable size and style of boxes of condoms and lube.

It seems impossible to her for a moment, that condoms and lubricant should exist outside her more fully fleshed-out world of America. *Italians* use *lube*! It's obvious but still startling, almost as startling as the fact that said products have been purchased by Mr. Lansing.

She replaces her sunglasses, even as the afternoon darkens.

Mr. Lansing makes another stop, this time at a Chinese restaurant, and emerges with a sack of take-out. He turns up a leafy side-street.

She will have to be more careful, as she can no longer veil herself in the crush of the crowd. She waits at the base of the alley, cars and buses honking past, and watches him. He stops outside the tall brick wall of a villa, he presses a button, waits a few moments, and then Gretchen hears the buzz of a door being released.

A shadowed woman steps out, kisses him on the cheek, ushers him inside and slams the door. Gretchen stops in front of the formidable gate, peeks through the seam of its hinge. An ancient fountain tinkles, giving the interior courtyard the character of a remote glen. Dinner and condoms, and no Gita?

Gretchen heads back to the Lansings' hotel.

She is only just able to recall the route back: skirt the *Circus Maximus* and pick her way over the cobblestones around the Colosseum, cross a piazza, and follow the street to the end. She is reeling at first, but her feelings turn to anger. How dare Mr. Lansing have an affair! He has a loving wife, the ideal home situation, and here he is throwing it all away. She hasn't even had a chance to announce her arrival, and Mr. Lansing has already gone wrecking the stable thing she has been counting on. Fathers are assholes.

She considers telling Gita but quickly realizes that the enormity of it would desolate her. Besides, upsetting Gita would get Gretchen nowhere. She seats herself at the now familiar bar across the street and stares into the hotel's gold and glass lobby, blankly follows the formal movements of the boys at the front desk.

She tries to calm herself by thinking only of the radiance of the sun on her arms, but her thoughts stay darkly romantic, all brimstone. She wonders how any relationships work, when even warm and lovely Gita can't keep her husband from straying. Little wonder that she couldn't make things work with Rajan, even with such sustained effort. Maybe he's glad to be rid of her. Rajan fell in love with someone who sparkled in conversation, who spoke readily and dewily, but the real Gretchen is pensive and terrified of being thought boring. Rajan fell in love with a girl with straightened hair and screen makeup that gave her the complexion of an inner petal, but the real Gretchen has greasy skin at the sides of her nose and stays skinny through fucked-up eating habits because she doesn't like to work out. Rajan fell in love with a girl who seemed unapproachable, but the real Gretchen would spend all day with him if he would have her, and during the night would lie awake staring at him and wonder what it would feel like when he left. How does anyone remain the person who was fallen in love with, not lose concentration and reveal her gray and boring center?

Gretchen stares blankly at a magazine. An awning above her flaps. Buses pass in poisonous gusts.

Eventually she musters the force of will to pass through the hotel's sliding-glass doors. The interior is like a scrubbed tropical paradise, all stone and flowing water and automatic doors leading into silk-flower jungles. She approaches the concierge desk. There are two attendants—a middle-aged man and an assistant closer to her own age. She selects, of course, the younger man. "I'm meeting a friend here. At least I think she's staying here. Gita Lansing?"

She has turned on her full charisma: the young Italian has trouble meeting her gaze. "Yes. You asked about her yesterday, *signorina.* Is she expecting you? Would you care to wait in the lobby for her?"

"No, I'd rather go up to her room, if that's okay."

The man checks his computer. "I'll be happy to call up for you."

"Yes. That will be fine. Thanks."

The young man is in the middle of dialing when Gretchen hears her name.

Gita has just exited the elevator. She wears a towel around her hips, and a sunhat obscures her face. She dangles a pair of swimming goggles from her hand. "Gretchen?!" she repeats.

Gretchen shrugs and smiles. "Yep."

Gita drops the goggles to the carpet and folds Gretchen into her arms. "Oh, honey!"

"I came . . . I couldn't do this alone," Gretchen says into Gita's hair.

"Oh! Oh, Gretchen!"

They stammer a few shocked phrases at each other, until Gretchen pulls back and looks into Gita's eyes. "This is crazy, isn't it?"

"I'm so glad you're here. And look at your hair color!"

Gretchen fondles her hair and wonders what to say.

Gita speaks. "There's so much to talk about. But let's wait for a moment. Have you just arrived? You must be starving. I'm going to the hotel pool. Why don't you come with me, and we'll order you some food."

The pool is below ground, but lit from above by a skylight. Gita is curious about everything—why is Gretchen there two days later than planned? how was the flight?—but shies from the issue of Rajan's absence. Once the subject of Rajan seems unavoidable, and Gretchen is about to speak of him, Gita dives into the pool. She swims a few laps and then perches her chin on the ledge as she kicks her toned brown legs beneath the shifting blue light. They have ordered wine from an attendant, and take sips from glasses on a tray.

"Gretchen," Gita says, "I don't want you to worry that I am unhappy at you. I am delighted you have come. A ticket to Rome is not something to waste."

"I'm so relieved. You have no idea. Do you think Raj will freak out that I'm here?"

Gita traces a circle in the water with her leg. "Freak out? Because what, you used a plane ticket that would have been to waste otherwise? I don't think so. Don't worry about my son. I don't know that I'm even going to tell him you are here. He's been so foolish."

"What has he told you?"

"Not much. Just that you two had broken up. He is not the type to open up about something like this. He is like a bottle—more my generation than yours."

"Is he coming here?"

"He says he is too busy. He is in L.A. now, trying to set up. Between you and me, though, I bet he will be here before the summer is over. He does not, for example, even own a bed. He will miss comforts."

Gretchen lies back and tries to relax, but then sits bolt upright again. "I'm sorry, this is totally weird. Is it totally weird?"

Maybe it's just a trick of the light refracting from the pool, but Gita seems to roll her eyes. "I said I'm happy for you to be here. This is a relief to me, you know? Come take a lap."

"I don't have a swimsuit."

"Just wear your underwear. There's no one else here."

"No, I don't think so, I'll just stay here."

"Don't be so *American.*" Gita had always occupied herself with making Gretchen comfortable, but now that solicitousness has dropped. She's become defensive, Gretchen realizes. Smiling rigidly, wondering how Gita's own situation has changed, Gretchen strips to her underwear and slips into the pool.

The Lansings made reservations for a late dinner at a restaurant near the Spanish Steps. Gita suggests she and Gretchen retire to their separate hotels and reconvene at the restaurant, joking that the first time Gretchen will see Mr. Lansing will be over appetizers.

Gretchen is the first to arrive and waits in an alleyway nearby, leaning against a doorway. The white linen shirts in the front window of a men's store catch stray streetlight and glimmer like ghosts. Even when she hears familiar footsteps approach, Gretchen resolutely maintains her focus on the closed shop. Liking the image she projects—styled young woman, peasant dress and narrow, tragic shoulders—she lets Mr. Lansing stare at her for a few moments before she turns around.

He looks at her, smiles as blankly as he would to any fellow American, and then the smile drops and his expression intensifies. "*Gretchen?*"

She nods.

"We figured you'd be here days ago, if at all. So you haven't blown us off?"

Gretchen steps forward. "Definitely not. Don't even ask about the specifics. I've already been through it all with your wife."

He shakes her hand, until his handshake becomes a hug that crushes for an instant then is gone. "I think you're right—it's probably best that I don't ask. Nice hair, by the way."

Gretchen shrugs and laughs, throws her hands on her hips. "Well!"

"What a coincidence!" Mr. Lansing winks. "All of us in Rome."

Gretchen orders a salad with cherry tomatoes and porcini mushrooms. Mr. Lansing sips a glass of wine and doesn't touch a plate of roast chicken. Gita, once she arrives, demolishes a side of lamb. When Rajan was around, family dinners typically started with Mr. Lansing dominating the conversation until his son's boredom became too evident, at which point Mr. Lansing would fall into a moody silence through which he regarded his wife and son with contempt. Now, however, there is no Rajan to hold him back. Mr. Lansing periodically cuts off his speeches to take a drag from a cigarette, leans his chair back on two feet, and laughs at the improbability of their being together. Gretchen suspects his jauntiness is an act: he didn't smoke before.

"So I figured," he says, absently tapping the rim of his cup with his fingernail and emitting a long plume of smoke before returning his attention to Gretchen, "the Italians really know how to live. Sure, they're behind most of Europe. But they still enjoy all the benefits of the EU, only work thirty-five hours a week, take all of August off. I figured . . ." Mr. Lansing breaks off and stares at the gold band of his cigarette, suddenly engrossed. Gretchen wonders whether he's nervous. "I figured that I'm finally at a place in my life where I have the clout to decide my own workweek. Essentially, I've doubled my productivity from where it was a decade ago. I could, therefore, make twice as much money or just maintain my standards of a decade ago and work half as much. So I made that choice. Few Americans would, I think."

Gretchen glances at Gita. Mr. Lansing's quit. Why is he pretending he still has a job? But Gita is inscrutable.

He continues, "And I admire that about you, that you're not slaving at an internship this summer, or restarting your acting career right away, and instead you're using your youth to travel."

Gretchen nods as she spears a mushroom. She never would have lasted doing an internship, it's true. She examines Mr. Lansing as he talks. His hair is wiry, almost inorganic, and his green eyes are ensconced in the dramatic crags of his face. He's got Rajan's athletic frame, though, unlike Rajan's, his shirt pouches over his belly. All the same, the buff hints of a fledgling tan have blossomed on his face, and Gretchen sucks in her breath at the unwanted yet insistent flicker of attraction, considers the possibility that should she not be able to win Rajan back, she could fall into a glorious and unhappy affair with Mr. Lansing himself.

Mr. Lansing gestures to the world outside the window of the restaurant. "So what are you going to *do* here?"

Gretchen shrugs and smiles. *Who have* you *been screwing?* "Not sure, really. Spend time with you guys, if you'll have me."

"Of course we'll have you," Gita murmurs.

"Rajan has to be missing you this summer, having you off wandering Rome by yourself," Mr. Lansing says.

Even as her feelings swell, it amazes Gretchen that Mr. Lansing could be so reckless with his suggestions. "I hoped he might be here when I arrived," she says. It is an initial offering; she hopes they will talk about Rajan for hours.

Mr. Lansing shrugs and grimaces, as if to comment on his son's unfairness. "I thought he'd be here already, too—that he'd have flown in when you did, maybe. But he's always doing his own thing. These opportunities only come once in a while, you know, parents in Europe who are willing to sponsor you. Dinners like this"—Mr. Lansing gestures to the table as Gretchen forks a salty lettuce leaf into her mouth—"are the benefits of staying with family members. But he's his mother's child."

"Oh, most nice, dear," Gita says. "Pin it on your Gita."

"I just don't see why he wouldn't come right away. See, he's just expressing another symptom of the overzealous American work ethic—*apropos* of our previous conversation." Mr. Lansing grins broadly, waiting for Gretchen's admiration. He might not, Gretchen recalls, be too bright.

"I don't think we're going to get back together," Gretchen says, wondering why she smiles as she speaks.

"Of course you are," Mr. Lansing says. "I refuse to hear any more about it."

"Oh, we are, huh?" Gretchen says flirtatiously. "How? Give me a plan. I'm listening."

"Well, um . . ." Mr. Lansing defers to Gita, who just stares back with amusement. "You'll just . . . I guess it depends on why things went wrong, doesn't it? Why did things go wrong?"

"He thinks I didn't love him enough, but I do, and he won't listen to me."

"Oh. I'm sure he'll come around."

Gretchen jabs a morsel of bread into the olive oil coating her plate. She senses Mr. Lansing's sympathy, even as she knows he won't express it directly. She wonders if she'll cry soon. "So what's the grand Italy plan?" she asks brightly.

"We don't really know," Gita says. "We've been to Italy plenty of times, so we are here just to relax. I am shopping and spending time at the pool. Joel, well, who knows what Joel does with his days. But with you here, maybe we will do real sightseeing again. You have never been here, no?"

"Right. I've always wanted to, of course. Everyone wants to."

"You are to be our project! All the major sights—Vatican City, Pantheon, Villa Borghese, all that. You are going to love it here. It is everything you have heard."

They chat about the sights of Rome for the rest of dinner, Mr. Lansing throwing out a place name and Gita commenting exhaustively on it. After paying the bill, Mr. Lansing rises and wanders out of the restaurant. Gretchen settles into her wicker chair, waiting for him to return. Gita, however, gathers her shawl over her shoulders and kicks her feet into her sandals. "Ready?" she asks.

"Oh!" Gretchen says. "We're not waiting for him?"

"Oh, no, we occupy ourselves."

Gretchen walks Gita home in the cooling evening. They are quiet with each other, but when they say good-bye Gita kisses Gretchen's forehead, says she understands what Gretchen is going through and that everything will be all right. They plan to meet in front of the hotel the next morning.

When they do, Gretchen is taken aback to find Gita straddling a *motorino*. Gita glances down at her leather-clad legs and hitches her helmet tighter under her arm. "You probably think I am to be crazy. What a surprise! Leather goddess Gita."

"Wow," Gretchen says. "We're not in America anymore, huh?"

"No, thank God. Let's go." She adjusts her black pants, sits higher on the cream Vespa, and pats the seat behind her. "Come on, get on. We're going to have an adventure."

Gretchen hesitates—she's nervous to board a motorbike, and she's also undone by the dramatic change in Gita's appearance. Then Gita suddenly laughs at herself and peers at the vehicle like it's a wild animal.

Gretchen rests her weight on the back of the seat. "I've never done this before," she says.

"Here," Gita says, "take the helmet. I'll ride without. Wind in my hair and all that."

"How dramatic," Gretchen says. Gita laughs automatically. Gretchen wraps her arms around her soft torso.

"What have you seen?" Gita yells as they speed down Via Aventina.

Gretchen smiles under the helmet. What *has* she seen? But of course Gita is referring to landmarks. "The Colosseum, Circo Massimo, Palatine Hill. Those ancient baths nearby, too."

They slow down for a light. "Via Appia Antica?"

"Vee what?" Gretchen has to yell to be heard through the helmet.

"Via Appia Antica. The Appian Way, you could say."

"No, haven't seen it."

Gita suddenly veers. They race along a bowered street, light flashing to dark as they speed through dappled sunshine. Gradually the clogged traffic of central Rome gives way to smaller roads and, finally, dirt and paving stones. Gita pulls the Vespa into the grass. "Let's get off and walk for some way. Full genuine Roman road."

Gretchen follows her onto the broken path. She kicks off her sandals and feels the grit of old Rome beneath her feet. Gita walks a few feet ahead, staring at the sky. Ruins hem the road, tall and ragged brick pillars, stones cut by tendrils of rubbery grass.

"It goes all the way to Naples," Gita says. "The central artery of the heart of the empire. So say the tour guides."

"It's like this all the way down?"

"More or less. I walk here on the mornings." She flashes Gretchen a brown smile. "Never walked all the way to Naples, though." Gita waits for Gretchen to join her. When she does, the unevenness of the flagstones puts Gretchen closer than she intended to be. Her shoulder presses Gita's back and she's subject to a flood of sensations: the heat from her torso, a whiff of her deodorant and the flavor of her skin, the rise of a curl of hair above her neck, and she can understand, easily, how Lansing once fell in love with her. Gita is self-possessed but not vain; she invites infatuation.

"This is my favorite part of all of Rome," Gita says. "The city does not run on in this direction, knew to stop. There are tall buildings, and then there are fields and ruins and birds and grass, all this grass. You can get something basic." They hear a roar in the distance, and the fat belly of a plane rises from behind a green hill. "And then, you see an airport. There is contradiction and beauty here, you know?" She looks at Gretchen shrewdly, almost accusingly. "You are making me all serious. Do you have this effect on everyone?"

Gretchen shakes her head and laughs, but she bites the inside of her cheek. She does have that effect on everyone, and she doesn't know why.

As they walk farther Gretchen begins to feel the full cut of Gita's statement, and a depression wells inside her. She and Rajan stopped having fun. Maybe she's just not a fun person. She's desperate to prove Gita's evaluation false, to supply an excuse for her sullenness. Guiltily, she realizes Gita can be made a companion in her unhappiness. "There's something I have to tell you," Gretchen says.

"Oh, yes?" Gita prompts.

"I—God, I don't know if I should even be telling you this—when I was trying to meet up with you guys, I ran into Mr. Lansing first, actually. He was . . . I'm pretty sure he was going off to see some other woman."

Gita lowers her broad sunglasses. "Oh. That."

Gretchen stops walking. Not *Are you sure?* or *None of your business!* but *Oh. That.* "I'm sorry, Gita," Gretchen continues. "I just thought you should know."

"And you figure I'm not aware. No, I know. It is fine."

"It's fine!"

"Yes. Don't be so American. Come on, let's go. We can catch the Galleria Doria Pamphilj before it closes. There is a fantastic audio guide." They mount the Vespa and leave the ancient road, Gretchen again hanging on behind.

The Lansings booked Gretchen her own suite in their hotel, and although she has been there only a few days her mini apartment already provides some solace. The curtains are reassuring in their tackiness, the tiny kitchenette bland but familiar. When she clicks on the overhead light and sees that the faux antique chandelier still brightens the same electric-blue fabric of her bedspread, that her clothes are still strewn on either side of the cleared currents of her walking patterns, when she still smells the familiar scent of old cement and rotting paint that will soon be replaced by sweet air when she opens the great double glass windows, when she sips espresso and sits on the bed and peels off her clothes and adds them to the piles around her, she feels she has awoken to a familiar slice of light after a long troubled sleep, that at least some of her new life is already known.

She strips to her panties and bra, lies down, and looks over her own body. She is satisfied with it, knows that many men will be interested in her physical presence. Will Rajan Lansing again be one of them?

Mr. Lansing is having an affair, and Gita doesn't care.

Gretchen sits up and takes a gulp of her espresso, feels the brown liquid scald her mouth, swallows and savors the flash in her throat. She puts down the cup and picks at a shred of cuticle on her toe. The Lansings existed only as parents before. Sure, they had their own complexities, but in front of Gretchen they were focused on the lives of their son and his girlfriend. But now the Lansings' interests have spilled into new areas. They're no longer partial and steady. They bear the potential to let each other—and Gretchen—down as much as her own parents did.

Gretchen catches a strong whiff from her suitcase, and so spends the afternoon in a nearby laundromat. She could have sent her wash to the hotel laundry, but she didn't want Mr. Lansing to see her clothes appear on his bill. Besides, the process of cleaning has always calmed her. She positions herself on a stool in front of a giant washing machine, watching her garments twirl in flashing patterns of red and white on a sea of black. It subdues her, that clothes can be washed in Boston or Rome and look the same for it, that she can step on an airplane and be anywhere else in the civilized world within a day and wear the same clothes and be the same person. That the small realities stay knitted together! She hears a click from deep inside the machine and her clothes begin to spin, faster and faster, until the colors are indistinguishable.

Gita appears at the entrance to the laundromat. "I saw the note on the door and thought, no, she couldn't really be off washing! What are you *doing*? Who comes to Italy and spends the afternoon in a laundromat?"

"It's okay, I'm almost done. Should be just a couple more minutes until I can put them in the dryer."

Gretchen feels Gita's hand on her back. "Do you want to be alone?" Gita asks.

"No, no, of course not," Gretchen says.

Gita sits next to her. "If you're worrying about me and Joel, do not," she eventually says. "We're all complicated. My husband is no different."

"I know, I get it."

"Men haven't the engineering to be faithful. My life became much easier once I accepted that."

Gretchen thinks again of Rajan. Her boyfriend was faithful, she's sure of it; why hadn't she counted that blessing? "Do you think that's always the case?" Gretchen asks.

"I don't know, honey. But when you make someone to be your everything, you are losing control of your own happiness."

Yes, Gretchen wants to reply, *but I wasn't happy to start with.*

"I just want you to be content," Gita says. "You are like my little daughter. I am here to help."

"And I'm here for you," Gretchen says.

Unexpectedly, Gita heaves herself up so she perches on the dryer next to Gretchen. She's sitting needlessly close, with her hands drumming the metal sides. It is the pose of a teenager; Gretchen sees a woman ready for some Girl Talk. "You really are the only one who can to wear all the peasant clothing that is so popular now," Gita says. "Even the tiniest girls can't pull it off like you do."

"Thanks."

"What do you *eat*," Gita asks, "just carrots and protein?"

Gretchen laughs because she's supposed to. "I'm totally the biggest pig you can imagine. Fries and all!" Actually, she can't remember the last meal she ate. And, as if to prove it, she feels a stroke of light-headedness.

Gretchen's clothes stop spinning, and she stoops to transfer them to the dryer. Gita pivots to give her room. The mortar of the old blue tiles of the laundromat floor has gone to dust, and Gretchen has to shift in her sandals to keep her balance. She feels very authentic for the moment, like an old Sicilian *donna* slogging through her daily chores.

"Listen, Gretchen," Gita says. "You are twenty-two, and in Rome. Joel and I care for you, and we are happy to take care of you financially while you are here. Yes, who knows what is going on with my fool son. But try not to worry about it so much. And certainly don't worry about Joel and me. We're going to be just fine—as we have been fine for years. Drop your clothes in the dryer and come shopping. And next time, have the hotel do it."

12

The hotel library is a vaulted room, lit to roasting by a row of glowing windows. Gretchen has taken to pulling an armchair against this wall of light and spending the post-lunch hours reading and perspiring. She speeds by the dusty cloth bindings of the great books series and heads instead for the antique slate annex strewn with *Glamour, Cosmo,* photos of fresh-faced blondes hooking their thumbs through low-rise jeans. The magazines have wandered from America in tourists' baggage, are slick and wrinkled from the purses of the girls who left without them. Gretchen comes across a Levi's ad from which the model has been snipped, presumably for some teenager's dream book. She pokes a finger through the rectangle cut from the glossy paper, sees the austere wall of the former villa on the other side, then sighs and moves on to the next page.

The urbane tourists who frequent the hotel skulk into the library wearing sunglasses and hats and seize books by the armful, all to avoid being seen associating with other Americans. Gita is the most flagrantly incognito hotel guest. Today, she actually cracks open the glass doorway and peers in before entering. She has flattened her shiny black hair and flipped it into the back of her dress. Once she has determined the library is empty, she speeds to the contemporary fiction section and slots a handful of books onto a shelf; she has either taken a special interest in authors beginning with Z or is misfiling. Gretchen can't keep from laughing. Gita scans the library and on seeing Gretchen slides her sunglasses onto the top of her head. "Hello!"

She perches on the arm of Gretchen's chair and rests a noncommittal hand on her shoulder. "What are you up to?"

"Mmm . . ." Gretchen glances at the glossy pile at her feet. "Reading."

"Anything good?"

"No, but I can tell you how to get a beach-ready body in three weeks."

"Totally unnecessary. I'm already there."

Gretchen laughs, but not too heartily. Though Gita's muscles may play at the surface, she has nonetheless given up to roundness. Gretchen crosses her legs. Her toenails are cracked and dry; she feels a sudden need to hide them. "What's the afternoon plan?"

"Coffee in the Trastevere quarter with Mr. Lansing. You would like to join us?"

"What else have I got to do?" Gretchen asks, holding up an *Allure*.

"Of course." Gita laughs and then stops abruptly.

"Look, I want you to tell me if I ever get in the way," Gretchen says.

"Are you kidding? I'm just glad to have someone to girl-talk with. It would be so boring here without you."

* * *

When she mounts the Vespa Gretchen realizes she has been looking forward to riding again, to clenching the smooth machine between her thighs, ceding control to Gita and being responsible only for holding on. She's thrilled by the minute of danger at Gita's back, feeling her freshly washed hair fan behind her.

They zip across the tram lines, over the stark banks of the Tiber and into Trastevere. Gita weaves through a clutch of haphazardly parked cars and deposits the *motorino* on a corner. Gretchen follows her into the trendy slums of the far bank.

Trastevere is all winding medieval streets with acute turns, hanging balconies and plazas that spring forth like sunrises from narrowing alleys: the bohemian quarter is made for pursuits and love affairs conducted in narrow corners with raised skirts. They amble through Trastevere until they cross a length of sun-sliced paving stone. Gita and Gretchen come upon Mr. Lansing seated at the edge of a restaurant patio and embrace him. He sips an espresso while Gita chatters of their excursion to find him. He follows her with what seems nominal interest, but at the same time his gaze does not wander—like someone watching a movie on a plane, he is engrossed in something that doesn't quite interest him. Gita has arranged herself to advantage, legs splayed to one side, her face turned three-quarters to her husband. They run the conversation in sprints, Mr. Lansing talking at length and then ceding to a monologue of Gita's, until both turn and inquire a point of Gretchen. She answers quickly. When Gita makes an insightful comment about a film they all saw a couple of evenings before, Gretchen watches Mr. Lansing's hand dance over hers and return to his lap.

"So what have *you* been up to all morning?" Gretchen asks Mr. Lansing. She winks—ever since she found out about his dalliances she's been teasing him; she doesn't know how to address a cad any way but flirtatiously.

"Hmm . . . a few hours of nothing. Same as I've been doing this whole trip. Wandered the Janiculum. Ate a pastry. That's the sum of it." Mr. Lansing looks to his wife first and then allows the full light of his smile to brighten on Gretchen. "I understand you spent yesterday doing the washing."

Gretchen shrugs. "You know, just researching for all my maid parts when I get to L.A."

"Oh, you deserve much better than maid parts."

"Is that so?"

Mr. Lansing throws his hands behind Gretchen's and Gita's chairs, coming perilously close to spilling his cappuccino onto Gita's top. "Maids are for TV movies and porno. Not a great career trajectory."

"Do you have a better plan? Some friend who can help me out?"

"Hmm . . . why does it have to be a friend? What makes you think I can't help you out directly?"

"Are you holding out on me, Mr. Lansing?" Gretchen jabs a finger into his chest, then turns to Gita. "Is he holding out on me?"

Gita shrugs, concentrates on a gang of teenagers lounging about the *piazza*'s central fountain.

"I might be able to do something. But what can *you* do for *us*?" Mr. Lansing says.

"Joel . . ." Gita says. He's randomly salacious; Gretchen knows how much it bothers Gita.

"I'm fantastic company. That's what I can do for you," Gretchen says.

"Hmm . . ." Mr. Lansing says. "Let me consider. Okay, deal. That's just about fair."

Gretchen grins, and inwardly frowns. It puzzles her that she's so tempted to trifle with Rajan's father. She wonders at herself, yet is thrilled to be flirting successfully. She closes her eyes and faces right into the sun.

"We're going to go to this great seaside apartment we love for the weekend," she hears Mr. Lansing say. "Don't worry, I've emailed Rajan to let him know where we'll be in case he comes around. You *are* going to join us, right?"

The next day the three of them load their luggage into Mr. Lansing's convertible, circle Rome on a highway that eventually turns off toward the coast, then zip along a tree-choked road to San Felice Circeo. Gretchen has folded her body so that her bare feet press into the glove box, and smacks gum as she fiddles with the BMW's radio. Mr. Lansing hooted when she called the front seat, and directed Gita to the back. Gretchen and Mr. Lansing carry on a spirited conversation over the whip of the wind, chatting about where he rented the car (a specialty importer), the Rajan of a few months ago, the Harvard and Cambridge College graduations. Gita is resolutely cheerful, like the good kid who hadn't ever expected to be in detention. She taps along to the music that Gretchen keeps changing.

Once, when Gretchen glances into the backseat, she sees Gita glaring at her. Gretchen swallows a wrenching thrust of worry and returns her attention to Mr. Lansing. She doesn't look back for some time, and when she finally musters enough courage she finds that Gita is again smiling and collected.

The trip is short, especially at Mr. Lansing's speeds. They race along desolate olive orchards, skip through towns little larger than intersections, zip past a gaggle of Algerian prostitutes on the freeway, and finally spring into Circeo itself, a seaside town approached by a winding road that wraps its walled circumference like stripe on a mint.

They unload in a small *piazza* overhung by baleful rooftop cats and sheets drying from apartment windows. Gretchen hops over the side of the convertible, landing in front of a medieval stone building. "Where to?"

"Second floor."

Gretchen doesn't want to linger at the side of the car, politely clutching her pink leather bag and waiting for the couple to unload the trunk. So she just heads up the loose stone steps.

She hears a jangle and turns to see Gita toss the keys. They come so fast that Gretchen has to catch them as she would a pitch.

Gretchen makes her way up to the second floor. A metal-banded wooden door is set deep into the stone wall, like the entrance to a mill. A mortuary of brown potted plants clutters the doorstep. Gretchen has to lean to reach the old iron lock.

The apartment is a swanky ruin, broken tiles and exposed brick and leather sofas. French doors give onto a balcony with a view of the sea. "Oh, Mr. Lansing," Gretchen says once he arrives, crossing to the doors and laying her hand on the worn handle, "this is *awesome*."

"*Oh, Mr. Lansing!*" Gita says as she enters. "Let's have some wine. *Dìo!*"

Gita prepares *bruschetta* in the kitchen while Mr. Lansing and Gretchen let themselves onto the balcony. Gretchen strips down to her bikini top. Mr. Lansing rolls up his sleeves. "Thanks for inviting me," Gretchen says after a suitable silence. "You guys don't know how meaningful it is for me to have you around right now." The background roll of the waves and the muted calls of the gulls lend her statement a gravity, as though the Lansings have forever corrected the course of her life.

Gita emerges with the lunch and some Chianti, the dregs of a barrel kept in the kitchen. The first duty of the afternoon, she declares, will be to buy more. Gretchen dodges the food, takes a sip of wine, and watches with some amusement as Gita and Mr. Lansing position themselves. Gita lands herself next to him on a rattan loveseat, kicks off a sandal, and drapes her leg over his knee. Mr. Lansing, his eyes flicking to Gretchen, stiffens. He gulps his wine like someone about to spit out for the dentist and lays his hand rigidly on Gita's leg. Gita gives Gretchen a wink and performs a kiss in her direction. Mr. Lansing has shifted his gaze to the sea and sees nothing, but Gretchen sees it all.

Gretchen has the maid's room, tucked under the staircase. She retreats there to nap, and when she wakens discovers that she is alone in the apartment. She finds a message scribbled on the back of a receipt, informing her that Mr. Lansing and Gita have gone to the beach for an afternoon swim. Gretchen is glad not to have been put in the position of declining. A few glasses of wine have made her erotically sluggish, and besides, she regrets her earlier flirtation with Mr. Lansing and wants to give the couple time alone to regroup; she has undoubtedly hurt Gita's feelings. She wanders the luxurious ruin of the apartment, slides her hand along the base of the craggy banister, pours herself another glass of wine. She puts on a jazz disc and examines the art on the walls, her arms clasped politely behind her back, like a museum patron's. What makes this couple keep ticking? Gretchen is unable to resist snooping. She opens chests and sifts through the blankets inside, examines the wineglasses, even runs a hand into the sconces that line the wall above the antique dining room table.

Noncommittally, Gretchen mounts the creaking stairs and peeks over the railing that forms the border of the master bedroom. The large hewn-wood sleigh bed hasn't been made since the Lansings last stayed here. An armoire hangs open; dress shirts lay crumpled on the floor. What looks to be a magazine peeks from a suitcase. She mounts the remainder of the stairs, takes a long look about the room, and then slides out what winds up being a plastic-sleeved catalog from an American teen clothing store. Guys in board shorts playing in the mud, two boys in a hammock, hairless legs hitched one over another, stripped and freckled, staring insolently at the camera. A shirtless pair, parkas tied around their waists, one slapping the other's chest—my buddy's hot, but I'm no fag. A few girls as incidentals, clustered around a hunk and trying to pull down his shorts.

Gretchen replaces the catalog and approaches the bed. The sheets are raw brown cotton. Gretchen touches them with horrid fascination: Rajan's parents undoubtedly had sex here. She pulls back the comforter. No condoms, no odd stains. Just the vague scent of perfume—both musky and fruity, undoubtedly Gita's. And then—she can't locate the urge, the fatal combination of lust and curiosity and nostalgia—she gets into the bed and pulls the comforter over her. It is heavy and instantly warm inside, rank with the smell of Mr. Lansing. His scent is almost like Rajan's, only slightly soured. She fans her hair out over the pillow. Her heart is suddenly racing. She is angry at Mr. Lansing in rare flashes, but at those moments she is livid. She scratches at a pillow as if to rend the fabric, throws it across the room and gets out of the bed.

That he sleeps around. That Gita isn't enough for him. Even his flirting back at Gretchen is so disappointing. She throws the armoire further open and riffles through the stacks of clothes, looking for evidence of debauchery, for further fuel for her anger.

Then she hears Gita's voice in the courtyard below. She shoves the drawer closed, slams the armoire shut as she rockets down the stairs. She leaps onto the sofa and picks up her wine, is scrutinizing the shape of her glass as the door opens.

Mr. Lansing is alone, his tan arms straining around a cask of wine. "Hello," he says happily and breathlessly, glancing back down the stairs as he drops the barrel on the kitchen floor. "Have you been lounging around the whole time?"

"Yeah, lost in thought, you know." She smiles sheepishly—what a dweeb I am.

Gita appears and wilts onto the couch next to Gretchen, wraps her fingers around her wineglass. "May I take a sip?"

Gretchen extricates her fingers from beneath Gita's and nods. Gita gulps. "Ah," she says. "Ten liters of that should do us for a few days. So Gretchen," she continues unrelentingly, drumming her fingers on the top of her foot, "you should definitely check out the beach. Lots of cute Italian boys."

"Can't help thinking of Rajan. It sucks," Gretchen says.

Gita laughs. "Uh-huh. You're in a new country, though, dear. There's time enough later to feel like you're married." She looks at the fireplace with a sudden mania. "I'd love a fire tonight. Why don't we turn the air-conditioning on high and do a fire?"

Mr. Lansing sits across from them. "Calm down, Gita, calm down."

Gita sniffs into her wine. "Don't tell me to calm. Someone needs to be passionate around here."

Gretchen retreats to the kitchen, opens the fridge and stares into it, seeing nothing. Gita is acting so strangely—she used to be the perfect matron, but now she's a child. Without the subduing influence of their son, Gita is willful and Mr. Lansing is flirtatious. Gretchen sees in the disparity the spark of their original attraction; but how have they been able to keep it up? Is it by avoiding each other for days at a time, even while on vacation? Is it by taking on new lovers? Could she be cut out for some similar future? Gretchen and Gita have shared so much, but she still wonders about the hidden corners of Gita's life. Whether she has her own secret liaisons. Whether she signed a prenup.

Gretchen closes the fridge mechanically. She hasn't eaten in a day, and still can't imagine putting food in her mouth. She stands at the entrance to the kitchen and watches the two of them. Gita sulks on the couch while Mr. Lansing strokes her hair. To see a middle-aged man mollifying his wife fills her with a fire that she's unsure of: Anger, pity, superiority? Melancholy about her own family history? "I'm going down to the beach," she calls out cheerfully. "Looking at some Italian boys couldn't do any harm. Just a peek."

Circeo has one Internet café, a small plastic-walled station at the water's edge. Gretchen picks her way down the steep beach path and wanders inside.

A response from her mother:

From: Triciaonstage@amweb.com
To: gbaxter@cambridgecollege.edu
Subject: RE:

Gretchen. I was surprised by your last email, all your going on about Rajan. He sounds great, but also typical. Trust me, there are more Rajans. You're lost so far inside him that I can't see you anymore. It's like this quote I wrote down from *Twelve Lessons Every Woman Should Learn* (recommended): "The lucky of us will be solid and uniform and peacefully loved. It is youth's disorder to depend instead on some larger energy."

You're probably afraid to be a little smaller than you used to be? Well tough, that's what love really is. You accept the boringness because that means things are good. Take it from me – I've made a lot of mistakes, your father among them, and I'm telling you that you're risking going way too far here. Do you have a calling card? Get one and call me and we'll finally chat.

George is fine. Not getting much work. I'm keeping everything together, like always. Don't worry about Humphrey.

-Mom

Ps if you don't give me your new email address, how can I keep writing when this one expires?

It was a mistake to open up correspondence with her mother. She recognizes the familiar attempt at friendship, the chummy sister act, and although Gretchen's desperate for sympathy, she can't stomach it from this source. She never wanted Tricia to be her friend. And now she can sense her mother's exultation to be telling her daughter what to do again.

To: Triciaonstage@amweb.com
From: gbaxter@cambridgecollege.edu
Subject: RE: RE:

Mom, thanks for the advice, but it just makes me realize how hard it is to make you realize what I'm going through. Probably because I'm so far away or something. Forgive me if I don't write for a while. -Gretchen

While she was sending the email another came in. She stares at the From line for a few seconds, her hand over her mouth, then clicks.

To: gbaxter@cambridgecollege.edu
From: rajincharge@mailhome.com
Subject:

I heard from a friend of Ale's that you're in Rome. I know you're really close to my parents, but this is over the line. I'm going to assume it's not true unless I hear otherwise from you, or from them. -Rajan

Gretchen orders a large beer at the bar next door and takes gulps of it, numbly watching a group of five young men surrounding the hood of a car. Four of them look intent on the motor but are really just chattering, and the fifth is bent over it with a wrench. She wishes that she were one of them, that she were a seamless fifth of a little society, that she were teased and loved and had a seaside town to limit her.

She pays for her drink and approaches the boys with a supermodel's walk, peering daringly under the hood as she passes. Taken aback, the boys stammer at one another. She saunters to the beach, lies down on a strip of brown-black sand, and plays lounge music on her headphones. She should feel serene. But she can't lie still for long. What is she going to tell Rajan? Is he furious, or just confused? She sits up and hugs her arms around her knees, stares out at the ocean.

Boats dot the water, their sails flashing white before the murky silhouettes of tankers at the horizon. Gretchen watches them dart over the blue chop, then shifts her gaze to two boys on the pier helping a girl into a rowboat. Just last month, Gretchen remembers Mr. Lansing telling her, a local girl drowned in these waters. As she almost falls from the pitching vessel, this girl squeals and grips the slender muscles of her companions' arms, her fingers deep in their underarm hair. Gretchen imagines herself as this girl, wonders if she could ever squeal as freely. The girl flails more wildly. Gretchen sits up, suddenly alert. Getting off a boat docked next to this one are Mr. Lansing and an African woman.

Mr. Lansing clambers to the pier. The woman moves more slowly, her head held high even as the hem of her wrap drags through a puddle of saltwater. She carries the expression of furious pride that Gretchen remembers seeing in the Algerian prostitutes they passed as they approached Circeo; she is a banished queen.

Gretchen watches them pick their way down the dock and slip into the medieval town.

It is past dinnertime when Gretchen heads back to the house. She meanders through the old town, stares in store windows and examines the community boards. Then she trudges up the stairs to the apartment. Gita opens the door holding a full wineglass that is halfway to opaque with fingerprints; she's been refilling for some time. "Come in," she slushes. "Mr. Lansing is not here. He left right after you did."

They sit around the empty fireplace, suck their way through a bowl of cherries.

"Gretchen," Gita says after a long moment, "you can't know how glad I am that you've come."

"I've been enjoying myself, too."

"Very, very glad." She shrugs and smiles.

"Is everything okay?"

Gita shrugs again—there have been too many in the last few moments for Gretchen to go on believing her casual manner—and continues. "Yes. And no. I've never known totally 'okay' since I married Mr. Lansing. There's always something to be concerned about, something to try ignoring. Don't get me incorrect—my life feels more full with him in it. But it also makes me . . . sad. That's it—I'm more full and more sad."

Gretchen nods and pours herself wine. She wonders if Gita's open-mindedness is an act—if pretending to be comfortable in every situation is opening her up to getting hurt all the more deeply.

Gita likes having Gretchen around because her husband is remote—Gretchen gets that. And yet she can't shake the feeling that by getting even closer to Gita she is making her situation with Rajan odder and odder, that he will be all the more freaked out when they finally rejoin. "Have you ever considered divorcing him?" Gretchen asks.

Gita smiles at her. "I know you come from divorce, that this seems . . . an option to you. But not for me, not for us. We cannot end it. And besides, I do not wish to."

"But don't you think—"

"Hush, child."

Gretchen reclines on the couch and rests her head against Gita's shoulder. The idea of leaning on Gita seemed like perfect solace, but the reality of it is awkward; her neck winds up bent. "I'm so glad I still have you in my life," Gita says.

"Me, too." She pauses. "I got an email from Rajan today."

Gita straightens, and Gretchen is glad for the excuse to release her head and sit up. "You *did*?" Gita asks.

"Yes. He seems shocked to hear that I was here with you guys."

"What did he say?"

"Just that."

"Nothing about coming, nothing about seeing you?"

Gretchen shakes her head.

"He's so . . . hard to figure. It's no easier for his mother."

"Have *you* heard anything from him?"

"No. But I have not checked my emails for days."

Gretchen's eyes water. "I don't know what to do. I've been so irrational in the past, but it's clearer now, and I don't know how to let him know how much I want to be with him."

"Give him some time. I can't imagine a more beautiful, smarter girl for him. You're not like all the silly ones. He needs something harder. You're something harder."

"I don't know if I should tell him I'm here."

"I'll email him, if you like."

"No, let me do it."

"Then do it tonight. He needs to know. The further you let it go, the more awkward it is to be."

"I know. You're so right. I'm sorry."

"Don't be. Just let him know that you're here. I'm going to call him tomorrow and tell him what we've been talking about. You should tell him before I do."

Back at the Internet café Gretchen finds an email from her mother.

To: gbaxter@cambridgecollege.edu
From: Triciaonstage@amweb.com
Subject: RE: RE: RE:

Received your message about not wanting to talk. Should have expected as much. Thought you'd like to know what's happened to your brother, though, while you've been moaning about your love life.

http://haventribunestar.com/article=03148.html

—mom

Gretchen clicks on the article and reads it twice.

BOY HOSPITALIZED BUT STABLE AFTER PARTY BEATING

DeShawn Powell, *Haven Township Tribune-Star*

HAVEN TOWNSHIP—A 15-year-old local boy was seriously beaten late Saturday night at a party in a subdivision on downtown's eastern side.

Humphrey Baxter was taken at 6:35 Sunday morning to Haven Township Presbyterian Hospital by a friend's mother and her roommate, Haven Township Deputy Police Chief Javier Lott said. "He's in serious condition," Lott reported. "He has broken ribs and some internal bleeding." Hospital officials contacted police.

Police informed the boy's parents, and investigated the home at 211 Baywood Road in Harbor Oaks, just north of the Washington Carver Housing Development, where they found signs of a party at which alcohol had been served. As of 5 p.m. Monday, no arrest had been made.

The woman who dropped the victim off at the hospital, Brandy Dixon, has previously appeared in county courts and lost custody of her teenage son, a friend of the victim, to the boy's father, who declined to comment on the situation. She has recently taken out an Order of Protection against a long-term acquaintance, Carl Sidton of 104 SR 530, unit #1. Lott was unable to confirm whether any witnesses had placed Sidton at the scene.

Anyone who has further information about this crime is encouraged to contact Haven Township Police.

Her brother—beaten! That anyone gets beaten seems so beyond her current situation. What is her family doing living in a place where those sorts of things happen?

A full minute ticks by in the Internet café before she finishes scrutinizing the photograph her mother sent with the article. Humphrey lies in a hospital bed, a cast on his knee and another on his arm, bandages wrapped around his torso. The stitches on his face aren't visible, but she can see the hints of the angry scar at his hairline.

This kid's so unlike the brother she remembers. Humphrey at nine was round, flat-haired, and pink-faced. He wore T-shirts with cartoon characters on them and maintained a horde of secondhand stuffed animals in his closet. He once stood in the bathroom doorway while she was getting ready to go out and nattered about a half-elven ranger. They are children of very different Tricias, Gretchen and Humphrey: her mother was a reckless twenty-something in New York, his mother a burned-out worker who constantly reminds everyone about the ashes of her dreams. Gretchen remembers Humphrey as withdrawn, older than his years, a reader and a thinker, who cultivated a steadier life in his mind. He would become the skinny guy at the window of his dorm room late on Saturday night, his face cast a minty green by his computer screen.

But the scandal of the beating! And that photograph! Shaggy-sleek hair falls on his forehead in chunks and careless waves. Two lengths of leather and one of nylon alongside the hospital bracelet. He stares right into the lens. The kid in the picture is no model but he could be a member of a pop act; he could have been her costar on *Mustang*. He is the summer-camp counselor all the girls vaguely wanted to wrap their arms around. And he has been beaten.

He probably messed around with one of his friend's moms and got roughed up by her boyfriend—it's an astounding story, the stuff of movies and tabloids, and it stars her brother! Her pang of outrage proves fleeting, replaced by pitiless wonder at this, the scandalous man her little brother has grown into.

She prints out the article and hurriedly sends the draft of an email she has been rewriting for days:

From: Gretchenzbeanie@webfree.com
To: Ale@post.cambridgecollege.edu
Subject: Forward this please

Hey Alessandra,

I bet Rajan still has me blocked from his email account, but I need to get him a message. Please forward this to him (rajincharge@post.harvard.edu). Don't try to talk me out of it, please, just do it. And make sure you erase this part, otherwise I'll look crazier than I already do. How are you?

Lovesick,
G

Rajan,

I don't have any new words to add to what I said before. We've said it all tons of times, and I don't want to start boring you on top of everything else. But . . .

I really don't know how to say this, but yes, I'm in Italy with your parents. I couldn't imagine not seeing you, and I looked forward so much to traveling together, to seeing if we could work things through. Wanted to be where we would have been and think of you. Part of me thought I would sit down on the plane and find you there. But, obviously you're not here, so I'm in a weird position.

God, don't get mad, it's all out of love for you . . . I know how hard it is when a family breaks apart, Rajan, and I just want you to know I'm doing everything I can to help the people I love feel better. You said my affection for you seemed brittle, and I'm just trying to show you it's not. You need to come out here. We all could use you. I love your mom, and your dad too, and being with them just reminds me of how much I care about you.

I miss you.

I love you.

—your Gretchen

Gretchen leaves the Internet café without the printed-out article, has to go back to retrieve it.

On the walk to the apartment she thinks: *I'm such a bitch. I implied the Lansings were having marital problems just to get Rajan to write back. My brother got beaten and the first thing I did was email my ex.* Oh, Humphrey. She feels right in having banished her parents from her life—they were just a competitive mother and an absent father—but now she feels a deep regret at having abandoned her half-brother to the life she escaped. She was the one person who could have understood him, made him realize he wasn't alone in his feelings.

She finds Mr. Lansing and Gita on the apartment roof. The sun has gone down, and the only lights are the glints of moon on the neighboring windows and the orange strips a citronella candle casts on their throats. Gretchen allows Mr. Lansing to fix her a martini and hands him the article about her brother in return.

Mr. Lansing examines the photograph while Gita reads the article. When he comments on his wife's engrossed expression, Gita reads the article aloud.

"Oh," he says. "God, Gretchen. Baxter. This Humphrey's your cousin?"

"My brother. Well, half-brother."

"You never told us about him. What else do you know about what's happened?"

"Nothing. I'm not in touch with my family."

Gita's eyes are wet. "That poor kid. Both of you had such difficult raisings."

Gretchen nods.

"Is he tough?" Gita asks. "Is he able to cope with a life like this, in a place like this?"

"Cope with Haven Township? I don't know. I've never been there. He's sweet, though."

"He's probably still in danger, don't you think?" Mr. Lansing says. "From this Sidton fellow?"

"You have to call him," Gita says. "Right now."

"I don't have a phone number. It's literally been years since I've spoken to him."

"That poor kid."

"He doesn't seem that injured," Mr. Lansing muses, angling the picture under the moonlight.

Gita laughs at Mr. Lansing once, and then her face turns hard. She speaks to the sea. "Not *that* injured."

"You know what I meant," Mr. Lansing grunts. "He doesn't seem like a total victim."

"Is your mother capable to take care of him?" Gita presses. "I know she doesn't have money, not much, and she works . . . oh, dear." Suddenly, Gita is crying.

"What are you crying about?" Mr. Lansing asks.

"You want to help," she says, shutting her eyes against her tears. "You want things to work out. You want to help people like that. Or *I* want to help people like that. Maybe you don't."

"What do you think I can do to help him?" Gretchen asks.

"You should fly there," Gita says. "You are someone of more power than the rest of your family. You can help him like his mother can't."

"I thought of that," Gretchen lies. "But I don't know what I'd do. I can't just cart him away. I don't even have my own place to live."

"You could both live in Haven Township for a while," Gita suggests.

Gretchen shakes her head slowly. Then she is surprised to hear Mr. Lansing clap.

"Just for the summer," he shouts. "Think of it! Rajan would kill me if he knew I was suggesting it, I'm sure." Mr. Lansing smirks. "But you could bring Humphrey here. You have to."

"You're too generous," Gretchen says.

"No, he's not," Gita says. "Joel does not give to charities. This is his form of giving. And it would be no more hard than having you here. I think it's a good idea. I would love to help care for him."

"He'd have to go back to Florida eventually," Gretchen says slowly, "but do you think it would help? We could have him for a few weeks?"

Gita nods. "If your parents are willing. The more the merry. Is that how it goes?"

"I know how thugs work," Mr. Lansing says, his words cutting over his wife's. "If there's going to be any retaliation, it'll be in the next few weeks. Let's get him out of there. Away from that tawdry woman and her restraining-order husband. God. Let's bring him out here." He drums his thick fingers against the ledge.

Gretchen looks at Mr. Lansing and wonders what he could possibly know about thugs. But the idea of bringing her brother over is appealing—they could occupy each other's days, and she'd both fill the Lansings' need for distraction and do Humphrey some good. "You're serious, then?" she asks.

"Yes," Mr. Lansing says. "We're serious."

The next morning Gretchen wakes early and heads to the beach.

Her first task is to write a card to her brother. She drops a photograph of her and Mr. Lansing at the Pantheon into the envelope (Mr. Lansing is all but cropped; only his arm remains), and express-mails it. Then, at the edge of the water, aided by the surf that makes itself heard whenever her music player is between tracks, Gretchen relaxes enough so that by the time the Lansings arrive she is able to greet them with an unclouded smile.

13

From: HumpSkate92@amweb.com
To: Gretchenzbeanie@webfree.com
Subject: RE: RE: Writing you back . . .

Hi Gretchen. i got your card and your email and theyre cool. i dont usually write emails so you cant think this is what im really like but i wanted to let you know that im happy you wrote to me. yeah im stuck in a hospital and i cant believe you heard about it. i guess sometimes it takes big things to bring people back together.

everythings fine here. i mean, like i said im in a hospital so thats not fine, but it doesn't hurt much and florida's not so bad as you probably think. but i think youre right that i should try to come see you. ive never been away anywhere so youll have to tell me what to do. the nurses want their computer so i gotta go. write back soon. Humphrey.

Mr. Lansing has to send a few faxes, and since San Felice Circeo has never known a fax machine they make plans to go back to Rome for the weekend. Gretchen and Mr. Lansing start to pack while Gita retreats to the roof to enjoy her last rays of sea-reflected sun. Gretchen doesn't have much to deal with: her morning is devoted to puzzling over how to transport a water-logged bikini. Eventually she decides to fold it into a plastic bag, wrap the bag in a towel, then sling the contraption over a shoulder. Mr. Lansing spends most of the morning in his T-shirt and boxers, reclined on the rattan sofa, his hand idly stroking the hairs of his inner thigh as he watches a variety show.

"I think we've finally gotten one hundred percent lazy," Gretchen announces, after changing her mind and wedging her bikini into the front pocket of her suitcase. "A whole morning to pack a couple of bags and we're only just going to finish in time."

Mr. Lansing turns his head enough to reveal his smile before returning his focus to the orange women on television. His chest shudders as he suppresses a burp. "I like lazy," he finally comments.

"I can see that."

He lets the remote fall to the floor. He stares down at it, befuddled. It's one of his favorite games: fake drunk. "Oops."

Gretchen drops her bag and falls into a chair, propping her legs over Mr. Lansing's. She's not attracted to Rajan's father most of the time, but having the soft bottoms of her feet against the hair and weight of a man's legs makes her sigh in contentment. "Well, *I'm* done," she says.

Mr. Lansing glances at the white strip of his flesh where a watch would be. "I haven't even started," he muses.

"You're just like Rajan sometimes," Gretchen says. "A total slug."

"How are you feeling about that wayward son of mine these days?" he asks.

She knows what kind of answer he wants.

The night before, she took a long walk with Gita while Mr. Lansing stayed home and watched television. She went on about how sure she was that she still deeply loved Rajan—though even as she spoke she wondered if she really meant what she was saying, or was just performing the remembered affection. During those two hours Mr. Lansing watched four dubbed American sitcoms, while Gretchen did nothing but investigate her feelings about Rajan with Gita.

But to Mr. Lansing she says, "I don't know. He'd better get his ass over here soon, that's all."

"Damn straight." Mr. Lansing looks right at her. "He doesn't know what he's got."

Gretchen's eyes tear, until Mr. Lansing adds: "A free trip throughout Italy. I mean, what is he thinking?"

"That's right," Gretchen says.

"You've always had more sense than that boy of mine. Maybe we should adopt you," Mr. Lansing says. "We could just have you be our daughter and be done with it."

Gretchen digs her toe into the side of Mr. Lansing's calf. She likes the look of her glittery red toenail against the tan of his leg. "Yeah, but then if Rajan and I get back together, it'll be incest."

Mr. Lansing blinks at her. "Well, we *will be* in Rome. You'd be Drusilla and Caligula."

"I'm just sitting here," Gretchen says, throwing her hands in the air in mock exasperation, "waiting for my brother-lover to return from war."

Mr. Lansing squints at her and considers for a moment before continuing. "He sent me an email. He asked for the number of my travel agent."

"Really? Why didn't you tell me? When?"

"Just got the message this morning. And before you even start, don't tell me you expect him to have enough foresight to tell us any flight numbers."

"Did he mention me?"

"You? Why would he? He did say something about 'that cunning bitch.' "

"Very funny." She feels an upswell of tears.

"No, seriously, he did mention you. Said he knew you were here. Didn't seem upset, not that I could tell."

"Can I see the message?"

"Nope. Private."

Mr. Lansing gets up and stretches. When he does his shirt rides up on his belly, and Gretchen can't help but stare at the black hair on his distended abdomen, the twin swaths that converge in a wolverine line arrowing into his shorts. Body hair is so primal, so distracting; she finds it hard to remain composed. "Finally packing, huh?" she says.

"Uh-uh. Not yet. Let's leave later, anyway—I have some errands to run in the town."

"Oh. Okay. Care for company?"

He pulls on pants and kicks his feet into his sandals. "No, thanks. Be back soon."

She follows him, of course. Waits a good minute first, spying out the window from within a curtain fold. Once she sees him leave the most distant *piazza* of the town she dashes down the stairs. She scans the beach path, but when she doesn't see him she checks the other direction and spots him, halfway down the hill and bearing toward the new town. That area has no good restaurants, no old architecture, no sand. Locals live there; she and the Lansings have never bothered to go. Gretchen follows him, avoiding the path and flitting among the trees instead.

Mr. Lansing walks at a good clip, and Gretchen is winded by the time she can maneuver to see him again. He stands before the outdoor stand of a gelato vendor, leaning against a paperboard display of ice cream flavors and tapping his leather wallet against the counter. The vendor disappears and reappears a moment later with a regal Algerian—the same one Gretchen saw getting off the boat. The woman approaches Mr. Lansing, her hands hitched under her breasts and her legs pressed together. They exchange a few words and then—Gretchen has to lean forward into the sunlight to see—Mr. Lansing extracts a couple of euro notes from his wallet and presses them into her grasp. All this in the presence of the vendor, who busies himself combining half-empty tubs of gelato.

Then the woman leads Mr. Lansing away from the stand and toward the outskirts of town. The street is fiercely illuminated in the morning light, so Gretchen waits until they are far along before following. The vendor leers as she passes, flashing a furry smile.

Mr. Lansing and the woman pause, exchange a few words, pass a key between their hands . . . and then they head in separate directions. The woman disappears into a small stucco home abutting a video store, while Mr. Lansing turns down an alley.

Gretchen pauses under the bright plastic awning of the video store. The alley is unpaved, mud and greasy puddles doing much to subdue the sunny cheer of the day. Mr. Lansing skirts past two old African women conversing loudly and clutching ripped grocery bags. As Gretchen tails Mr. Lansing one of them smiles a twilight smile, an alarming thickening of her lips that reveals a marbled rectangle of gray and pink flesh. "*Ciao*," Gretchen murmurs as she passes.

She missteps and lands a foot in an oil puddle. When she pulls it out she sees that she has dirtied the white plastic of her flip-flop. She hisses. How dare Mr. Lansing lead her down here! How dare he have affairs at all—and with a prostitute, no less! She feels personally disrespected by it, that her own intimacy with him has been cheapened. Mr. Lansing stops in front of a shiny pine door. He hesitates, runs his fingers over the sharp edge of the lock plate. Then he slots the key into the lock. The door opens and Mr. Lansing disappears inside, shutting it soundly behind him.

The building is unadorned. Gretchen would have assumed it to be under construction if Mr. Lansing hadn't just let himself inside. She approaches closely enough to peer into a corner of the front window. The room she sees is dark, just shy of black. Objects clutch the stray light and seem to glow of their own accord; near the door glimmer a phosphorescent plastic chair and a stack of water bottles. Somewhere at the far side of the house a crank turns and a faded blue window canopy rises, allowing more shards of light to enter. The house is cluttered, arranged with no nod to order: toilet paper in the kitchen, clothing laid out on the couch; it is not meant to be visited.

Gretchen risks exposure to get a better view. In a hallway deeper inside the house she sees a slender shape cross the uncarpeted floor, followed by Mr. Lansing, who takes a seat on a shapeless couch.

If Mr. Lansing happens to look toward the entrance he'll see her—she can't risk staying where she is. She makes her way back up the street and withdraws to the entrance of the video store. The old women down the street stare at her and jabber. Spooked, Gretchen hugs herself.

She sees a store offering phone service and Internet access—as well as a view straight down the alley. She ducks inside and rents a computer, continually glancing down the street as she opens the web browser.

From: rajincharge@mailhome.com
To: Gretchenzbeanie@webfree.com

Gretchen,

I almost think I shouldn't write at all these days, because sometimes I'm mad as hell and other times I'm just sad that we had to break up. I can't imagine the email that could do justice to all my feelings. Look, it's okay that you're there with my parents. I guess. But it also seems that it's just making things even harder. I am going to come. In a couple of weeks. I think it would be smarter if you weren't there. But at the same time, I kinda wish you will be. How's that for fucking mature? Do me a favor and don't write for a while, okay? - R

After reading the email a few dozen times, Gretchen pays for the computer rental and heads back outside. He's offering her happiness and ripping it away at the same time. How the hell does he expect her to respond to that?

She tries to calm herself by examining the sun-faded movie posters in the window of the video store. It is past noon now, and the streets are newly full of Circeo's underclass. Finally she sees that the door to the house down the alley has opened. She slips between buildings and peers through her sunglasses.

Mr. Lansing emerges first, holding one of his sandals in a flailing hand as he wedges his foot into the other. Then a young man trips out of the entrance. Algerian by the looks of him, twenty if not under, tidy chest and trim waist, the wet stain on his T-shirt visible even from a distance. He hazards one glance up the abandoned alley before he dashes away. Mr. Lansing gives him a slap on the ass, and then the boy's gone.

Keeping cool during the ride back to Rome pushes Gretchen to her limits. She finds it excruciating to act as if nothing has happened, but what option does she have? Go into a blazing show of prudery, with the sole effect of alienating Mr. Lansing? Instead her shock expresses itself in all the insidious ways common to polite society: for the rest of the day formality to even her grandest attempts at ease. She excuses herself to take a walk as soon as they arrive back at the Rome hotel.

It's not the homosexuality of Mr. Lansing's affair that has stunned her, even though the sight of the young man with the stained T-shirt lingers in her head, casts shocking vibrations over her other thoughts. It's rather the ballsy decadence of what the Lansings have arranged: not only is Mr. Lansing unreliable and unfatherly, Gita is willing to share their bed with (or maybe entirely turn the bed over to) a young man. Young men? There's so much changed now.

She wishes she had never come to Italy, never put herself in this unnatural position.

She calls Alessandra from a pay phone—she can think of no one else—and gasps strangled phrases into the receiver until Alessandra finally cuts in.

"Well, it's an activity in Italy, not a lifestyle," she says. "*Fare ma non essere*, you know what I mean? Activity, not identity. Guys are gay for half an hour in bed, spring out, and aren't anymore."

"But Mr. Lansing's not Italian," Gretchen says.

"But he's still in Italy. It's probably why he's even *there*. Lots of local guys fool around in their teens and twenties and then get married. It's been changing, but Rome's still a little southern Italian town, honey. Just with a subway and a pope."

"I can't believe Gita would put up with it," Gretchen says.

"You always said she was so unconventional, despite all the Ann Taylor—this is probably part of it."

"I kind of get it," Gretchen says, her tears drying somewhat as she turns analytical. "She's got some big thing about giving men as much freedom as possible. Just between you and me, she *never* talks about her own family. I think she thinks they were just way too restrictive. And maybe she's afraid that if she doesn't put up with everything, she'll lose Mr. Lansing."

"So. You got your plane ticket back yet?"

At dinner in the hotel restaurant the Lansings discuss which other cities to visit, the competition between the *Roma* and *Lazio* soccer teams, where to get the best pizza. The conversation is resolutely cheerful and therefore exhausting. Afterward Gretchen excuses herself to go upstairs but withdraws instead to the bar next door. She orders a beer and watches the bubbles flash white as they travel up the golden fluid. She takes a big swig to disturb them all and see them begin anew.

She wonders: *What would it feel like to have a cock? To be with another cock?* She glances at the men around the bar, her face aflame. She's never been a free spirit when it comes to sex—she usually can't get the broader implications out of her head (*Are we doing this often enough? What if he goes soft? He's shooting inside of me, and even though I'm on the pill it's as if he's getting me pregnant, pregnant!*—none of these particularly sexy thoughts). Maybe if she just had a blunt penis and the will to use it as much as possible, she would have as much fun with sex as her boyfriends seem to.

Gita and Mr. Lansing are probably heading to bed now. She imagines the momentary swish of his undershirt going over his head before the room goes dark.

Does Mr. Lansing still have sex with Gita, too? How often does he sleep with guys? What would Rajan do if he knew? Jesus, what *would* Rajan do? She can't imagine. He's open-minded, but this isn't some third party, it's his *dad.* She takes a gulp of beer. At the very least, she knows, she's uncovered a secret here, something to report to Rajan if she decides it's at all appropriate to do so.

Mr. Lansing is no Gita; he will never allow Gretchen to get inside his head. But she imagines that he's acting against years of small repressions, justifying that he paid his dues through his solid years of earning money and raising his family, and that now he's owed some selfish time. He's showing an indulgence typical of teenage boys. It makes understanding him easier—she's had enough experience with immature guys to forecast how they will act—but it makes her sad for Rajan, that his dad was never more of a model for him. The oblique reference Mr. Lansing made to marriage at dinner, that "most wives just don't understand infatuation, what it can do to someone," made her skin crawl. Infatuation. To actually use that word, at his age!

A stool scrapes against the stone floor, and when Gretchen looks over she sees that Gita has sat at the other end of the bar. As she orders her drink she glances over at Gretchen with an urbane and closed look, but Gretchen can recognize a woman ready to Talk. Smiling wanly, Gretchen scoots over a few bar stools to sit next to her.

"Hi," Gretchen says. A dozen next sentences float in her head.

Gita picks up a peanut and plays with it, sliding the greasy seed between her fingers. She puts it down and licks the oily salt. Gretchen decides to wait for Gita to break the silence. "We," Gita finally says, "just had a little fight in the hotel room. I consider myself a world's woman . . . but sometimes I, even, get angered at all these behaviors."

"It makes you mad that . . . he's with guys?"

Gita registers Gretchen's knowledge with a sideways glance as her wine arrives. "A boy? Yes. They are all legal, he says, and he is only kissing. Normally I do not care. It only reminds me of my own freedom, you know? But in front of you, it is shocking you, I know, and now that you are here I see it through your eyes, and wonder—ach, what are you doing, Gita, why is your life like this?"

"I never would have predicted any of this back in the States."

"Really? He is still the same man."

"I know—I mean, I could imagine what he *was like*, but I just . . . I don't know, I had no idea, that's all."

"Before, I had no real difficulties with Joel's behavior. In some ways I consider this the . . . truest relationship I could have. He does not hide what he desires from me, even his most deep desires."

"And he obviously cares for you," Gretchen says. "I guess that once you see what he's doing and accept it, there's no dark secret that could ever pull you apart."

Gita nods without looking up from her glass.

"But there must be limits," Gretchen says. "Aren't you ever afraid that he's going to find someone else? Leave you for some guy?"

Gretchen can't stop staring at Gita's jewelry, suddenly: it shines at her from a thousand directions. The hand that pulls out a cigarette is weighted with two thick, knobby rings. "As I told you, Gretchen, I do not worry myself greatly with Joel's desires, but I do occupy myself with them. Does that make sense?"

Gretchen shakes her head.

"He may like men, but he doesn't like to be someone who likes men. Rajan's father is not a 'faggot.' " Her eyes flash.

"Okay."

"You see, you are disgusted."

"No, I'm not. I promise. Just shocked."

"Yes, okay," Gita says, sighing.

"So Mr. Lansing has never had a . . . boyfriend?"

"No. That is something I could not support. Impulses of the sexual kind are fully acceptable. Nothing of more matter—or less ridiculousness—than that."

And, with the relieved look Gita shoots at Gretchen, they are closed back into a tight ring. Gita sees Mr. Lansing's attraction to boys as his vulnerability; if she exercises it correctly and prevents it from blossoming full-scale, it will actually keep them together.

But when Gita speaks, it is as if to a stranger: "I am tired and going upstairs."

Gita leaves her glass half-full and returns to the apartment. Gretchen finishes her beer and Gita's remaining wine, pays the check with the money Gita slapped on the counter, then wanders off into Rome's center.

In the *Campo dei Fiori* Gretchen finds a café seat at the edge of the square and orders a large glass of wine. As it arrives she stares unseeing at the seam where the terra-cotta of the café tiles meets the stone of the street. She tries to steady herself, but she can see the wine's surface ripple to the pounding of her blood. She takes in mouthful after mouthful.

A group of German backpackers at the next table engage her in conversation. She smiles winningly, turns on her full charm even as she appraises them and concludes that none is worth pursuing. They eventually move on, and when Gretchen turns to order another glass of wine she sees that the café interior has turned tranquil. It is well past midnight. Gretchen chats to the waitress briefly, then relocates to a new post in the café's back room. She imagines Mr. Lansing and some African boy holing up in this café in winter, a log burning behind the copper and glass of the fireplace. Then she imagines Mr. Lansing and Gita breathing against each other beneath the beach apartment's heavy brown sheets.

The café has almost emptied out. In fact, Gretchen realizes with a start, she is the only patron left. The moment she realizes it, though, an American boy shambles in. He's gawky and Hispanic, his hair hanging down the side of his face in shiny waves. His T-shirt has seen days of continuous wear and the hem of his shorts has scalloped at the edges, the threads hanging about his calves. She smiles at him as she tries to take a sip from an empty glass.

When they have sex it is in his room at the hostel, her shins bumping the blue-painted metal rail at the base of his bunk. She clutches for that same rail when she weaves to her feet and shimmies her panties up. She sobered while they were having sex, and all she wants now is to be sitting in her bath. As she staggers out of the hostel she glimpses the carbon-copy receipt from some backpacker's plane ticket in the wastepaper basket and remembers with a shock that her brother arrives the next morning.

PART THREE

HUMPHREY & GRETCHEN

14

GRETCHEN

How can she be back in another airport? She's waiting in one of a row of plastic chairs, her feet planted on cherry carpet that extends in all directions, listening to looping announcements ignored by everyone. *Le porte stanno per chiudere.* As a nervous joke, she's scrawled Humphrey's name on a posterboard. It's propped up against the edge of her chair, and an Italian man who walks by ogles her and shakes his head, as if asking himself what organization could possibly have sent *her* to pick up a stranger from the airport. She moves a row deeper into the seats and lights a cigarette.

A stream of young American men passes through the arrivals door. They amble along, resolutely comfortable, as if intent on proving that this foreign lobby is actually an Ohio living room. They hitch tremendous backpacks on only one shoulder, their expressions dazed and their hair still betraying the shapes of their airplane seats. Gretchen watches them pass in their faux camp-counselor T-shirts, their frayed sandals. These guys exhibit a shambling innocence that their European counterparts lack; they make her think of tight and typical families, of younger sisters and brothers who sell cookies and shoot spit wads. She trusts these young men, even as she is unmoved by them. She thinks of Rajan's family, and of her own lack of family. Rajan had been her one link to guileless American boys, and who knows if she'll ever have him back.

Another flight has arrived. Gretchen scans the passengers. No Humphrey.

Then more American boys file into the arrivals lobby. Gretchen scrutinizes each one, and lingers on a slender guy with ravaged dark hair and a limp. His nose is swollen and hooked. A scar on a cheek. He scans about with wounded and widened eyes. Tough but vulnerable. A long torso to match her own. She holds up the sign: her brother has arrived, and she's going to save him.

Some things are the same: he still stares boldly at her when he starts a sentence, and by the end of his thought his gaze has shyly wandered to the ground. At random moments he glances at her with adulation (may he never lose that!). He still walks widely, his feet turned out, like he's about to either charge or scuttle away. But most of him is different: his taciturnity, his toughness, the fullness of his lips. They have returned from the airport and are sitting on a dusty floor in front of the American School's main office, their bare legs splayed to soak up as much coolness as possible from the tile. Humphrey is pressed against the copier; an arm rests on top of a paper tray. They have come to get registration material for the fall semester, so Humphrey will have the option of enrolling after the summer's travels. But the director of Studies is in a meeting.

"So what are the things you want to see?" she asks. They've been timid to talk about what happened in Florida, so Gretchen has prattled on and on about Rome.

"I don't know, Gretchen. I don't have a guidebook. I haven't even emptied my backpack yet." She is put off by his use of her name. He's mysterious and formal, not like a kid brother at all. She takes his hand and pulls them both to their feet.

"Come on, we'll enroll you later," she says. "I brought some lunch."

They walk out the front doors and crunch across the white gravel of the school's parking lot. Some American girls are lounging by the gate. They appraise Humphrey as he and Gretchen approach. She wonders what they see. Humphrey looks like her, but his hair is darker, and of course he has that newly bent nose. Gretchen takes his hand in hers as they march past the girls. She savors their interest, their confusion.

Other siblings would have too much baggage, too many histories of fights and pettiness. But Humphrey and Gretchen have the opportunity to create their relationship. They will be best friends, of a fashion. Or maybe Gretchen will become the parent her own mother was never able to be.

They wander onto the Appian Way, lie amid tall clumps of wild grass. Gretchen is amazed anew that such a road exists, that unnamed monuments sit unenshrined in the soil, crop up out of the wildflowers. It is in such a place that she will make Humphrey close to her.

They share a bottle of wine that Gretchen hauled in her straw bag. She asks if Humphrey is allowed to drink at home but he just raises an eyebrow, uncorks the bottle, and pours them two glasses. Drips of Montepulciano make spotted red stains on the yellow stalks of grass. They lie back, munch on bread and cheese, sweat and stare at the sky. The blue ages to gray at the horizon; peaks of ruins lurk at the periphery of their vision. Gretchen turns and stares at her brother. "Are you going to tell me about Florida?"

Gretchen watches him take a sip of wine and stare into the atmosphere. In full daylight his scar is a seam uniting pieces of his face, flesh that used to be apart now joined by a red tributary. It is revolting and enthralling. "I fell in love," he says. "I totally fell in love with this girl."

Gretchen waits for him to continue, and when he doesn't she says, gently, "Hardly a girl, Humphrey. A woman."

He shakes his head. She wishes he would talk freely. She feels like she knows him so well, already; doesn't he feel the same? "It's not who you're thinking about," he says. "Not Brandy."

"Brandy's the one with the husband?"

"Yeah. Carl was never her husband, though. Just boyfriend." He laughs. "Abuser, really."

Gretchen nods, silent. Laughing is still his only way of expressing feeling. He's such a *boy*. "So who did you get a crush on?" she prompts.

"This girl. Chantal. But she was the girlfriend of my friend Wade. Who's Brandy's son."

The connections should be simple enough, but Gretchen has trouble getting her mind around them. The puzzle doesn't fall together correctly.

"So I like this girl Chantal, and Wade doesn't like that. And this one night, at this party, I get trashed and wind up falling asleep at Brandy's house."

"The party was at Wade's *mom's* house?"

"Yeah. And Wade tells Carl, knowing that Carl's going to go ballistic, all to get back at me."

"Jeez, Humphrey. And just because you were there, he beat you up so badly?"

"Dude was insane. Totally bonkers."

Gretchen ponders where to go next. Humphrey has been smiling the whole time he has told the story, making it into an amusing anecdote. She wants to make him face the grimness. "It doesn't make sense to me. Wade's still your friend. I don't see why he'd do that."

Humphrey finally turns to her. "Really? You don't?"

"I just imagine it's a lot more complicated than it sounds."

"I guess so," Humphrey says. "Who knows what they had going on. Brandy was as messed up as Carl. But she was really good to me, too. She liked having me around."

"Do you miss her?"

Humphrey shrugs but says yes.

"And Mom wasn't around much, huh?"

"Mom was around some. She had one weekend day off, usually. But during the school week, yeah, I was kind of up to myself. And Dad . . ."

Gretchen snorts. "Man needs to be put on antidepressants."

"He totally does. It's all dedicated motherboards and USB this or that and nothing else."

"It's like being raised by a single parent, huh, even though they're married?"

He wrinkles his nose at Gretchen's prepackaged analysis. "It's okay, though, Mom worked really hard to . . . she really does her best?"

Gretchen pauses. She's waiting for him to decide if their mom really does her best. He picks up a dry piece of grass and fashions a ring around his finger.

"Maybe she's changed," Gretchen says. "Maybe it was different for you."

"You two just plain hated each other, huh?"

"Mom just never liked me much, Humphrey. I really can't tell you why."

"She says you challenged her."

"She talks about me?"

"Not much. But when she does she says you challenged her."

"I was a *kid.* Do you see how ridiculous that is? Saying that your *kid* challenged you?"

"I know, I know, I'm just trying to say what she might have been thinking."

"Well, no, thanks. No, thanks." Gretchen adjusts herself on the grass. A flame of anger has risen in her, and she has to struggle to keep it in control. She hadn't planned to talk about herself today. She rips up a tuft of dry grass and watches the fibers float away.

"So!" Humphrey says. "What do you do around here? Is this, what, just business as usual for you, going off to Italy?" College graduates are clearly unknowable beasts to him; anything could be typical of them.

"Well, you know . . ." she starts. She could tell him everything or nothing; both seem like good courses. She decides she will tell him everything, but only eventually. "I've never been to Europe. People should go to Europe."

"Cool. Why Italy, though?"

"Um . . . you know. I broke up with this guy. Well, actually, he broke up with me. It sucked. I'm not used to that." She licks her lips. "And he said I took him for granted, that I didn't care enough, that I was all words. That's a common complaint of Harvard students, that we're all words."

"I thought you went to Cambridge College."

"Yeah. But it's pretty much the same." She sees Humphrey following her intently. "So his parents are here, in Italy," she continues, "and they've become my best friends. Sorta. I just had to be with them. They were my family, you know? And Rajan's supposed to come here, and I want to see him."

"Rajan? What kind of name is that?"

"Indian."

Humphrey nods. Gretchen is sure that he's imagining something like an Apache, all feathers and peace pipes, and she wonders how to correct him.

"He won't be totally freaked out because you're here with his own *family*?" Humphrey asks.

Gretchen pauses, horrified that Humphrey should have so easily picked up on her greatest worry. "We've been together a long time," she says. "He gets me. He's not freaked out."

"That's a big thing, huh? Just showing up for someone."

"Yep. But I love him. That's the kind of stuff you do when you're in love."

She's been way too pedantic, and sure enough Humphrey looks disbelieving, newly closed off from her. He doesn't get it, she tells herself; he doesn't get the lengths you go to when you care about someone.

15

HUMPHREY

Gretchen told me the boat was going to be a "cruiser yacht," so I'd hoped it would be polished wood with a bunch of masts with parchment-colored sails and some guy standing at the creaky wheel with a pipe and a concerned expression. Instead it's a big hunk of curved plastic, and I think that maybe it drives itself. Even though I keep asking to, we haven't put the sails up even once. Mr. Lansing says it sleeps eight but it's only barely big enough for us four, and when it's bad weather and we all have to sit at the inside table our knees knock. There are cup holders everywhere, scrubbed and gleaming like something out of the hospital. I've spent most of my time on deck. We've left Rome and we're heading up the Mediterranean. I saw a movie set in ancient Greece back in Florida, a couple days before the beating, and I keep imagining the sharp prows of shield-studded ships crossing through this same blue water.

So, yeah, I'm in Italy and that's crazy. I've never been to a foreign country before, and I keep trying to play it cool but it trips me out anyway. I'm thankful that Gretchen's here to look out for me, and that Carl and Wade are nowhere near, but at the same time, even after the initial insanity of arriving in a new country wore off, I've felt freaked out more than anything else. There are lots of things I don't get, for example why the Lansings want either of us here. Maybe Mr. Lansing is just really nice and his son got old so he wants a younger kid around. Mrs. Lansing seems like she's best friends with Gretchen, but there's this weird competitive vibe going on with them, like they might actually hate each other. Whenever we all four hang out Gita and Gretchen are just beaming . . . like beaming too much, as though they couldn't be more thrilled with the situation but that actually the opposite is true. I know there's shit I don't know, but honestly I don't want to find out, because that could mean an end to this kind of perfect setup. Gita keeps asking me these total mother questions, like have you had sufficient to eat, and is the bedding comfortable enough, and shouldn't you be doing some summer reading?

It's nine o'clock, so I guess it's dinnertime. I drop the anchor and pull open the "hatch" (Mr. Lansing likes to call it that even though it's got a silver handle and is the size of most doors—for the record, he also likes to wear a cheesy hat with a gold anchor on the front) and hurl myself inside. I let myself fall onto the plush rug and just lie there, feeling the softness on my bare belly, because we're on a boat and so you're allowed to do shit just because you feel like it. The interior's like the inside of a genie's bottle, cramped and sloping with big colorful cushions and a low table. Dinner's olives and cheese and caviar and bread that we'll snack on for hours. It was the same last night, too, because Mr. Lansing didn't want to buy gas for the stove. He'll spend massive amounts of money, suddenly turn stingy, and then start spending again. He's sitting alone at the low table, picking at some chickpea muck. I'm at his feet, but he hasn't looked at me yet. He likes me, in a way that makes everyone shut up and not say anything. At least Mr. Lansing's goofy about it, not creepy. I'm like his nephew or something.

He hasn't got his shirt on. Mr. Lansing's got one of those backs that are wide at the top and stay wide all the way down, like a big block of salt. His shoulders are red, and his skin is papery. I've never had a conversation with a businessman before. After I got over the shock of how rich he is, he's really boring. Gretchen seems to adore him, though. I guess she thinks he can do something for us, with all his money. I don't know. I owe everything I'm doing to Gretchen. She got me out of Haven Township, away from Wade and Carl and Brandy and Mom, and now I'm dependent on her. I like her, so if she wants us to be friends with Mr. Lansing, I'll be friends with Mr. Lansing.

"Hi, Mr. Lansing," I say, sitting opposite him and grabbing an olive. I figured he would have asked me to call him by his first name by now. But no. He likes me calling him "mister."

He looks up, startled. I've disturbed some intense daydream. "Humphrey. Hi. How is it on deck?"

I shrug, spit a pit into my hand. "The sun sets late around here. It's weird."

He likes it when I say stupid things. The crepey skin on his belly shifts and slides as he chortles.

"Are you cold?" Mr. Lansing asks.

I shake my head no, but I must look upset because he goes to get a blanket from the couch anyway and puts it around my shoulders. "I know you've had a rough time recently," he says. "But you're far away now. No one's going to hurt you here."

He's used the tone people take on for strays. I hate it and I just want to get away and be by myself, but we're stuck together on a boat and for whatever reason he's made me his favorite. So I smile and say thanks.

* * *

A couple of hours later. We've pulled the folding table up on deck and we're playing cards. There's some jazz music. They're all drinking wine and I've got a glass, too, but I'm only sipping it because I don't really like that they've served me any. I just want people to be adults, responsible adults, but it's like as soon as you're marked as deviant everyone magically knows and they figure, oh well, might as well throw in the towel. It's my turn to play. Gita's my partner and she sucks. She keeps trumping my tricks. I put a queen of diamonds down on Gretchen's ten and look at Gita, like please don't, but then Mr. Lansing goes with a throw-away and it's her turn and oomph, here it comes, a queen of spades. Gita smiles as she pulls the cards away and Gretchen's giggling though she's trying not to. I slam my hand down and pick up the glass of wine and say "Damn! What are you doing?" in a cartoony voice and Gretchen's on the floor laughing and Gita looks around, really not knowing what she's done wrong.

"What?" she says. "What is it?"

I start to explain to Gita, but she's not going to get it. I decide just to have fun by keeping Gretchen laughing, because winning the game is going to be impossible. "Jeez," I say. "I'm sorry, but jeez." I don't say it meanly. Gretchen's actually having trouble breathing, she's laughing that hard.

I smile and shake my head. Losing can be fun if you play it right. I look over at Mr. Lansing. He's squinting at Gita, like he's a little embarrassed. Then he looks at me and winks. "Quite a partner you've got there."

I roll my eyes. "No kidding."

Gita puts her cards down and crosses her arms. She frowns, and when she does you can see that she's not as young as she seems. Her face wrinkles all over whenever any part of it moves, like the skin of a ripe plum. "Perhaps I will just stop playing, then."

She's so pretty in an older woman way, and so defenseless, that it's impossible to stop picking on her. She's easy to take down, and you figure when someone's got that much going for her, what's the harm in jabbing a little? "Give me your cards," I say. "I'll play both hands."

I've gone too far, because they don't laugh as much anymore. Mr. Lansing puts his hand on Gita's. "No, honey, stay in. We want you here."

"Me and Humphrey are going to do fine," Gita says.

"Your lead," I say, popping an olive in my mouth.

There's no official sleeping arrangement. Usually I haul a cushion out on deck, because I sleep better with no one around me. I place the pad on the textured plastic surface. When I lie down, I hear the slap of nylon cord against the mast, and the sky looks blacker than any sky I've ever seen. At sea you really become aware of how far apart the stars are. It's also the same night sky you see back in America; I didn't expect that.

I hear movement near me and look up. It's Gretchen, wearing a light nightdress. I stand and join her at the prow. "It's nice, huh?" I say, because that's what you're supposed to say when it's your first time in Europe and you look at the sea at night from an expensive boat. But there's actually not much to see.

She puts her arm around me and keeps looking out at the water.

"Are you thinking about your ex?" I ask. I say it softly, make it clear that I don't expect her to answer if she doesn't want to; I really don't want to be the annoying younger brother.

"More or less," she says. I wonder how complicated that "more or less" is.

"Anything you want to talk about?" I say.

She shakes her head. "Are you having an okay time?" she asks.

"It's beautiful. I just can't believe I'm going to have to go back." I'm lying; it is beautiful but mostly it's lonely. I've been beaten and now I'm wandering the world alone, and my sister's fun but she's alone, too, in a way families aren't supposed to be. I want to go home, but nobody's home; nobody's ever really going to be there. It's true that I hate the thought of going back, though. I can't imagine the first day of school in Haven Township. Better to stay in this totally foreign place, even if it's tripping me out.

"You don't *have* to go back," she says. "We could try again to enroll you at that boarding school in Rome. They have scholarships. If anyone'd qualify, you would."

"Really?" I consider it. "But Mom would never say okay."

"She would if you asked hard enough."

If I left . . . Mom and Dad aren't close. Without me to bind them, they'd probably split. We'd be free agents, all of us solo. "I don't think I'd do it. It's an idea, though. We've got some time before the summer ends, anyway."

We stare at the water. I hang my head over the rail and watch the moon-white tips of the waves breaking before the bow. Then I look up at Gretchen. "So you and Gita are having trouble, huh?"

She doesn't look at me. "I'm surprised you picked up on that."

Is she serious? "Of course I picked up on that. Sometimes you two like barely look at each other. The way you talked about her before, I thought you were best friends."

Gretchen turns away from the water and stares at her feet. "I think she's depressed," she says softly.

"Really?"

"I'm pretty sure Mr. Lansing's having an affair."

"Damn. That's messed . . . So are you going to tell Rajan?"

Gretchen takes a deep breath and lets it out between her teeth. "I'm not really talking to Rajan right now."

"What do you mean? How are we tooling around the Mediterranean with his parents if you're not talking to him?"

"We've sent some emails, but I haven't actually spoken to him for two months." Not "a couple" of months. "Two." I bet it's two to the day.

"Do you have hope for you guys?"

"Kind of. It's really just a hiatus. We're going to get back together."

"And you're just trying to get in good with his parents in the meantime?"

"Yeah. Like that." She raps her fingers on the pulpit edge. "But it's hard, actually."

"Why's that? It seems like we're all having a good time." Although sailing around with Rajan's parents without telling him doesn't seem like the best way to get on his good side. I'm probably just not understanding something. We're both a little drunk, and our hands are stained with caviar juice—if this is all really for someone else we should be suffering, and we don't seem to be suffering.

"Look. I'm keeping me and the Lansings a family," Gretchen says.

I whistle. "Twisted." Then I say, "Any luck getting Rajan to write to you again? Because that's probably the first step."

"I'll think of something."

"Huh." I can't stop looking at her; she's crazy and maybe a little evil. "Wow." I pause, then say, "Let me know if there's any way I can help."

She's quiet for a second until we laugh, nervously at first and then hard and helplessly. The world is shrunk and blurred by my crinkled eyes: the water, the stars, the shapes of Mr. Lansing and Gita beneath the curtained window below—all of it is far away. We laugh for a while, no real source for the humor, just pure release. Gretchen stops laughing first. I'm left chuckling alone as I arrange myself on the deck.

We sail into a new port every few days. Sometimes we sleep in hotels (me and Gretchen in one room, Mr. Lansing and Gita in another) and more rarely we anchor and spend the night on the boat. Sperlonga, the Cinque Terre, Sanremo . . . I'm super brown by the time we get to France and, I like to think, pretty sophisticated. I make an effort not to sulk about Florida, because I'm in Europe on a boat for free, and that's awesome. We're all getting really good at cards, even Gita. Well, actually she still kind of sucks, but I'm the best, so we've stayed partners. She's started making fun of herself, too, and I like her a lot more now. She's got this funny way of saying "*Ech?*" in a really high voice whenever we all play our cards too quickly and she doesn't follow, and it's pretty darn cute. Sounds like a fisherman's wife.

We pull into the dock at Villefranche-sur-Mer, which has an old wall covered with flowering vines, a medieval port, and a train track running over the ridge of the mountain behind. I'm amazed people actually live here. I've made myself cabin boy, and hop to the dock and tie up the boat. I secure the rigging while Gita goes to buy provisions and Gretchen and Mr. Lansing check their email. We all plan to meet up at a pizzeria near the waterfront. I arrive first and sit there sipping a sparkling water, watching the old rusty boat of a diving school make its maneuvers in front. The sky is a sharp color, setting off the plumes of blue-black smoke spewed out by the old boat.

Gretchen and Mr. Lansing arrive next. They sit down and are as silent as they always are after checking messages, like they're still carrying on private conversations with whoever emailed them. I take care of ordering because I took French, and this is just like unit 4, "*Dans la Rue*," when Gilles prefers red wine to white and Dominique will take a peach. Mr. Lansing is the first to snap out of his reverie, right after the pizzas come. "So, that's some news about Rajan, huh?" he says.

Gretchen keeps running her serrated knife over the same spot of her pizza. "Rajan?"

"Yes. Did you write back to him? Funny he thought we're in Rome. He's got to get that ticket changed, but luckily Alitalia flies to the Riviera." He takes a gulp of the yellow sparkle of his beer. "Where *do* you think we'll be in a week?"

Gretchen shrugs then says, eventually: "Nice? Marseille?"

It's so clear that she has no idea what Mr. Lansing's talking about, that she didn't get any travel info from Rajan. I wish she would just fess up. I watch Mr. Lansing for clues. He's just rocking back in his chair and holding his beer. He has this disrespectful air that I've come to associate with older American men abroad, where his comfort and loud expression come first. So what if he breaks the wicker chair? So what if someone wanted to sit at the table behind us and can't because he's reclining into that space? So what if he falls and embarrasses us all? He rocks back and looks at Gretchen, sipping his beer and chortling the way he does. I hear the gurgle in his throat and imagine what the threads of his saliva look like, the wet web inside him that makes his breathing so noisy. I've gotten so fucking morbid and weird, I hope it doesn't show. Gretchen just keeps cutting her pizza into slices. Her sunglasses make her look intense and anonymous, a fighter pilot. "He didn't mention you," Mr. Lansing finally says.

"No?" Gretchen says. She still doesn't look up. She's an actress, and she's good; I know that by now. It's her intention to look upset. I just wonder why. I bite into my pizza and watch.

"Is everything okay with you two?"

"Did he ask you to say he didn't mention me?"

Mr. Lansing considers. "No."

"Huh," Gretchen says. "Huh." Both *huhs* seem whole declarative sentences, like they hold layers of penetrating meaning. But I don't think any of us, Gretchen included, has any idea what she's getting at. I'm desperate to ask what's going on, but I lean back and stare out at the water.

"So what's the story?" Mr. Lansing presses.

Gretchen pushes her sunglasses back into the lights of her hair. "Rajan and I like to surprise each other a lot, that's all. I'm sure he meant to burst into the scene. You know, carrying flowers or something." She smiles winningly at Mr. Lansing. There is not one touch of reproach in her voice, which of course makes her all the more reproachful—*How dare you spoil Rajan's surprise!*

Mr. Lansing shrugs. "He should have told me not to tell you, then. I just assumed he emailed you separately."

"So what *is* the story?" Gretchen asks, suddenly eager. Her enthusiasm is engineered to shut down this conversation. "Tell me everything. When exactly is he coming?"

Mr. Lansing winks. "Nine-thirty tomorrow morning. In Nice. But I can't tell you any more now that I know what's going on, can I?"

Gretchen and I escape after lunch, while Mr. Lansing goes looking at shops, probably to buy Gita something. We follow the flowery wall along the beach. I stare at the throngs of people on the sand. So many of the hot women are topless, and I'm glad we bought me sunglasses so I can stare as much as I want. I've been testing myself ever since that night at the party with Wade, wondering if what we did makes me queer. I've never met someone who was, and I don't think either of my parents is, and it doesn't make sense that something could come up inside of me that I didn't get from somewhere else.

You don't suddenly become a different person when you're fifteen. That shit just doesn't happen.

These women are undeniably hot. Tan and lean bellies that spread hard like violins, small breasts that lift. Soft brown nipples. I enjoy how being attracted makes me feel. I'm in a totally good mood, walking along the beach with my sister, beautiful women on one side and an erection in my pants.

When Gretchen speaks there's upset in her voice. I figured she was going to be ecstatic to hear about Rajan coming—I didn't realize she wasn't feeling as sunny as I. "What the hell am I going to do?" she says.

"What do you mean? You keep doing what you're doing, and when Rajan arrives you two will make up and figure something out. You *want* to see him, right?"

"Of course I want to see him," she snaps. "That's not the point. When I do see him, though, what will have changed? All that'll have happened is that I manipulated my way into mooching—into our mooching—off his parents. Our problems will still be there, you know? I won't have proven anything to him."

We walk. I should ask pleasant questions to keep her talking, but she hurt my feelings when she snapped at me. After a while I start blathering about the forest above the beach, how the trees are so thick and black, how I want to go exploring there sometime. She doesn't say much so finally I speak up: "You should email him again. If he's going to get upset, better sooner than later."

Gretchen shakes her head. "You don't get it. I'm talk. Talk is what I do. It's my profession, and it's how Rajan and I have always operated. We discuss things, we chatter endlessly, and we haven't done anything with our lives. My last real role was five years ago. And he's never even had one."

I don't get why this is suddenly about her career. Maybe

Gretchen's just way smarter than me. "You've been in college. That's hardly—"

"The point is that we've set up a habit. I love him but we'll keep having problems unless we're more in the moment, you know? Unless we actually *show* each other what we feel. Unless we're spontaneous and romantic and a little crazy and a lot less boring. I'm going to do this. If I lose Rajan, then I lose Rajan. I've already sort of lost him, so I'll just be where I am now. But this could be what saves us. And I need to try that."

"What are you going to do?"

"I don't know, Humphrey! I've just got until tomorrow and I fucking don't know!"

I can't stand her mad at me. I've been fine so far, calm and unmopey, but it's been a brittle calm, and if she keeps this up I'm gonna explode into misery. "You know what? I'm going to go sit on the beach for a little while," I say.

I want her to say, "No, stay with me," but she just says, "Okay." I hop off the ledge down to the hot sand.

I watch some French boys play paddleball. They invite me to join, but I've got some shit to figure out, so I just shake my head and shift my gaze to the ocean. There's one big cruise ship out there, in the deepest part of the port, and I wonder where its tourists are from.

I find Gita on her way back from the grocery. She's got a bunch of plastic bags in each hand, and smiles frailly, like she's too encumbered to keep on looking elegant. I take half the bags and walk with her to the boat, stand over the rocking hold as she passes me the food. She sighs when she finishes, leans against a pylon. She's wearing a tight button-down short sleeve, and it's got these dark patches where she's been sweating. Gita never showed up for lunch, so I ask if she wants company to go get something to eat. She looks a little surprised—of the four of us, me and Gita are the only pairing that hardly ever happens—and then she nods.

We get her a falafel sandwich and poke around the old shops in the medieval part of town. Some gay guys at a café check me out. I ask Gita if she wants to get a drink, and she does, so we sit at an outdoor bar a ways down from the guys, whom I concentrate on ignoring. I ask her what she bought for the boat, and she asks me what it was like growing up in Florida. She says "good for you" a lot. Gita gets out Mr. Lansing's money to pay—it leaks out in so many small ways, Mr. Lansing's money—but when the waiter comes I order myself another Coke and her another beer. When Gita looks at me I say, "Come on, we're having a good time."

The second round of drinks is almost gone and Gita's teaching me curse words in Hindi when I ask, "How did you and Mr. Lansing hook up?"

She gives me a shocked look and I panic until I realize that she enjoys being shocked. "First week of business school. I went to college in India, and hadn't ever been to America before. He showed me around Boston. I didn't know anything. I pronounced Filene's Basement as 'Philenas Basameantay.' "

I have no idea what either of those places are. "How long ago was that?"

"Ech? Oh. Wow. Eh . . . twenty-five years."

"You must have been super young then."

Gita pushes her sunglasses more snugly over the network of creases around her eyes. "I've always seemed young."

"What did you like about him?"

"You're a very curious little boy."

"I'm sixteen."

She pauses, probably debating whether to answer. "You were asking how he was different then?"

"No, I wasn't."

Gita coughs.

It's after drinks that I do it. We've wandered deeper into the old part of the town and are traveling down a dark alley that dives below the thick stone buildings. Ancient chiseled rocks chop into the air, making the passage look like the lower level of a castle. It's narrow and storybook, lined with old wooden doors and crossed by the paths of stray cats.

I wonder how to make a move. I've never done it before; I've always been the target, not the aggressor.

Since a large puddle of old water covers the stone of the alley, we have to walk single file across the only dry stretch. I let Gita go first, and watch the cork and leather of her sandals as she crosses. She's so careful not to get the hem of her linen pants wet and I'm distracted by that, but since I've already decided to go ahead with my plan, my hand is suddenly holding hers. I can feel myself shutting off, getting glassy, like this is the last time I can do something like this and hope to feel anything genuine ever again. She stops and one of her feet slides so that it is covered in black water.

She stays totally still. Then she places my hand back at my side. "Don't do that, Humphrey," she says.

I stare back at her and wonder if I'm supposed to kiss her now. "I'm sorry."

"Why would you do that?" she asks, sliding down the wall to sit on a doorstep.

"I don't know," I say. The truth is it seemed like the one thing I had to offer.

"You don't have to do that," she says. "That's not why I like you. You don't have to do that for anyone unless you want to." She pats the space of stone next to her.

I sit on the opposite stoop instead. She figured me out right away, even though I thought I could fake it. I don't have anything over anyone. I slap my head a couple times.

"Humphrey! Stop that!"

I hold my head, rub my hair and feel like crying. Then Gita is next to me, hugging me. "What's this about?" she asks softly.

"I have something to ask you for," I say.

"And you thought kissing me first would make it easier?"

I look up and see she's smiling. Not at me, but because she cares for me. The relief that comes feels really good. "That's crazy, huh?"

"Not crazy, no. But not true. I can see these have been top-turvy months for you."

I nod.

"You don't owe people anything, you know this?"

"Yes, I know."

Who knows what she was about to say, but she stops when she sees me roll my eyes. "What was the favor you were asking me, Humphrey?"

"I . . . I love Gretchen," I say.

"I love Gretchen, too."

"And she loves your son."

"Yes, I believe she does."

"I need your help. They have to get back together."

"Really? Who says this?"

"You don't see it? Come on, they're totally in love."

"You haven't even met my son."

"Can't you talk to him? Make him come around?"

"Humphrey. We can't just make people fall back in love."

"I know. But she's so unhappy without him."

"And you think if they got back together she would be a happier girl."

"Yup."

"And a happier girl will keep you around."

"That's totally not part of it," I say, as though I'm all that sure.

"You don't have to do things for people for them to love you."

"I *know*, duh."

"Humphrey, I'm going to say something important to you, because you are old enough. Your sister thinks she can always change people her way. Sometimes it will work, and sometimes it won't, but it's not a good way to be. Until she learns to be satisfied she will keep pushing. Mr. Lansing and I know it, and look past it because we love her, but do not let her force you into doing things."

"She didn't ask me to talk to you, if that's what you think."

"I bet she didn't. And she did all the same."

"You're sounding like there's nothing you can do to help."

"Humphrey, let me make this very clear. We like having you. You don't have to do a job to stay."

I like what she's said, but I can't get my original mission out of my head, even though I know it's not getting me anywhere. "Well, maybe you can still talk to Rajan tomorrow or something."

"Yes, okay, Humphrey. I'll talk to him tomorrow."

I gesture toward the puddle. "I'm sorry about that."

"Don't be sorry. We will forget about it."

16

GRETCHEN

She hasn't gotten the Lansings to where she needs them to be; she knows that. They've been pleasant with her, have evidently enjoyed her company and her brother's, but they haven't closed ranks around her and pledged to help her fight. Did she really expect them to, to choose her over Rajan, to put her desires over their son's obvious reluctance?

Whatever words she should deploy next won't come. She's had years of acting, of throwing herself into foreign and tenuous positions, of going to sets and shoots and schools that force her to mold to new shapes, and she's always succeeded. Yet this challenge is too great.

Maybe tiny Villefranche isn't giving her enough space to think. She walks along the harbor until it turns to scrub, follows a trail up the green hills. She turns around once, and spies a young man Humphrey's size disappearing into the old city. The real Humphrey is napping at the hotel—so is most everyone on a Mediterranean afternoon—but this boy puts her to thinking. She's certain she isn't putting her brother into danger. Surely Mr. Lansing would go only for anonymous boys; he wouldn't dare make a pass at Humphrey, especially under her watchful eyes. No, her brother's safe, and he's out of Haven Township, and they're helping each other. They're doing good for each other. She pokes along the side of the road until it narrows and she's on a trail above the water, skirting the estates of forgotten aristocrats. She pauses far above a private beach and watches the miniature form of a waiter in a polo shirt. He's something out of a diorama, beautiful stuffed fabric.

If only she didn't have to sort through her own emotions; if only she could experience a feeling and its cause would spring to mind organically. Does this bad feeling mean she should get her brother out of there? But she has to stay long enough for Rajan to come. It should be simple: Gretchen and Humphrey remain cheerful parts of the Lansings' lives until Rajan arrives. But the logic of the situation has been stretched too far. She's piled up layer upon layer of calculated choices, created a situation in which she can't behave naturally because nothing around her has come into being naturally.

Gretchen edges out on a rocky promontory. The ocean wind pulls at her skirt, fills her hair with salt and wet. She's keen, suddenly, to feel the chill of the water, to be in one of those blue fathoms fading to black, to worry only about swimming and surviving and nothing else. She pulls off her shirt and skirt and stands in her underwear above the distant water. Gauging the depth of the water, she considers leaping. And then she has done it. As Gretchen hits the water she realizes that she's been wondering whether she might die when she strikes the surface.

She swims the hundred yards to the boat and dries off on the deck. The water left a red slap over her eye. She's given up on retrieving her clothes and is lying in her underwear on the decorative wood planks of the aft deck, the clap of rigging against the mast almost enough to distract her from her thoughts. She falls asleep, and when she wakes it's to a coolness, a spritz of cold vapor on her face. She opens her eyes to a field of gold: a glass of beer. "I opened one of the big bottles and I can't drink it all," Humphrey explains.

"You're sixteen, remember that," Gretchen says. She wraps a towel around herself.

"Hmm," Humphrey says, taking a sip. "You're sunburned."

"I guess I am." Gretchen's voice trails off. She wishes she didn't feel serious anymore. "I like it on this boat," she says brightly.

"I see that."

"I'm thinking of asking Mr. Lansing if we can stay for a while longer. Would you be up for that?"

"I don't know, shouldn't we head back to Rome and apply to that school?"

"So you're considering it?" *But Humphrey,* she wants to add, *don't you see that would mean we'd miss my chance with Rajan?*

"I'd like to give it a shot, yeah."

"Well, we'll be here just another week. It's only September what, second or something? I'm almost sure schools don't start until late September."

"Gretchen! It's not like I'm starting some language course. This is *high school.* We can't just wing this."

She takes a slow gulp of beer. "Of course. I'm sorry. We'll head back as soon as we can."

"You're sorta my mom right now. I don't need much, but you have to help me make sure that the important stuff happens."

She clinks her glass against his. "Okay. Got it, child. *Message reçu.*"

Humphrey swings his legs over the side, kicks his heels against the hull. He looks thirteen. "So, Gretchen!" he says grandly.

"Yes?" she says. She lies back down; the sun makes her sleepy.

Humphrey glances down the hatch to make sure the boat's empty, and giggles. It's a forced cackle, horrible and flat, that of someone affecting indifference. "I talked to Gita about Rajan."

"You did what?"

"Gita. I pulled her aside and asked if she would talk to him for you."

"Humphrey!" She imagines herself throwing her beer into the sea or at Humphrey, yelling *Why the hell did you do that,* but she only sighs. She realizes this is what she wanted, and it's desolating. One more reason for her to hear from Rajan soon. She's coming closer to either bliss or the end of hope. "You shouldn't have done that," she says.

"I know. But I like you, and this is what you want to happen. I could tell."

"No, it's not." She's glad she's wearing her sunglasses.

"Okay, sure, 'No, it's not.'" Humphrey glances at her and then stares down at his body, flicks some sand off the hair of his forearm.

Gretchen smiles. She's saddened to get Humphrey so deeply involved in her own affairs, but at the same time he's such a sweetly willing accomplice. "Don't worry about this stuff," she says.

"Yeah, sure. '*Don't worry about this stuff, Humphrey.*' "

"I'm serious. Rajan has to come around on his own. You just sit tight and enjoy yourself. The Lansings have been married for twenty-five years. They get how relationships work. They know what to do to save us."

"Oh," Humphrey says. He tightens his lips like an admonished child.

She has to be careful here, she reminds herself; she's gained the authority of a parent and no one's going to be checking her decisions. "So what did she say?" she asks, a tension rising in her belly.

"I think she's going to help," Humphrey says. "What do you want me to do now?"

"Just do what you're doing. The Lansings love you. Keep hanging out with me. Don't get yourself in any trouble."

"What do you mean, 'trouble'?"

"You know, don't involve yourself in anything intimate." She screws up her face: *Intimate* is one of those words for avoiding talking about sex.

And sure enough, Humphrey screws up his face and blurts out, "Frickin' hell."

"Why?"

"Mr. Lansing. Is he a fag?"

"Don't say *fag*."

"Is he? Or does he just like some guys?"

"I'm not sure about the distinction here."

Humphrey grunts.

"Look, don't worry about anything," Gretchen says. "Leave Mr. Lansing out of this. Just be yourself. Once Rajan arrives, he'll see me, and you, and that his parents are so happy hanging out with us, and we'll work on bringing him in. We'll all be like one family."

"What we're doing sucks. We're being totally manipulative."

"No, what 'sucks' is that no one's giving me a chance to prove myself."

"Well, it's their lives, Gretch. Not ours."

"Fine," Gretchen snaps, shutting her eyes. "I don't think you get it. This is my family. You and the Lansings, you're all I've got. Mom doesn't want to hear from me, I don't have a job, nothing. Just leave all this shit alone. You don't have to do anything."

"Oh, stop," Humphrey says. "Of course I'm going to help. I'm trying to, what is it, play the devil."

"Yeah, Humphrey. Just play the devil."

They pretend to fall asleep. Gretchen opens her eyes and stares at her brother.

That night Mr. Lansing suggests a harborside restaurant, orders a cauldron of mussels, and shows Humphrey how to use one shell to pluck the flesh from the others. Gita, a hill of discarded shells already before her, stares at a shard fallen from Humphrey's sole tortured mollusk. Her eyes flick to Mr. Lansing, chortling as he tries to get his thick fingers around a slippery specimen. She expertly plucks out another limp orange organ and pops it into her mouth. Gretchen has wondered when Mr. Lansing would tire of having them around, but he roars with laughter when a mussel slips out of Humphrey's fingers and onto the floor. Gita, however, is silenced and pissed.

"So, Gita," Gretchen says, "what have you been up to today?"

Gita smiles, a gray line. "Very little."

Gretchen sits back and takes a sip of wine. There's no need to talk anyway, she tells herself. Gita's probably angry because she thinks Gretchen ordered Humphrey to talk to her. So what? She didn't do anything wrong. Rajan's on his way. Everything's been set up; she can do no more. A wind is blowing in off the water, and she enjoys its coolness on her skin as it passes up her loose sleeve.

Gita excuses herself to the restroom while Gretchen involves herself in watching Humphrey. He is unaware of her: she feels like a mother musing over her son. He has finally grasped how to eat the mussels and, suddenly aware that he and Mr. Lansing have been focused only on each other, winks at Gretchen as he tucks his sun-bleached hair behind his ear. He opens his mouth enough to reveal a yolky mussel trapped between his teeth.

Mr. Lansing lights a cigarette and passes the pack to Gretchen, who lights one from his. They lean back and puff. Humphrey takes the box in his fingers and fiddles with the wrapper. Gretchen and Mr. Lansing stare at each other, in the abrupt intimacy of smokers recently lit up. He has an expression like he's bored by most of life, like he has resigned himself to small pleasures. She figures Gita was once a small pleasure, as was Gretchen herself. Having Humphrey around is another. They could all easily be discarded. Gretchen takes another drag and keeps staring at Mr. Lansing, tries to telegraph her awareness of his passive desire, make clear that she will never leave her brother alone with him. He winks at her. He winks a lot; she wonders what meaning this one is intended to convey. He is like so many other older men: he gives a barrage of clues to what he's feeling but is never actually demonstrative.

Gita comes back, and staggers as she pulls out her chair. She is both overly engaged and off center: a fit is about to come on. "So, Humphrey, you seem to have grasped how to do it, no?"

Humphrey holds up a shell and grins. Gretchen is unsure whether he is being guileless or cunning.

"You know how to just pluck it out of there. Well, you have a very good teacher," Gita continues. "Mr. Lansing is most experienced in the arts." She leans forward, bleary and blinking heavily. Humphrey runs a hand through his hair and crosses his arms over his chest.

"Subtle, Gita," Mr. Lansing says. "But not quite Bette Davis, are you?"

"Oh, yes, this is *funn-y*, is it not? *Bhainchod! Chootiya!*"

"You taught me what those words mean," Humphrey says brightly, as if to start a more polite conversation about Hindi anatomy.

"It's time for a scene," Mr. Lansing says, shaking his head. "We've been overdue."

Gita clinks her wineglass so fiercely against Mr. Lansing's that it splashes a crimson crescent on the tablecloth. Gretchen pulls the box of cigarettes away. She and Humphrey exchange a glance as she uses her napkin to wipe wine from the pack. "Okay, let's all have a scene," Gita says.

Mr. Lansing tsk-tsks. "You're fighting unarmed."

"Come on," Humphrey starts. "Let's just—" Gretchen lays her hand on his knee.

"This is a battle game, hmm?" Gita says. "A game to you, when I am all the time here, trying to maintain a *life*." Her voice constricts on the word *life* so the foreign syllable comes out like a shrill blast of air from a balloon. The only other restaurant patrons, a Spanish tour group under a broad white umbrella, recommence a now-stilted conversation.

"The Indian knack for melodrama," Mr. Lansing says, facing Gretchen. "Amazing. No one feels as deeply as whoever's speaking."

"I am not *trying* to cause a *scene*, here," Gita says. "I am not the one turning our *family life* into a *scene*. But if I'm the only one who has heart, who cares about what's going on—"

"You're trying to tell me that, what, *I* don't care what's going on, when I'm the reason we're all traveling around the Mediterranean? Did you ever make the kind of money for this? Who bought your clothes? Whose boat have you been on? Look at them—" He points to Gretchen and Humphrey, who shrink away as if behind a tapestry. "They're appreciative. Stop being so sensitive. Let's have some fun here, okay? Enjoy life."

"It is not only you who is upsetting me. I find a selfishness all around."

"What's going on in your head, Gita? You've got to clue us in if you want us to follow you."

"I think Gretchen needs to go home. We all need to return to our lives."

Mr. Lansing looks about the table. "Why don't we eat more later. I think we've had enough for now."

Gita screws up her napkin. "Yes, we've all had enough."

"Atta girl," Mr. Lansing says. "Now stalk off."

Gita stalks off.

Mr. Lansing is smiling, and Gretchen isn't sure if it's a polite cover or the result of real pleasure. "Perfect," he says. He tops up their glasses with what's left of the bottle. "Perfect."

That evening they sleep in a hotel. Embarrassed by the scene at dinner, Gretchen skirts Humphrey at the sink as they brush their teeth. Gita's dismissal hasn't begun to sting yet, but she knows it will soon. She eagerly slips into her crisp white sheets. It is a blissful feeling to stretch into a real bed, and Gretchen realizes that she's been looking forward to shutting out the world and going to sleep.

Humphrey doesn't seem as eager to fade away. Gretchen props her head against the pillow and stares at him. He's still in his swim trunks from an evening dip, sits cross-legged on the room's only chair. His now unnecessary Haven Township High School summer reading is propped open on his knee. Gretchen suspects he's focusing more on the hangnail he's chewing than on *The Awakening.* He glances up every few minutes to see if she has fallen asleep.

When she next opens her eyes the lights are still on. The clock at her bedside says 1:30 A.M. Gretchen looks at the chair. His book is there, but Humphrey is not.

17

HUMPHREY

I'm finding it hard to sleep. I'm finding it hard to read. Most things are hard right now, actually. Not that everything's so exhausting, but at the same time nothing's *easy*, you know? Sometimes it's a thrill to be unknown and able to build myself to be however I want, but more than anything else there's the jittery sense that there's no fallback, that it's all best behavior, all conversations with people who don't know me. After what happened with Wade, Carl, and Brandy, I wanted to get away, but now that I've escaped . . . I dunno. Now I want something familiar. Gretchen and I are getting there, but we're still sorta new, too, and I'm not sure how to make sure she likes me.

I inspect the book I'm supposed to be studying. I've been feeling the slickness of the cover, smelling the pages, flipping through and enjoying the breeze on my wrists, anything but reading it. Gretchen looks dead-tired, so it's not as though I can ask her to go out with me. But then I'm like, this is some small town in the south of France. I'm probably never going to have the chance to get here again—I don't want to spend the night in a hotel room reading about olden times.

I'm still on the same page when I see that Gretchen's fallen asleep. I leave the light on so that the change to darkness won't wake her, then I throw on a shirt and some jeans and I'm out the door.

Mr. Lansing and Gita have the better room facing the ocean. I listen at the door: I hear words, but not sexy voices. I knock. Gita answers. She looks cranky; I know what the answer to my question will be before I ask it. But I go ahead anyway. "Do you guys want to go out, like take a walk?"

She looks at me long enough that I know she's choosing between radically different responses. Potential outbursts flash and disappear way back in her weary eyes. "Joel," she says, "do we want to go out and, *like*, take a walk?"

She stares at me while we listen to Mr. Lansing shuffling around in the background. Gita might care deeply about me, or she might wish I never existed, or she might not give a shit one way or the other. She's lost somewhere inside. Mr. Lansing appears behind the partially open doorway. He doesn't have a shirt on; he's got the body of a sea lion. "Hi, Humphrey," he says. His tone is a little impish, like I shouldn't take what he's saying to heart because someone's listening on the other line. "What are you doing up?"

"I couldn't sleep, so I figured I'd check out the town. Do you guys want to come?" I don't really want to hang out with him, but I figure inviting him along will make sure he won't send me and Gretchen away.

Mr. Lansing looks down at himself. He's wearing only boxer shorts. "I don't think so. But you shouldn't go off wandering on your own."

"It's a town full of weenie French guys," I say. "I'm going to be fine."

"Stay close," Mr. Lansing says, holding my gaze until he shuts the door.

* * *

I do stay close. I head first for the medieval alley where I asked Gita to get Rajan and Gretchen back together, then eventually seat myself at a bar that has red velvet everything and no Americans. Turns out the owner is German, and prefers speaking English to French anyway. He's a roly-poly guy with a beard and no other hair, and he serves me a beer without any question. I chat with him for a while until the bar fills up, and then I check out the people who have come in.

A bunch of them look classically French, with pasty complexions and skimpy clothes, and a lot also are probably from Africa even though they're speaking French. I'm there just to watch and that's fine. Until this girl comes in, Algerian or Egyptian or something, probably seventeen, with what look like her grandparents. She orders straight tonic water and looks bored as hell. She's got these long legs and really thick black hair that you could lose a hand in. I wonder about the best way to come on to a girl you haven't met. In the movies you have the bartender send her a drink, but the idea of actually doing that feels stupid. How the hell are you supposed to know what someone you don't know wants? Besides, if she's with her grandparents, can you have the bartender just send over more soda water?

The girl scans everyone in the club, person by person and then back again, and by my accounting she looks at me more than anyone else. So I glance at her, then I take a swig of my beer and look away, and when I look back our gazes fit together. The owner realizes what's going on and starts coaching me. "Joost stahrt danzing. I vill poot on zhe music."

He starts playing some dance music from years ago and I figure, what the hell, so I get off my stool and start rocking, my beer in my hand. The girl won't look at me, I think she's embarrassed for me;

she involves herself in her grandparents' chatter. I'm not going to give up, though. When she finally looks at me during the second song I can see that she's beautiful, big eyes and this tiny waist that I could almost span with my fingers. She chuckles a little, but kindly, and I know what I must look like, a very American-looking teenager making dorky dance moves with a beer in his hand. But I also know that I'm cute now, and I raise my beer and nod that she should come over, and she does. Her grandparents are staring, like no you're not, and that gives me some extra illicit energy. I can feel the beginning of a hard-on.

Her moves are even dorkier than mine, all unsynchronized arms and legs. She's dancing like some lifeless sea monster, tentacles trailing slowly in the currents. But she's so hot. She's self-conscious, holding her hair back with one hand and smiling as if at her own inanity, and I want to cup her chin in one hand and tell her she's beautiful and kiss her. We dance a few feet away from each other. She won't look at me, but I'm getting cocky that she came over at all, and I edge closer when the next track starts. It's clearly a song that she likes, and she looks up with such a burst of white teeth that my heart stops a little. I tell her my name. She just shakes her head but is beaming and starts to move more, swaying her hips and arms as if my hands were pushing them.

A couple more songs and we're kissing as we move. Then her grandparents come over and she has to go. I don't get a phone number or anything. I watch them leave, and as they pass through a red curtain I see someone at an outside table fishing olives out of a martini and catching glances of me through the gap in the curtain. Mr. Lansing.

I smile and wave because that's what you're supposed to do, but inside my pulse says I'm about to fight and I wonder what the hell he's doing here. I know I'm going to need another beer so I get one and then go join him at his table. "You decided to go out after all," I say stupidly.

He nods and I can feel the weight of his gaze. There's always something masterful about him, like everyone's his creation and he's already decided what we're gonna do. I like it sometimes, but not tonight. I scan down the road, trying to catch another glimpse of my girl. She's long gone.

"You like her," Mr. Lansing says. I wonder why it sounds like I'm in trouble.

"She was pretty damn cute," I say.

"She *was* cute," Mr. Lansing says, looking at me curiously.

I don't like him calling her cute, but I don't know how to undo the bad feeling he's just caused. "Where's Gita?" I ask, I guess to get back at him.

Mr. Lansing shrugs. "Sleeping. She's not as young as she used to be."

"Does this feel weird for you, to be out here in France, without your friends or anything?"

Mr. Lansing sucks the olive out from between two hairy fingers. "How do you like France?"

I nod and say it's fine and we're quiet for a while. I try not to watch him slurp the martini juice off his thumb. Then we get another round and eventually we're talking easily again. I can't say anything interesting to Mr. Lansing, and yet he wants to hang out with me. That's a weird kind of power, and I like it. I feel his gaze on the hard lift of my chest and I sneak a glance down at myself as I grab my beer and I think, it *is* an attractive chest. I've never been hot before. It's been a weird summer that way. I've gained something that is mine alone, and that's pretty awesome. I know that Mr. Lansing's intentions could be totally innocent. I also know that it's been a while since I've come across innocent intentions.

Mr. Lansing still looks tired. His cheeks have gone all gray and puffy. After I finish my beer he asks if I want to go for a walk and I say yes. We move down the quiet, narrow streets. When I look up there's the unbroken black of the buildings on either side of the stars. We pass the gay bar and as the guys outside stare at us I wonder what they think, whether they've decided Mr. Lansing is my father or my lover. We go farther into the town, splashing through the puddle where I tried to hold Gita's hand. Mr. Lansing spits out a curse when his moccasins get wet.

Then we're outside the town, on the path that goes high above the water, into the rocks and the trees. There's no good reason to be walking away from civilization at one in the morning, I know, but I've had three beers and I'm curious what's going to happen. Curious and also afraid: the combination produces something in me that I guess is desire.

Mr. Lansing's puffing after we mount the first rise. I sit on a rock to wait for him to catch up, twiddle a pine needle, and look at the moon caps on the water. He sits next to me and looks at the water for a while. I massage my knee because it's started to throb a little.

Then I feel his hand on my back. It just lies there motionless and moist, like a starfish that has crawled onto me and died. I can sense a general heat from his palm, but have no idea where the fingers are. Then they're moving, pressing into the muscle of my back, and he says, "Come here."

He turns me on the rock so that I'm between his legs, my back facing him. He's just giving me a back rub. He's just giving me a back rub.

He lights up and offers me one and so then we're both smoking. I can picture his cigarette bobbing between his clenched teeth, the end glowing. He's started rubbing my back again and it feels like he's digging something out, like he expects to find jewels hidden under my muscles. I don't know how Gita puts up with anything like this.

But when I take a deep breath and try to think of nothing it almost feels pleasant, being touched, even by a hand that hurts.

"You don't mind?" Mr. Lansing says.

I shake my head.

"Of course you mind," he says. "You totally mind." His hands keep pressing.

My cigarette has gone out. I chew on the rolling paper. "Do you want me to fucking mind?"

He keeps massaging.

"I mind. Stop it."

He keeps going so I shrug him off and stand up. I grab his cigarette and relight my own off it. We look at each other in the darkness. His body is outlined in silver by the moon, his nose glowing before the cigarette embers.

"I don't like guys, okay?" I say. I mean what I say. It's even more than that; this whole scenario has shades of Wade; I think I really *hate* guys. But even as I look away I can feel his eyes on my body. I like being liked. And I know that saying I don't like guys makes me wanted even more.

"Come here," Mr. Lansing commands.

"Hell, no," I say. But then I walk over and place my foot on the rock, at the space between his legs. "All I want you to do," I say, "is put your hand on my leg. Put your hand on my leg."

He pauses, then I hear him shudder. His hand is on my calf. I shudder, too, and I wonder if I'm going to cry. Then I swallow the feeling and I'm cool inside—I feel like I could do anything and not cry, now that I've decided not to. I stand still for a few moments, one leg cocked on the rock, posed like a runner warming up. Then his hand starts to move. I don't want him taking control so I straddle the rock so my gullet is right in front of him. I imagine him biting into my throat, drawing blood, like a hunting dog after a stag. I hold my neck before his mouth and he kisses it. His lips are thick and awkward on my skin. I feel the grit of his stubble against my jugular. His breath is hot and intense, though, and I hear throaty little gasps as he sucks my neck. He's desperate for me to kiss him. I won't kiss him. He grasps my hips. I pull his hands away and place them at his side. "Don't touch me," I say.

He shudders again, and keeps shuddering. I'm worried he's having some heart attack or something, but then I realize it's from expectation. I sit down so that I'm facing him. "Don't touch me," I repeat.

He shakes his head, suddenly annoyed. I've been authoritative too long, maybe unconvincingly. He's taking deep drags of his cigarette. His eyes seem closed, but they could be open, as slits. Then he shakes his head. "Wow, Humphrey," he says.

"Let's go," I say. I'm not playacting anymore. I'm desperate to get back to the hotel, to Gretchen.

He waits a minute, then stands, and we head down the ravine back into town. We don't say a word. When the elevator opens at his floor he shakes his head and shoots me a look, like we'll definitely be hanging out again. Then the door closes and I tremble a little. I slot my key card in slowly so as not to wake my sister. The lights are off now, the windows tightly shaded. I crawl into bed and watch the black space where I assume Gretchen is sleeping and thank God that she's there.

18

GRETCHEN

The first place Gretchen goes looking for Humphrey is Mr. Lansing's room. She pauses before knocking, momentarily concerned about waking someone. But it's one in the morning and her fucking brother is *missing.* She slams her hand on the door. No one answers so she slams it again. The chain slides, a bolt unlocks, then relocks, then unlocks. The doorknob jiggles and finally opens. Gita is behind the door, groggy and in her underwear. She squints. "Who are you?" she asks.

"Who am I? What the hell do you mean, who am I?" Gretchen pushes the door open, and it snags Gita's wrist. "Is that supposed to be a joke?"

Gita aborts a protest over her banged wrist and peers at Gretchen. She shields herself from the hallway light as if from a blow. "No, sorry, my eyes . . . it's so bright in the hallway."

Gretchen steps in and closes the door. She is thrust into the pitch black with Gita. "Have you seen my brother?"

"Your brother?"

Gretchen listens in the darkness, suddenly alert. The air is hot and still. "Is he here?"

"No," Gita says. "Your brother is not here." Gretchen's eyes adjust. She can see Gita retreat toward the bed. She's obviously tired, but the slump of her shoulders betrays more than that: she's deeply miserable, and hungover.

"Is Mr. Lansing here?"

She hears Gita flounce onto the bed. Her voice comes from within a pillow. "No." She raises her head, and for a moment her voice is clear. "I'd suggest you find your brother."

The bars are all closing, their owners reclining on steps or mopping the street, chatting with the last booze-cheerful patrons. Gretchen peers into each window. Her own haggard reflection is superimposed over the faces of the dimly illuminated customers. She's in her cotton nightdress with a sweatshirt pulled over and, she notices abstractedly, isn't wearing any shoes. She's only just aware of the slick suds on the cobblestones beneath her feet, of the shadowy imprint left by a now absent trash bag. She concentrates on the morning coolness, and she concentrates on her brother.

After clearing the town, Gretchen darts across the tracks of the empty train station and down toward the water. She skirts a looming stone wall, hopping over as soon as it gets low enough. She lands heavily on the beach and crouches until the tingle in her ankles dissipates. The sand is cold beneath her feet, and the same color as the night. The flowering vines along the wall are only intermittent glimmers. She takes a deep breath and yells Humphrey's name.

The waves continue to crash on the shore. There is a low murmur of vehicles from the main strip of the town.

She passes along the beach, sticking to the wall. A shape looms in the darkness and she recognizes the cube of the lifeguard watch post. She places her bare feet on the first splintery rung, pulls herself up until she is at the summit, and surveys the neon-edged beach. The ink of the sea is undulating but otherwise unbroken. The stone walls are illuminated in staggered globes of yellow. The forested coastline is unlit.

Should she contact the police? She has no idea where their office is, or how to dial an emergency number in France. And she senses that others wouldn't share her dread, that her own remorse is propelling her hysteria. She will have to keep searching.

The road can be identified only by the gleaming silhouettes of parked cars. She tracks along it and away from the town until the seaside trail begins, snakes off into the star-eclipsing bulk of the trees. Gretchen picks her way across branches and loose stones. All she can see are the glowing sleeves of her own sweatshirt as she lurches forward through the darkness. There are noises in the brush to either side, rustles of retreating animals. She feels vulnerable and alien, all bare ankles and outstretched arms.

She crosses a copse of trees and then is again soaring above the shore. She can see her way now, for the moonlight plays directly on her path. Would they really have come this far out? As she creeps forward she remembers Humphrey's being so enchanted with the woods, Mr. Lansing saying he hadn't been yet . . . but in the early morning? Gretchen imagines the two of them alone. That she didn't stop this from happening . . . She shakes, a combination of the night chill and a flash of self-loathing strong enough to make her want to collapse into the sharp bed of pine needles. But she continues along the path. Stop and listen. Move, stop, and listen.

The trail curves into darkness again. Brambles overhang the path. They snatch her hair, scratch across her face. The ground beneath her has changed to grass and sharper rocks; she is no longer on the trail. She tries to return, but the brambles grow thicker and she knows she has again gone in the wrong direction. There isn't even any grass now; she tries to cut back, but a tree blocks her path. She picks another direction and continues.

Eventually, pain cuts through her numbing anxiety. When Gretchen stops to feel the bottom of one foot, her fingertips come away wet. She climbs a boulder and cranes about, trying to orient herself. A treeless patch reveals itself and, imagining she has found the sea, she descends toward it. Newly frantic, she picks up speed and crashes through branches. Salt is in her mouth, and she doesn't know if it is from cuts or tears.

Then the ground slopes, and Gretchen imagines the beginning of the trail. But the slope steepens and then the loose gravel gives and she is falling. She skids for a couple of blinding, terrifying feet, her knees catch and scrape along a stretch of rock, and then she is falling again. The cold air is all around her, in her hair, between her legs. She's motionless and then flailing, and then she strikes the water. The surface punches her forehead first. Then the rest of her body slams into the sea and she's far below. She can't find her way; in her shock she is the cold and directionless dark. Before Gretchen can stop herself she gulps water, and the saltiness of it stokes and disorients her. She pushes hard with her feet, and comes out of the water sideways. The night sky is red. Her scalp aches. The fluid that has filled her mouth tastes of blood.

If she panics, she's in trouble. Gretchen treads water for a few moments, swims and breathes until she is able to reason again. She tries to think clinically: if she is facing land, she must also be facing north, which means Villefranche proper is to the left. She peels off her heavy sweatshirt and lets it sink. It is a long swim, and she keeps close to the rocks, clinging to them every few minutes to rest her muscles. Invisible seaweed and fish caress her legs when she does, though, so she pushes forward as soon as she can. She grits herself against the blank infinity beneath her. And then she is on the shore.

She pulls herself onto the smooth rocks of the beach, looks to the east, and witnesses the color seeping from the black sky. Rajan arrives this morning. Rajan. She can share all of this with him. He can decide what to do, and even if he doesn't make the right decision, at least he will have made it and not she. She doesn't want to have to plan anymore. She just wants her brother back, so the three of them can get out of here.

Could Mr. Lansing have taken Humphrey out of Villefranche entirely? Gretchen moves toward the marina, but she can see, even from her distance, that the sailboat is still there. Then she trudges back to the hotel, ignoring the gazes of the fishermen, the woman baker across from the hotel, the desk staff. Her wet nightdress clings to her thighs; her feet squish on the carpet of the elevator. As she extracts the key card from a wet pocket and fumbles with the lock she hears the elevator behind her whirr and wonders if the desk staff has called it to follow her, if they are outraged at her watery footprints. The door opens, finally, and she tumbles in, presses it shut, and leans against the wood.

Humphrey still isn't there.

She calls the Lansing room, but there isn't any answer. Then she glances at the clock: 5:45. Rajan arrives in Nice at 9:30. She can still make it to the airport in time, tell him everything on their way back. She hops into the shower, blow-dries her hair, sticks plastic bandages to her feet, and applies foundation to the scratches on her face.

The railway station in Villefranche is a cement box with all the monumental unsightliness of a highway exit, but the Nice station is a manor. This is a good omen, surely. Gretchen gawks at the national railway sign atop a glass balustrade, at the French flag clapping nobly above. She hails a cab and stares out the window, ignoring the taxi driver's solicitous glances into the rearview mirror.

The airport is small and the arrivals section manageable. It is smaller than the other airports she has recently been in, still anonymous but also intimate. She assumes a seat and waits. Even as her eyes remain riveted open, she's falling asleep. When the message board announces that Rajan's flight is *à terre* Gretchen stares at the words. It seems impossible that he's come to her. He's been such a presence in her imagination that he surely can't go back to being real. She clutches her purse and stares at the monitor, watches the words switch from *à terre* to *landed* and back again. When she adjusts herself her bandaged feet make plastic sighs in her shoes.

The doors open, and he emerges.

She had hoped for a visceral reaction to him, some surge from within that would inarguably decide how she should feel about the object of so much attention. But when he ambles through the doors she doesn't know what she feels. He's instantly familiar, like old clothing.

If anything, he has grown even bulkier over the past few months. A worn polo shirt stretches over his chest, dangles loosely over his waist. He has taken off his baseball cap, as if out of politeness, and the hair beneath is slick and flattened to his head. When he comes closer his eyes—Rajan and those green eyes, exotic flowers set within brown and black—fire a crude charge.

He doesn't notice her (he is, she consoles herself as her breath catches, not expecting to be met), and passes through the crowd to the curb outside. His nylon duffel, hitched over his shoulder, carries a scent of him and Gretchen is taken aback by the waves of complicated feeling that come over her. He's past her now, and she leans against the *Selecta* vending machine and watches him exit to the curb.

As he gets in line for a cab she doesn't know if she can do it, if she can approach him and supply the shock that will determine their future. She's come all the way from Villefranche to get him, and he's going to help her rescue her brother; it would be a failure to let him go. She propels herself across the lobby.

In the studied nonchalance of the newly arrived foreigner, he doesn't turn around even when she stands right behind him. She watches the two planes of his upper back and wants to hide in the crevice between and be part of his body. She lays a hand on his shoulder and he jumps; she would never have known it by looking at him, but he's aflare with nervous energy.

He smiles when he sees her. He smiles! How can he possibly have so familiar a reaction? She tells herself not to read too much into it: it's the same blank grin he would give if he were unexpectedly called on in a seminar. Then the smile widens into something more savage and he throws up his hands and speaks to the sky: "No, you're not! No, you're *not*!"

"Surprised?" she says. Her eyes are wide. Hesitant but confident, hesitant but confident.

He hiccups. His eyes are wet. "I thought, as I was waiting for my bag, you know, back there, that—shit! I can't fucking believe this."

"Is that a good fucking or a bad fucking?" *What?!*

"I was telling myself, I was saying, maybe Gretch will be there, and that was crazy to think, but I—" He hiccups again. "I didn't think it would actually happen."

"So you're not totally surprised."

"Oh, I'm plenty surprised." He takes his hat and curves it in his palm, then slides it back over his hair.

"Do you want to give me a hug or something?"

He hugs her, but she's not convinced. A girl asked him for a hug, so he gave one. He withdraws, pulls his hat back off, laughs into it, puts it back on. Is he thrilled to see her, or freaked out?

"Do you want—" She wipes her nose. She wishes she hadn't started crying. "Do you want to share a cab?"

She tells the driver to go to the train station, but Rajan corrects her. "Directly to Villefranche, *monsieur.*" Then, to Gretchen, "The least my dad can do is spring for a cab."

Gretchen has missed his way of talking: so stupid and yet so articulate, an intellectual Valley boy. They lean back against the black vinyl. Rajan is talking inconsequentially, waiting for her to start, but she just stares out the window. She doesn't want to explain anything. She hasn't figured out what would be too much to say.

"I'm glad you're here," he says. He raises a hand as if to touch her, then returns it to his lap. He's not pushing her; at least he knows her that well. She looks at him hopefully.

"A little weird, right?" she says.

"Yeah, a little weird, I have to say."

"I guess you'd like an explanation."

He props his legs up against the driver's seat. "Bare bones at least."

"I'm staying with your parents here. Me and my brother are." The mention of Humphrey sets off a wave of anxiety. She forces herself to maintain control: she's in a cab heading to Villefranche; panicking won't get them there any faster. She'll keep parceling out information until it feels like she's said too much.

He stares at her. His eyes look brown now. "What does that mean, you're staying with my parents?"

"You got my email. There's a *reason*. I'll tell you all about it. When we get there. I'm tired right now, and . . ."

"So it's what, the four of you in the hotel room? I did get your email, but I didn't think you'd be *staying with them,* at least not still. I thought you'd go to L.A. after all, or whatever, not stick around without me."

"I couldn't go to L.A. yet, not by myself. I couldn't imagine it without you. So I had a choice, stay in Boston or go somewhere else. I heard you were coming after all, so I figured I'd stay around to meet you because I"—some revelation might distract him from the shallow desperation of her story—"I missed you. I really missed . . . oh, God."

She's sobbing now, not for effect but purely and uncontrollably. She feels Rajan's fingers on her shoulder, and then she is inside his embrace, the two of them on one side of the cab. They're passing through a dense and ancient part of Nice, and when she looks over his shoulder she sees the cement walls blackened with pollution, the old blue tile street signs, and cries. She shudders and breaks against him. It's when she wails, short and loudly, a siren, that he begins to talk. "Stop, shh, come on, shh . . ." He strokes her hair, and then she feels the strokes stop. "What happened to your face?" His hand pulls up the hem of her skirt. "And your ankles? Jeez, Gretch."

"Oh, the scratches? They're nothing. I got them . . . My brother's missing, Raj, since last night. I went looking for him. It was dark, and I got caught in branches. I fell in the ocean, too. Maybe he's back now, maybe it's nothing." She's trying to sound collected, the slackening of her self-control sets her off sobbing again.

"What's been going *on* here?"

She wipes her nose on a wadded tissue and wonders how to answer.

The cab driver asks where to head once they arrive in Villefranche. Rajan pulls an old notebook out of his bag and the sound of the zipper near her head jolts Gretchen into sharper awareness. She stammers the location of the hotel and succeeds in collecting herself just as they pull up in front. She has to solidify her position with Rajan before he finds out about his dad and Gita. Finds out about his dad and Humphrey, too, maybe. Jesus. But she has to locate her brother before anything else. "Raj," she says, "I have to run up to check on my brother. I'm sure your dad's not here—he's probably eating lunch. I'll be right back, and then we'll go find him."

"I don't think I'm ready to see him yet, anyway. I just kinda want to take a nap. I'll come up with you now."

"Umm . . ." She can't think of a way to keep Rajan downstairs without explaining everything. But she can't help thinking that he would never speak to her again if he discovered why she feared for her brother.

They barely fit into the elevator. Gretchen's face presses against Rajan's bag as they go up, and she is again full of his scent. It steadies her somewhat. Let it just be her brother in her room, she thinks, not Mr. Lansing or anyone else, just her brother.

No one answers the door when she knocks. Then, as she is opening it, she hears a mumbled "Hello?" She races over to the bed and there he is. Her brother, whole and alone. "Humphrey, thank God, Humphrey, where were you?" She sits on the edge of the bed and puts her hand on his back. "Humphrey? Where were you?"

He doesn't move, doesn't open his eyes. He's got one pillow beneath his head and he's hugging the other. "Hey, Gretch. I'm tired. I wanna sleep."

She looks up at Rajan, who is wearing his charming introductions face. "Hey, Humphrey," he says, "Don't you want to meet me? It's your sister's boyfriend, Rajan."

Humphrey's eyes pop wide open. Gretchen, struggling to process Rajan's use of the word *boyfriend,* only distantly notices the peculiar mixture of fear and detachment in her brother's expression. Humphrey clenches his eyes back shut.

"Wanna give us a sec, Raj?" Gretchen asks. Rajan looks around the room, his grin still hanging on his face, then heads into the bathroom and closes the door.

"What happened?" Gretchen asks soothingly, running her hand up and down the stretch of comforter covering Humphrey's shoulders. "You need to tell me, okay? Please?"

Humphrey is quiet and then says, "Let it go, okay? I'm fine, I'll tell you later, just let me sleep!" He curses and rolls deeper into the blankets.

Gretchen gets up and stands by the armoire, staring anxiously at Humphrey, until Rajan reemerges. "Let's go get some breakfast. My brother needs some alone time."

Rajan yawns and looks longingly at the bed. "Are you sure?"

They eat breakfast at a café near the shore. Rajan is on his third *pain aux raisins*, and has started listing his failed auditions. Gretchen hasn't been following. He bores her, she remembers now; he often bores her. Every man she's dated has—is boredom something to be expected and enjoyed? She stares at his body as he speaks, loses herself in the morning light playing in the shine of his hair. "—kind of sucks, because they aren't really ready for anything like that, you know?"

She nods, and he continues.

Humphrey's safe. She wonders what he was up to last night. She wonders where Mr. Lansing is, if she can discover anything from him. She should, she realizes, find him right away. But that means Rajan will see him as well, and that means telling Rajan about why she's nervous.

Gretchen nods at whatever Rajan has just said, and then interjects, "So, Rajan, about why I came here . . ."

He looks at her quizzically. He has evidently processed the version she already told him and accepted it; her reasons for acting the way she did have been sealed and filed away. Why complicate it? "Part of what I wanted to do, why I came here . . . I figured you were right, that I haven't been as engaged in us as I could have been."

"Gretch, let's not get into this right now. We're here, let's have whatever fun we can scrape out for a while. We'll figure out 'us' later."

"I'm sorry I tried to kind of take over your parents. That sucks."

Rajan leans back, pastry in hand, and appraises her. For the moment he looks like his father, inscrutable and masterful. "They just took you back in?"

Gretchen shrugs. The move is heavy; it feels like it takes all her energy to lift her shoulders up and let them casually fall back down. She runs a finger down the prickly seam of a scratch on her cheek to distract herself from what she has been saying. "It's kind of like I'm their daughter, Raj. I was in a really bad place. They saved me."

She wonders if he's been wounded by her actions; when he's hurt, she usually never knows until days later, when there is an otherwise inexplicable bout of moodiness.

"Mom called me from the hotel yesterday and told me everything," he says.

"Oh! Oh."

"She wants a divorce. I had to bring some papers from the lawyer. I thought that it'd be best if I told Dad. She was just going to slap him with the papers as soon as I brought them, and I guess that'd be one way to tell him how upset we are—"

"She wants a divorce! Why?"

"He's been having affairs, Gretch. You know that."

"Um, I guess I did, but I thought they were cool with it."

"I guess she was, up to a point. But something changed. I don't know. I didn't talk about it much with her. I just got my ass over here."

"Oh, my God, Raj, you must be so sad."

"It freaks me out to learn that he's been with other women, but I always figured as much, I guess. At the same time he's still my dad, you know? I don't want to see him get completely screwed."

"Oh, Rajan." He said *other women.*

"It's fine, it's totally fine. Don't worry about it."

"Of course I'm worried about it. These are your *parents.*"

"They've been acting divorced for years. It's really no big deal. It's just an official acknowledgment."

"But still. You must be a wreck."

"I'm pissed more than anything. I mean, I'm beyond the age where this matters too much. But my mom'll be all alone, you know? And the rest of the family, the cousins, everyone . . . you don't do this in Indian families. They always judged her for marrying a white guy, and, well, they'll have been right all along." He leans forward. "But here's the thing. My parents officially reside at the Miami condo, because there's no state income tax. And there's this law in Florida that as soon as they're married twenty-five years, they split the assets, no matter what."

"And you think your dad doesn't know?"

"I'm sure he doesn't know. Their twenty-fifth anniversary was last night. I got a hysterical email from Mom right before I left for the airport—he forgot about it, didn't give her a card or flowers or anything. All you guys did was eat mussels or something. If he knew about this law I'm sure he would have divorced her already. He's being such a fucking fool. I'm so embarrassed, you know? That he's my father. I'm like, *Dad,* get a grip!"

"And you're the best one to tell him about this? Are you sure?" Gretchen asks.

"Yeah. And I'm going to fucking enjoy it. I mean, I'm doing him a favor, but all the same I'm going to enjoy watching him squirm."

"It's just, you're their kid, shouldn't you not be so involved?"

"Shouldn't I not be so involved? Gretch, listen and look at yourself. My mom's a wreck, which you should have noticed. She can't even keep herself together. I'm just going to tell my dad what's going on and get us out of here."

"So you're not here to, you know, play paddleball with me on the beach?"

Rajan shakes his head. "I'm flying back out tomorrow."

She and Humphrey must fly with him back to the States. Forget Europe, forget the Roman school.

"We should find him, then, huh?"

Rajan nods, goes to the bar to pay the check.

"So you're not mad at me?" Gretchen asks when he returns.

He kisses the top of her head. "I love what you've tried to do," he says. Gretchen sighs into the kiss, raises her chin so he can transfer it to her lips, but he has already moved away, is staring darkly at the sea.

19

HUMPHREY

I'm not sore, not really. But I do feel like there's an outside in me, that now there's a space where there never was space, that an emptiness has been created and I'll never return to my old shape. I showered a lot this morning. When I pulled up the comforters and put the pillow over my face so only my nose poked out, I was able to sleep. I have no idea what time it is; I drew the curtains as soon as I came in.

I turned the air conditioner way up when I got in to feel the chill, and now when I roll in the bedsheets it's like I'm a little tunnel of heat. It seems the whole worth of me, that I can create this cozy space in a freezing room. I've been taking in the carpet—it's gray-green, with a red thread at odd intervals. I try to figure out exactly how regularly the red comes, but I can't find a pattern.

I wonder if I'll ever have to get out of this bed. I can get room service. I can eat all my meals here—it's on Mr. Lansing's credit card. But the idea of his paying, of his interacting with me in any way ever again, throws me for a tailspin. I breathe into the pillow and scrunch my eyes but I'm awake now so they just roll back open.

* * *

So, last night. I was in the initial freak-out about Gretchen being gone at four A.M., and still a little drunk when the knock came. I opened the door partway and it was him. I felt this initial quake of fear, made bigger by the fact that Gretchen was missing, and I was both upset and relieved to have him there, because maybe he would help. That hope faded pretty quick, though, because he was still wearing the same clothes from yesterday and looked fried.

"What's going on?" I asked, poking my head under the door chain.

"Hi Humphrey, open the door," he said.

"Have you seen Gretchen? I think she went to go look for me and now she's gone."

He shook his head. "Open the door."

I closed it. There's no way I should have been opening the door to him. But I needed to go look for Gretchen, and I couldn't if he was blocking it. I put on some clothes (what I thought were unsexy ones: a beaten-up polo that smelled like armpit and jeans that had last been washed in Italy and had begun to stiffen), then unhitched the chain and opened the door. Mr. Lansing was leaning against the far wall of the hallway; he hadn't bothered to knock again. He was just staring at my door and, now that I had opened it, was staring at me. "We've got to find Gretchen," I said.

"Where is she?" His lips curled around the words.

"I don't know! That's why we have to find her."

He came toward me and put his arm around my shoulders. "Don't worry. We'll go get her."

I pulled free and led down the hallway. I wondered for a second why he was around at all, and then I realized Gita probably kicked him out of their room. He and I had become the new couple, thrown together for good or bad. I headed for the stairs so we wouldn't have to face each other in the elevator.

The desk clerk asked us if everything was fine when we walked past and we both said yes at the same time, me quickly as I pushed open the front doors, Mr. Lansing more slowly and politely as he trailed after.

I couldn't find Gretchen anywhere. Those shutters, thrown open all day like in a storybook, were now shut and barred, the cafés closed and dark. We didn't come across anyone, really, except a drunk by the fountain in front of the church. Mr. Lansing waited on corners as I ducked down streets, sat on a bench as I tried the church door. He was really good the whole time, respectful and patient. I sat down next to him and desperately didn't want to be with him. But I even more desperately didn't want to be alone.

"She might be taking a walk. She might be looking for you, or maybe she's given up. We could check your hotel room again," Mr. Lansing said.

"This is all my fault," I said. "I shouldn't have wandered off with you." I sighed a little and he grunted, as if accepting apology. But I hadn't meant to apologize; I had meant to offend him.

"You might have left her a note. Then again, you're sixteen. You're old enough to handle your own affairs." He said it slowly, like he was trying to convince himself.

I got up and wandered toward the boat, because that was the last place I could try.

I threw open the hatch and peered in. Of course she wasn't there. I sat on the edge, halfway between the cold wet outside air and the stuffy heat of the day still trapped in the hold. Mr. Lansing leaned next to me. He was smoking again. He didn't seem tired anymore, and instead he was intense, staring at the faux-wood planks of the boat. Then he was staring at me. "You're a cutie," he said.

I wanted to say *please don't* but I couldn't find the strength right then. I certainly looked unreceptive, though: I was scowling. I should have done more, I should have said something strong. I couldn't stand the idea of him touching me again. I dreaded the shutting down of my personality. So much of "romance" must be this way, I was thinking, this cold submission and letting your boundaries be overcome.

"Come here," he said.

"I'm worried about Gretchen," I said.

"Come here," he repeated, really gently, like all he wanted to do was console me. And I bet he honestly did want that. But I knew that once he was holding me he'd want to do more. I shook my head.

He started smoking more quickly, puffing like it was keeping him alive, and I could see him turning mean. I dreaded the moment that he was going to start talking again.

I couldn't believe Gretchen wasn't there for me. I was mad at her, even though I knew she didn't ask me to come on to Mr. Lansing—I did that on my own. I'm angry that we couldn't have a relationship like other siblings have, one that didn't get fucked up like me and Wade got fucked up. I'm mad that she doesn't have a simple, clear soul, that she's not the person I could finally cling to and trust she was looking out for me. Yeah, she brought me plenty of adventure, but I was still alone, just with her. And I'm afraid that if I keep tackling the world alone, without depending on anyone, I'll become someone who can only be alone. Already I'm afraid that I won't be able to touch anyone without thinking of Brandy, of Wade, of Mr. Lansing. I'm being used, I've been used by everyone I've met. But even though I know that's wrong, being used is still the best thing I have to offer.

I kept telling myself, I'm a guy. Sex for us is supposed to be all about gratification. What does it matter who I get off with, as long as I'm getting off? There's nothing permanent to hooking up—I can always shower later. I tried to tell myself that submitting to Mr. Lansing would be an adventure, an experiment.

"You love getting everyone falling over for you, don't you?" Mr. Lansing said. He didn't sound as mean as I thought he would, but I felt a bigger onslaught coming up.

"What do you mean?" I asked. "No one falls over me."

"You're a tease just by existing. You tore up everything in Florida weeks after moving there. Leading that kid's mother on until her boyfriend had to step in. Winning Gretchen over so easily after years apart. You don't have to try to fire me up, it's coming naturally. So stop trying to tease me."

This didn't seem like something people could have an argument about. "I want to go home," I said.

"You don't have a home." He gestured toward the boat. "This might as well be your home."

"I want to go back to the hotel."

"There's no one at the hotel. You could go back to Florida, sure, but someone would have to fly you there, and I know enough from Gretchen about who your parents are . . . going back to them, that's really just a trap, isn't it? No, you're here, you've got yourself into this, and now you have to deal with what you've set up."

I stepped around him toward the dock.

"Honestly, what the *hell* do you think you're doing?" Mr. Lansing said. "Do you think you can just lead me on, just play around to get attention? You've started something here. The least you can do is finish it."

"I don't know what you mean," I said.

He took a long drag and exhaled. "You know exactly what I mean."

I shook my head, because I knew if I said something my voice would crack.

"Get over here," he said. I took a step toward him, just because of how strongly he spoke, before I remembered I didn't want to be near him. "I can take care of you. I can send you to the top schools in the world. I can make sure you get the best opportunities, that you meet fascinating people your own age. You could model, start a rock band, I don't care. I don't ask for much in return. I'm offering you *chances*, and that's exactly what you don't have. All this potential and no opportunity to use it. You've been throwing yourself against people who are unworthy of you. You're like your sister, not made for a normal life."

His words were hitting me despite my defenses, leaking in and around the seams of my decision to hate him. I was still scared that no one would ever really know me, that no one would ever care to. I didn't want Mr. Lansing to "know me," but he was right that no one was going to understand me at Haven High. And he was my best chance to get away from there. That's why I kissed back when he finally grabbed the back of my neck and pressed his lips on mine. There was a full day's growth of stubble on his face. I could feel it scrape away at the soft skin on my chin and my cheeks. His tongue was round and muscular, bathed in the bad taste of his cigarette.

He led me down into the hold.

Now, back in the hotel room, I can feel my eyes get tight and dry and then stingingly wet and I think, here it comes, the flood. But I don't start crying. I'm just clutching a loose nylon thread of the comforter and feeling it dig into my flesh. I stare at the dark glass of the window where the curtain has parted. I'm waiting to feel something but nothing's coming, just a glassy space slowly inflating inside. Aren't I supposed to be bawling? I'm all alone here, I've been through some crazy, tough shit, and here I am, calm as anything. That's what scares me most. I feel like I can't act normal if I tried, but I also can't act crazy and wounded, because that feeling doesn't come, either. I'm just an unnatural nothing, I'm all my experiences but none of my reactions, like what I'm feeling has been written down and then read aloud by a machine. A splash of detail comes unbidden from last night: I held the loose weight of his ass up in my fingers. The skin beneath his underwear was red and pebbled, as if rubbed raw.

I cried when he did it. It felt gritty, at once a familiar feeling and a shocking one, like I was pissing and taking a shit at the same time. I concentrated all my rage into my muscles, like I was enveloping him, crushing him. I fixated on the cushion under me, on the riveted line where the fiberglass hull attached to the couch. When he finished and threw the condom over the side of the boat I looked down and was shocked to see my own erection. My rage, the bolt of all this newness and foulness, had turned me on. I put my pants on over my bulge and staggered off the boat. I wish I hadn't seen his expression when I left, because the whole walk back to the hotel I couldn't get it out of my head. He wasn't scared or guilty at all. He was proud. Like he had done something bigger than get himself off in me.

I stand and go over to the window, because I haven't stood up in a while and I want to remember what movement feels like. I sway a little, like I'm injured, although all my parts feel fine. I throw open the curtains and the room goes white. My eyes scream and tear. The brightness makes everything in the room seem heavy and permanent—the rumpled sheets are from a tomb. I grab a soda and a bag of candies from the minibar and flick on the TV. Everything's in French except the music channel. I watch some hot starlet who just became a singer.

This isn't something I got into and got out of—I've got a secret now. I've never had one before—whenever I played truth or dare in California, I felt I had to make shit up because my life wasn't dramatic enough. But this . . . someday I'm going to get married, and there'll be a point when I'm gonna feel I'm holding back unless I tell her . . . God, there's a dark little bump in me now. I thought you could always pick up and move on, but this, I don't think there's anywhere I could go without it still being part of me.

20

GRETCHEN

Gretchen can't really feel her hand as it raps on her hotel-room door. The world has gone light somehow; substances give slightly when she touches them. Even the door feels soft to her, soft and yet firm, like the flesh of a mushroom.

She's back in love.

She hums a tune and toys with her hair as she waits for her brother to answer. She beams at the fluorescent ceiling light, gazes down the hallway to the sun-filled window at the end and imagines the glorious possibilities of the city outside. They'll be like a little family, she and Humphrey and Rajan, settling in L.A. on Rajan's trust fund and what's left of her financial aid. Rajan's back, he's glad that she cared enough to run to his parents, it worked. He can tell his father what he needs to, and they'll all take the next train north. Gita'll come around and join them. In Paris, maybe!

Why won't Humphrey answer?

She savors the lingering sensation of Rajan's weight against her in the elevator, the heaviness of his form, the heat that hit before he kissed her, the heat that remained after. *I've missed you so much,* he might as well have said, the way he held her.

When she knocks again, she hears a shuffle behind the door. It's Humphrey, dressed only in his briefs, pale in the bold sunlight. "Hey, come on," she says. "It's a beautiful day. Let's go for a walk."

Humphrey nods and shambles into the bathroom. "Just want to take a shower first."

She turns to follow him and sees that, yes, it's like she thought, his hair is still wet at the tips; he's only recently showered. She feels a surge of unfathomable panic, and her voice tremors. "Okay, Humphrey, if you want."

She pulls a chair to the bathroom door, sits and listens to the spray of water hitting porcelain. She hasn't heard the metal curtain rings slide yet, so she surmises her brother is standing in front of the mirror, checking himself out. "Hey, Humphrey?" she asks. "What happened last night?"

She can see his feet haloed by shadows under the seam of the door. "I went for a walk. I couldn't sleep, for whatever reason."

"Where'd you go?"

"You went looking for me, huh?"

"I was really worried."

"I was fine. Went to this bar for a little while, danced with this French girl."

"Cute?"

"Pretty cute, yeah."

Gretchen wonders how to voice her suspicions. "What did you do, have a few drinks?"

"We did, yeah. What are you worried about, that I drank too much?"

"Well, you know, you're young, you don't have that much tolerance yet."

A pause. "I guess I did drink more than I should have."

"Did you . . . sleep with her?"

"No. Jesus."

"Well, I've got Rajan waiting downstairs."

She hears Humphrey get into the shower. "Yeah? How are things?"

"Great. Really, really great."

"Awesome."

Gretchen gives the Lansings' door a dozen knocks, calls the couple's names into the wood. She rummages any number of borrowed key cards out of her purse—one of them is bound to open this door. She tries the cards in the lock one by one, but it keeps blinking red. Then the door opens from the other side. Gita's face hangs in shuttered darkness.

"What do you want?" Gita asks.

"Rajan's here," Gretchen says.

Gita nods. "I know. We're leaving as soon as he gives some papers to his father."

"Don't you think . . . don't you think it's unfair to make Rajan deliver them?"

Gita nods again, backs into the room, and sits on the unmade bed. "Yes. I should do it myself. But I can't. I'm . . . not well, Gretchen."

Gretchen sits beside her. "Are you sick?"

"No. I'm tired, very tired. This trip is not . . . what I've wanted. My husband has changed. I assume Rajan has told you what those papers are?"

"Yes." Gretchen tries to put her arm around Gita, but she shies away.

"Don't hold me, Gretchen. You are not my daughter."

"What?"

"You have acted selfishly. Everyone has acted selfishly." It comes out like a pronouncement; she has been arriving at this conclusion for some time. "I hate that you have made me feel I am only good for you so you can get to Rajan. I hate that I have had to compete with you for my own husband's affection. Now I have to compete with your brother as well—that is the final straw. I hate that you see my life as you do. You have not been my friend. You have been only your own friend."

Tears smart in Gretchen's eyes. "I love you, Gita. I haven't done anything that I thought would hurt you."

"You are a weasel."

Gretchen stands.

"I have done everything for you," Gita continues. "You came from nothing, and I understand that this struggle has made you hard. I admire you for it. But without my goodwill Rajan would not have stayed with you as long as he did. You would not have been allowed into our world. You have been my little chick. And you have turned on me."

"Of course I haven't turned on you!" Gretchen stands by the door. She recognizes the desperation before her. Gita is miserable, probably has been for some time, and so she's lashing out at everyone around her. Surely she's not still that upset with *Gretchen*! But Gretchen knows the irrational anger of the depressed—she knows it from her own mother. "I can't deal with this right now," Gretchen says, rubbing her eyes. "You're not making any sense."

"Then leave. Leave me here. But when I go to the airport, it will be with my son alone. I will pay for you and Humphrey to go home on a different flight. That will be my final gift."

"I don't need your money!"

Gita blinks at her. "Of course you do."

Gretchen backs into the hallway and grips the door handle. "I am going to *help Rajan*, your son, who's standing down there freaked out, because he has to divorce your husband for you."

"Oh, yes, help my son. He'll just *love* you for it. Child."

Gretchen slams the door closed.

Gretchen, Rajan, and Humphrey watch from the far end of the pier as Mr. Lansing loads up the yacht. He tosses a couple of coolers into the aft cabin, his cigarette slipping from his mouth and onto the plastic floor of the hull. He's wearing his poofy sailor hat, and surveys the boat with an authoritative air, his fingers nestled between two buttons of his straining shirt. He sees the three of them, straightens and squints. Spying Rajan, he waves his hat in the air.

"Oh, fuck no, he's not pulling that friendly-father shit," Rajan says under his breath.

Gretchen squeezes his arm. "Are you ready for this?" she asks.

Rajan just strides forward—she loves him for doing that—and Gretchen grabs Humphrey's hand instead. It shivers once as she takes it, and then goes limp in her palm. "Don't worry," she whispers to Humphrey. "I know you're tired, but this will only take a few minutes, and then you can take a nap while I get our tickets, and then we're out of here."

"Out of here, where?"

"Wherever you want," she says distractedly. She scans the boat, is relieved to see that Gita's not there. She must still be tanked out in the hotel room.

"I don't like Mr. Lansing anymore," Humphrey whispers as they approach.

"He is kind of a tool, isn't he?"

"Rajan," Mr. Lansing calls. "Come here, we're all going to take a ride." The words come out both hospitable and formal, like the introduction to a theme-park ride.

"Hey, Dad," Rajan says. He stands a few yards back, his arms crossed.

"What do you think of it?" Mr. Lansing asks. He has pulled another cigarette from his pack, and offers the box to Rajan, who shakes his head.

"It's great," Rajan says. "Expensive." And then, softly enough so only Gretchen can hear: "Perfect for sharing with random whores."

Mr. Lansing puts his hands on his hips and gives a forceful grin, as though determined not to let Rajan ruin everyone's day. He gestures to the yacht. "Come on in. I brought dinner stuff."

"Why don't we get something to eat somewhere in the city?"

"No. I've packed dinner."

Mr. Lansing boards the yacht, and Rajan follows him, arms crossed. His sneakers squeak across the fiberglass.

Mr. Lansing tries to hug his son, but Rajan blusters past. Gretchen skirts by, and it is Humphrey who winds up receiving Mr. Lansing's affection: he slings his arm around Humphrey's shoulders as he lands on the boat. "Good to see you again, boy," he says.

Humphrey's lips spread tight and red across his face, like a gash. He slips from Mr. Lansing's grip and heads for the bow. Gretchen sees Mr. Lansing's expression of odd tenderness, then Humphrey's squared shoulders, and then Rajan, his arms crossed over his massive chest, doing nothing to mask his dismissal of his father. There's a lot she doesn't know about, she realizes.

"Cast off!" Mr. Lansing calls.

Rajan took sailing lessons as a kid, so for the first time they will use the sails instead of just relying on the motor. Father and son each instinctively takes his own side of the yacht and barks terms like *halyards* and *stanchions* and *shrouds* at the other. Their movements are practiced: rigging passes easily from one hand to another. After each knot is tied, each winch turned, each sail unfurled, both men know which knot, winch, or sail must follow. But their meaty hands—one closer to muscled, one closer to stumpy—become fists on the sailcloth, grip the ends of nylon line like hilts. Gretchen is disoriented by their odd war game; all she can do is sit at the bow with Humphrey and watch them.

They've motored far out of the port but as there is not much wind, the mainsail hangs slack on the mast. Mr. Lansing looks meaningfully at Rajan and wordlessly heads into the hold. Rajan cuts off the inboard motor and follows; the door slams shut.

Gretchen and Humphrey sit at the pulpit of the boat, their legs dangling over the side. The air beneath the cloudless sky is hot and low, spreads over them like gauze. Gretchen doesn't speak for a while, and then finally says, "You're not just hungover, huh?"

Humphrey keeps swinging his legs. One of them strikes the hull.

"Do you want to tell me what happened?"

He looks at her and then out at the water.

"Does it involve Rajan's dad?"

Humphrey breathes some words.

"What did you say?" Gretchen asks.

"He fucked me."

"What do you mean, he fucked you? He fucked you over?"

"No. Right below us. Last night."

The sky is too bright suddenly; her eyes scream at the intensity. "Are you sure?" she asks. She hates her words as soon as she says them. She claps her hands over her mouth, and then says, "I didn't mean that, of course you're sure. I'm just really shocked."

"I'm totally sure, yeah. Just like I'm totally sure what happened with Brandy, and Wade, and Carl, yeah, I'm totally sure. I've been *fucked*."

"How could he do that to you?"

"It's not that hard to imagine, is it? What the hell are we doing here? The dude is heartless."

"Did he . . ." She can't say the word *rape*. She wishes she could, but she can't. There's a fury welling inside of her like blood from a fresh wound, but there's another feeling, too, something severe that's pressing down so fiercely that it's hard to breathe.

"Whatever," Humphrey says. "I'm fine."

Gretchen's on her feet. Her knuckles are white on the pulpit railing.

21

HUMPHREY

I see Gretchen freak out and sense I should be the same way, on my feet and yelling, but all I feel is sluggish, and if I'm alarmed it's at the fact that I'm not more worked up. Mr. Lansing took what he could, and I gave it to him even though I didn't want to. Can I blame him that much? Couldn't I blame myself as easily for not resisting more?

But I see her crying and clutching herself and I realize this is a big deal. This whole summer has been a big deal. I've enjoyed it and I've hated it, receiving so much attention. It's healing and it's damage, it's idolization and it's rape. And now it's all gone too far, and something has been taken from me. All I can think of is how dangerous it is, to wander from situation to situation and spend all your energy on trying your hardest to be great. Better to be awful and imperfect if it means sticking with something. I'm tired of newness, of being the focus just because I've got something that wasn't there before. Give me old and boring. There's nothing like that in my life anymore.

I feel like crying but I make it turn into anger instead. It's a false move, but the rage comes out so easy and so strong. "You owe me big time."

"I owe you? What does that mean?" She looks up at me all uncertain, her hair scraggly in her face.

Now I'm crying, for the first time. My mouth is scrunching up and the muscles hurt, like they're straining too hard. It's coming out so hard I feel like I'm hanging upside down; I see spots. "You *owe* me. To stick around and let me trust you and you care for me, and all that."

I've been pacing the edge of the boat, and now I'm at the motor set into the back. I look at it and realize that the motor's all I need to get back to shore. I turn the key but it doesn't start. As I yank the key back and forth Gretchen's standing far away at the bow, staring at me, her arms lifeless at her sides. Then there's a thump, and another thump, from the inside of the boat. Through the haziness of my tears I hear it and feel it reverb. Something's striking the side of the boat. Then there's Mr. Lansing's voice, muffled but unmistakable. "The law is on her side! The law is on your side!"

He says "your" like it's all the world. I hate him. I hate his indignation, I hate that he could be feeling anything more than remorse for seducing me. I hurl the door to the hold open but Mr. Lansing's already on the steps, barreling up. He's so pissed his hair is wet; his face is white, purple, and red. He slams past me, almost knocking me over, and storms on deck. Rajan spits cool words out after him: "No point getting angry. Should have looked up the law, asshole, instead of wasting all your time fucking whores."

Suddenly Mr. Lansing's standing behind me, has his arms on mine, is holding me between him and Rajan. His hands are slick on my arms; I've never seen anyone so angry. "Oh, yeah, fucking whores?"

And then he's gyrating, simulating what he did to me the night before, close to this very spot. His words don't make sense. He can't *want* Rajan to know he screwed me, right? But the salvaging power of a secret, of his dominance of me, has taken hold of him. I didn't fuck him; he fucked me, and suddenly what he's demonstrating makes emotional sense. I can feel him press against me, feel the straining muscles of his thighs.

Rajan's face is blank like someone just vanished, and then Gretchen's yelling into his ear and pointing to his dad. Rajan's face begins to fill back up, only with fury now.

I whirl and throw myself against Mr. Lansing, like I'm body-slamming him, but he's big so he hardly moves and I just press against him. It's uncomfortable and weird, but I only wanted to be the one in control. That I'm too weak to budge him gets me even more angry, so I start swinging. He's stunned. My first couple of punches land on Mr. Lansing's chest, and I can feel the convulsions of his fat beneath my fist. Gretchen screams, and that makes me boil more.

It feels awesome to hit someone. I've had so much fury swelling in me for months, I've been so careful about holding it in, that when it comes out it's like I've already pulled the string as far back as it can go and I'm just releasing the arrow. Mr. Lansing's on his knees and I've got my hands around his throat. He stares at me, his eyes bugging.

I hear thumps behind me, underneath the piercing sound of Gretchen's screaming, and then strong hands are on the back of my sweatshirt and I'm off Mr. Lansing. I throw punches in the air and stare at the red hands on his throat where I just was. When I simmer down the hands release me. As soon as they do I fly through the air and fit myself back over the red marks and squeeze as hard as I can. Me and Mr. Lansing are both gasping. The strong hands are on my sweatshirt again, and I'm flying. I skid on the deck and slam into the rail. Rajan is standing over me but glaring at his dad, his eyes blazing. "Fucker!" he yells.

"Stop it!" Gretchen yells to all of us.

I'm embarrassed and furious and want to make it stop so I scramble to my feet and throw myself at Mr. Lansing. But Rajan puts himself in the way so I've got my hands at his chin instead, pushing it back. I want to sink my fingers into his mouth, into his eyes, to push his mass of muscle into itself and squish him beneath my fingers. The back of his head presses into the limp fabric of the sail. I've got a hard-on, I can feel it push against him as we fight, and I don't care. I want to crush his muscle, feel his powerfulness crumble under my fury. But I'm not strong enough.

"What the fuck is wrong with you?" Rajan yells. He yanks my hands away and advances on me. He's gonna wrestle me to the floor, I know. I can't take being wrestled to the floor again, not by anyone. I back up, heedless of where I'm going.

His hands are on the front of my sweatshirt, and he's thrown me to the ground. My wounded knee hits the deck first and then my head hits the railing and I scream. I don't recognize my voice. I throw myself at him again and he pushes me down harder this time. I'm exhausted and I can't really breathe and I have these images of my fight with Carl going through my head, his big hands so like Rajan's except covered with black hair, and I'm resisting hard and the strong hands are on my chest, pushing down so brutally that I feel the sharp splinters of my rib bones. They creak like they're going to snap.

Then he's off me, and all I can see is the blueness of the sky, the blinding sun. I breathe for a few seconds, then sit up. Mr. Lansing has grabbed his son from behind and pulled him down into the seating area near the boom. Rajan turns on his father and the two big men face each other, hunched forward, arms cupping the space between them.

"What the fuck did you do?" Rajan yells.

A wind has come up, strong enough that the boom sways between them. All they must be able to see are sail and the other's feet as they edge from side to side. I try to leap forward but I feel thin arms around my chest and that's when I realize Gretchen's holding me and I give in to her. I feel her sleeve at my cheek as we watch. Gretchen keeps screaming for them to stop but I barely hear her for the loudness of my breathing.

Rajan makes a hard dive for his dad's legs, but he hits the boom on the way and his head rocks back. He busted open his chin and there's blood on the floor of the boat, running into the rivulets designed for breaking waves. The red runs along the grooves of the white plastic hull. The shock of seeing his own blood spilled, and maybe some missing teeth, makes Rajan pause. He crouches, blinking heavily, his hand over his chin. Gretchen gets up and heads toward him.

But Mr. Lansing can't see any of it. He pulls the boom back and throws it at his son. It should have hit him in the stomach and knocked him over, but since Rajan has hunched it nails him right in the chin, at the exact spot the blood has been spewing from. The triangle of open flesh on his face splits farther at the corners and becomes a great flapping crimson square, flinging drops and streams of blood as Rajan falls. I can't see his expression as he's flying backward, but his arms and legs are all askew like he has been falling for miles. A sharp howl and then a splash as he strikes the water.

Now both Gretchen and I are yelling. Mr. Lansing comes from around the other side of the boom and sees everything. In a moment he's over the side. He snags the railing as he leaps into the sea, though, and his skull smacks the hull heavily before he splashes in.

He's disoriented and slips under the surface, but then he's got Rajan around the shoulders as he treads. The halo of Rajan's blood is around them, like an oil slick. Mr. Lansing sputters and coughs to keep Rajan's struggling weight afloat.

Gretchen flashes past me. She's desperately turning the motor key, yelling that we need to turn the boat around. I take over and try. It turns but never comes close to starting. Fumes fill the air.

Gretchen's sobbing and banging at the motor as I continue to fiddle with the key. She throws a coil of rope to Mr. Lansing, but by now we're too far for it to reach. Then she starts opening chests and cabinets. She tosses a half dozen life jackets and a partially inflated dinghy overboard. There's so much orange plastic bobbing that it's weird and almost funny, like we're getting rid of junk. Mr. Lansing won't even try to grab on to a life jacket. He's doing all he can to keep Rajan afloat. His son's blood has soaked his face.

Gretchen finds a life preserver on a long rope and tosses it as I continue to throttle the motor. The ring flies over the heads of Mr. Lansing and Rajan and then catches against them as the drift of the boat drags it. Gretchen has pulled off her shirt and skirt and stands in her underwear at the boat's edge, like she's going to dive in to help secure it. "They'll pull you under," I say, surprised at the power in my voice. She steps back from the edge.

The life preserver has been bobbing against Mr. Lansing long enough that he finally notices it. He threads one arm through the ring and the other around Rajan. The position doesn't work, though, and when his grip slips he almost loses the preserver entirely. He lets go of Rajan and disappears under the water, resurfacing a moment later to grab his son back. Mr. Lansing's choking and gasping; saltwater streams from his mouth.

"Is there another preserver?" I ask, but Gretchen's already looking for one.

"No," she screeches.

I'm still jiggling the key when I see that the outboard motor's started. I pull the wheel hard to one side to circle around. But the boat's slow to turn and its speed pulls the life-preserver line taut, and now drag is pushing Mr. Lansing off. He's flailing to keep his grip.

"Cut the motor!" Gretchen screams.

"I don't know how." I look at the motor. All I see is a choke button, and I don't know what that means.

Gretchen's helping me try to figure it out, and then she stops. She's staring behind the boat, her hand over her mouth. Mr. Lansing has lost his grip and he's sinking. He reappears a few feet back, then disappears again. I can see the sun glint off the silvery buttons of his shirt, and then he slips under the surface.

Rajan, however, stays afloat. I wonder if maybe he has regained consciousness, but his head still lolls to one side. Then I see the cord wrapped around his chest: his father tied him to the preserver. Gretchen and I start to pull it in. It's hard work against the current, but eventually we get Rajan to the back. I put the ladder down and try to haul him up, but I don't have the strength. Instead I return to the wheel and guide us back to where we last saw Mr. Lansing. He's probably swimming out there somewhere, but we can't find him. I want to keep looking but Rajan is still unconscious and bleeding. Gretchen uses her shirt to bandage his jaw as best she can, and then it's all she can do to remain perched at the edge of the boat, leaning off the ladder so she can hold Rajan's head. And we're like that—me gripping the wheel, Gretchen bending low and awkward to keep her boyfriend's savaged head out of the water, Rajan himself bobbing unconscious—as we head to shore.

22

GRETCHEN

It takes place at a New Jersey cemetery, in a town where no one who attends actually lives. Gretchen watches with a dull curiosity as friends of the Lansings emerge from black cars and take their places around the casket. Would any of them have come to Italy to spend time with the Lansings; would any of them have come to know of the divorce papers, of Joel's lovers? The men wear suits they perhaps wore to their offices the day before, the women cover their highlighted hair with embroidered black scarves or the fabric of saris. Gretchen stands away from everyone, barely part of the ceremony. Gita is clustered by Mr. Lansing's black-garbed peers on the far side of the coffin, Rajan beside her. He doesn't look at Gretchen; he hasn't seen her since his father died. For both of them, in the throes of their sadness and guilt and relief, in that bitterness and chill and heat, the other can bear only the stink of death, of blows rained on Rajan and Humphrey's bodies, of a divorce announced minutes before Mr. Lansing's lungs filled with seawater, of thousands of dollars dispersed throughout Europe. Rajan's chin is heavily bandaged; Gretchen can see only half of his face.

The attendees shuffle to make a breeze beneath the strong sun, inconspicuously fan themselves with any loose material of their clothing. The coffin is sleek, chrome-handled, and requires four flailing handlers to deposit it into the earth. Mr. Lansing's body was recovered two days after the accident: the service is closed coffin.

Later that day Gretchen is again on a plane. That the people around her speak English is disquieting rather than reassuring. She can no longer cloak herself in foreignness. The two overweight women in spandex who barricade her into her window seat bombard Gretchen with questions—was she vacationing? does she live in New York? where is she going in the Sunshine State?—and the stiffness of her answers only fires them into greater heights of inquisitiveness. The women huff into their own private conversation shortly after the drink service, and when Gretchen disembarks at the airport it is in the frustrated daze of someone who has been grilled and found lacking.

She doesn't need to go to baggage claim, and the fact that she can stride forward while the other passengers wait by the whining conveyer worries her. She's not here for a weekend trip; she's here to live, and she has no luggage. That's the danger of thinking there's always something better out there: you don't have any luggage.

23

HUMPHREY

First thing I did when I got to Florida was get my license—I'm going to have to be able to get myself around. After that I looked in the paper, though, and even the cheapest cars cost too much. Eventually I'll have one of my own, just not now.

We had a good first few days, Mom and me, and then everything fell into the old routine. She'd come home late from work without much to say to anyone, and then she'd go to bed. I'm so happy to have Citrus again, but even that doesn't much undo the fact that I'm getting really ticked to have to live here. I hate the closet I live in. It's not a tiny bedroom, it's a closet. The door slides, not swings, and I can't stand that there's computer shit everywhere and I won't ever be able to invite anyone over. We might have proper silverware and real bowls now, but we've got nothing else like what homes are supposed to have, and Mom and Dad are just treading water. They should get divorced, but, unlike the Lansings, they couldn't afford it. They can barely make it together; I don't know how they'd get by apart.

Second thing I did was tell my mom and dad that I'm moving

out. Dad just looked confused, but Mom went ballistic. "You're only sixteen, how do you think it's possible to live on your own," but then I explained how it was really going to work, and she settled down some. It's like a divorce—my mom will get me half the time.

I've gone over to Brandy's place some. I know I shouldn't, but real school doesn't start for two weeks, and Gretchen's not here yet, and I'm lonely. When Brandy first answered the door her shoulders sagged, like I was one more punishment, some ghost all set to haunt the hell out of her. She's not doing too good. Dee moved out. My mom wanted to press charges against Carl, but he disappeared. He has family in Georgia and Mom wants the address, but Brandy honestly doesn't know it. Mom's sure she's lying.

I start spending more time at that little house than in my own motel-home. Brandy and I live together like a sexless old couple, watching TV and microwaving dinners. I never go out because I don't really know anyone and don't have any money (I should go see if Food Festival will rehire me, but I don't have the oomph yet). Outside of the lawsuit, we don't talk about Carl. I never go into Dee's old room. Since Brandy's still on worker's comp, all we do is sit on that ratty couch and watch TV or listen to the radio and play cards. The only one thrilled with the situation is Citrus, because Brandy has a backyard. He wanders around the overgrown grass and weeds for hours, yipping at lizards and rolling in dirt. He comes back with thick gobs of pollen in his beard.

Wade never comes by—the Department of Children and Families called to inform Brandy that Wade's dad took him out of school and down to Miami, probably to find work.

I wrote a half-assed email to Gita but I never got an answer—I guess she'd rather not be in touch. Can't blame her.

Brandy lets me take her car (Dee's old one—she moved to some big city and didn't need it) to go pick up Gretchen at the airport. I'm surprised by how good she looks. I figured we should all be carrying our demons like scars and stains, but she's sad and glowing pale. Me, I've got a tiny limp and this line on my cheek. Sometimes I like it, and other times it seems like the beginnings of a past, a heavy weight that's a part of me now. Gretchen gets in the passenger seat, kicking the old cans and take-out bags and receipts to one side. She gingerly rests her little pink bag on top of the layers of crumbs and wrappers covering the maroon carpet.

She doesn't want to see Mom. When I suggest it she doesn't say "not yet," just "no." So when I start the car I'm not sure where to take her. The only place I can think of is Brandy's. Half an hour later we're putting Gretchen's designer bag down on the bed in that room where I got beaten up. We sit there for a while, and I tell her that this is my first time back where it happened, and Gretchen covers her mouth. Not hysterical, just overcome. We're so quiet together now.

Gretchen eventually shrugs it off and arranges her few belongings on a shelf in the closet. She shakes the comforter, which only releases more staleness in the humid air. We go to the living room and sit on the couch and sweat for a while, and I ask her when we're going to start looking for a place.

"I don't have much money left," Gretchen says. "Airfares here are expensive."

I know for a fact that flights from New York to Florida aren't that expensive. She just wants to name a specific place her money went to, instead of all the incidental trips and expenses that ended with Mr. Lansing drowning. I nod at her. All I want is for there to be enough money that we can make it for a few months together. And there is. If we don't have to pay rent.

Brandy herself proposes it after she comes back from walking Citrus and sees Gretchen's bag in the other room. She says she's getting enough workers' comp from her hurt wrist that she can swing the whole rent if we want to stay. Gretchen buys the pizza that night.

When Gretchen finally meets up with Mom it's awful. They immediately fall into what Gretchen always described and what I vaguely remember, sniping at each other, jockeying around to find each other's weaknesses. Mom says Gretchen's selfish and how does she think she can waltz back into everyone's lives just because she feels like it, and then Gretchen says if she's selfish it's only because her own mother never wanted to see her succeed, and who is *Tricia* to be criticizing her after what she went through? It's true—I don't know how Mom can say anything mean to her, not yet, when Rajan left her and Mr. Lansing died and Gretchen has to do stuff like get me tested for STDs. And I see Mom's position, too—Gretchen won't give her a fresh chance. They'll never be close or even nice to each other. I love my mom, but I feel like I'll never be close to her, either. I like being with Brandy instead, because Brandy knows she's weak.

Gretchen and I share the same bed; we have to. The first night I think it's going to be fine—brothers and sisters share beds all the time, right?—but it's not. My heart goes real fast and I don't sleep at all. The next night I try sleeping on the couch, but there's no air conditioner in the living room so I end up going back to the bed in the middle of the night. Gretchen asks me what's wrong a few times and finally I tell her that it feels weird to sleep next to someone after everything that's happened. So then she tries sleeping on the couch. It's too hot for her, too, so by the fourth night I've resigned myself to sleeping alongside her. And after a couple weeks, it's gone from excruciating to tolerable. She even rolls in her sleep sometimes so that her hand's on my back, and that's okay, too.

Gretchen doesn't ever actually say she's sorry, but it's so clear how bad she feels that she doesn't need to. I know she could be in New York or Los Angeles or some other exciting place where she has friends, but she's not. She's here in order to be with me, to see me through school.

She's taking grad courses. She says it's to get a master's in performing arts, but I know it's just because she doesn't know what else to do. I'm worried she's going to decide it's not for her in six months and pick up and go, and then where will I be? So today, in the dim dawn light as she makes me breakfast in Brandy's kitchen, I tell her that I'm scared she'll leave. She promises me she won't.

Gretchen drives me to school, late enough that all the kids are already milling outside and comparing schedules for the semester. I slam the car door loudly so that everyone looks over. They see my cool older sister from that TV show, and me right next to her. She gets out and walks me through the students, and I can feel them scoping the two of us. A twenty-something in the middle of teenagers; she's the shit, and she's got her arm draped over my shoulder. She's beaming, but it's for my sake: I don't think I'll see her genuinely smile for a long time. But my smile is for real as I throw open the doors of the school and go inside. I don't look back as I go in. This is my last day of being the new kid, and I'm going to make the most of it.

ACKNOWLEDGMENTS

Thanks are due to my agent, Richard Pine, who is especially adept in those areas of book publishing for which I haven't the slightest knack. His level of dedication is rare.

Amanda Murray, my editor, has an eye for human detail, and suggested just the right revisions. (Note the lack, in the preceding pages, of any Roman schoolteachers named Marcella.)

Similarly, I can always count on my production editor, Loretta Denner, for her elegant prose sensibility.

Simon & Schuster publicity—Elizabeth Hayes, Julia Prosser, Nicole De Jackmo, Victoria Meyer—couldn't be better at what they do.

Darcy Cosper at *Swink* magazine was very supportive, and nurtured *The New Kid*'s earliest kernel.

I'm lucky to have a writers' group full of diverse talent. Gratitude to Jill di Donato, Matthew Robinson, Joanna Solfrian, and Michael Stearns.

Two veteran instructors led a terrific workshop at the Sewanee Writers' Conference: Margot Livesey and Erin McGraw, thanks for chapter 9.

Thanks, too, to my friends for having pursuits in fields that make them ideal fact checkers for *The New Kid*'s seamier details: Angélica

Cházaro, for aiding humankind while simultaneously studying the vagaries of Child Protective Services; Bede Sheppard, for his intimate knowledge of the peculiarities of European cigarettes; Sonia Inamdar, Haya Zuberi, and Ali Almani, for their bawdy Hindi; Massimo Sette, for his randy Italian; and Tyson Duane, for, once upon a time, wandering with me along Florida roads.

I am indebted to Tim Federle: in this book and beyond, he is my closest reader.